RESCUING JENNA (SPECIAL FORCES: OPERATION ALPHA)

BRAVO TEAM SERIES 5

ANNA BLAKELY

Cover by Lori Jackson Design
Copy Editing by Tracy Roelle
Proofreading by Christine Hall and Kim Ruiz

Dear Readers,

Welcome to the Special Forces: Operation Alpha Fan-Fiction world!

If you are new to this amazing world, in a nutshell the author wrote a story using one or more of my characters in it. Sometimes that character has a major role in the story, and other times they are only mentioned briefly. This is perfectly legal and allowable because they are going through Aces Press to publish the story.

This book is entirely the work of the author who wrote it. While I might have assisted with brainstorming and other ideas about which of my characters to use, I didn't have any part in the process or writing or editing the story.

I'm proud and excited that so many authors loved my characters enough that they wanted to write them into their own story. Thank you for supporting them, and me!

READ ON!
   Xoxo
   Susan Stoker

To my amazing editor, Tracy. Thanks for putting up with my craziness and still loving me, anyway. (Despite my crazy neurosis and last-minute edits!)

I also want to give a huge shout-out to the oh-so-talented Jenna Jacob...the original fiery redhead. Not only are you an amazingly talented author, you've also become one of my closest friends. I'm so very blessed to have you in my life.

And last, but certainly not least...to Kim R. and Christine H. Thank you both SO very much for helping make this final Bravo Team book the best it could be. I couldn't have done it without you!

Love you ALL to bunches!

XOXO ~

Anna

PROLOGUE

Jenna Shaw studied the blood on the front of her top and sighed. It wasn't the first time she'd gone home with blood on her clothes, and unless she changed professions, it wouldn't be the last.

The blood's owner—a seventy-two-year-old Veteran whose car had been t-boned when a teenage driver blew through a stop sign while texting—had suffered only minor injuries and was expected to make a full recovery. As it often happens in cases like this, the kid who'd hit him had walked away with barely a scratch. Jenna just hoped the hefty ticket in his pocket, along with the headache of a totaled car, would be enough to knock some sense into him.

With her mind back on the blood, she mentally ran through the steps of what needed to be done to keep it from staining. Not that she was worried. Having been an emergency room nurse for the past several years, Jenna had become a veritable expert in making stains, such as this one, disappear.

Exhausted from another grueling shift, she pulled her keys from her purse as she made her way through the dark parking garage to her car. A cool breeze sent a shiver racing down her spine, and she shifted the strap on her purse before crossing her arms and hugging herself to keep warm.

California winters were mild, to say the least, but it was barely after six in the morning, and the sun had yet to rise. If she was lucky, she'd make it back to her apartment and into her bed while it was still dark.

Spotting her car up ahead, Jenna suddenly couldn't wait to be in it and on her way home. With a little more speed in her step, she was rounding the rear bumper when a beat-up van seemingly appeared out of nowhere.

Tires skidded, the intrusive sound echoing through the garage. Startled, Jenna spun around to see what was going on just as the vehicle came to a hard stop.

While her tired brain worked to make sense of what was happening, a man in a dark hoodie jumped out and headed straight for her. Jenna's heart flew into her throat as the scene finally started to make sense.

He's going to hurt you.

She spun on her heels and ran for the driver's door. Her long, red ponytail smacked her in the face with the movement, but she ignored it and focused only on getting away.

She'd been kidnapped in order to be bait for Ellena Dawson—the killer's real target and Jenna's best friend. Though it all worked out in the end, it was an experience Jenna had no desire to repeat.

Fumbling with the key fob, her trembling thumb pressed the panic button. Her car lit up and the horn began honking in even intervals. A low, inaudible curse hit her ears just before she felt her purse being ripped off of her shoulder.

"Hey!" On instinct, Jenna faced the jerk and prepared to fight.

Scrambling to keep possession of the handbag, she

dropped her keys and wrapped her fingers around the thin, leather. She pulled as hard as she could. He pulled harder.

The shoulder strap burned against her skin as it was ripped from her hands. Jenna yelled, her voice barely rising over the incessant honking, but no one else was around to hear her. Shoving her hand into her scrub bottom pocket, she started to reach for her phone to call for help when the man slammed both of his large hands against her chest.

Losing her footing, Jenna cried out as she went flying backward. She turned mid-fall in order to keep from landing on her back. Instead, her left hip, thigh, and palms took the brunt of the fall. Behind her, the van door shut, and the thief and his getaway driver sped off, leaving her lying on the cool concrete between someone else's car and her own.

Fear and adrenaline left her shaken, but Jenna's anger was the driving force that pushed her back onto her feet. From the corner of her eye, she saw her keys lying at her feet. Bending over, Jenna picked them up, got into her car, and locked the doors.

Resting both hands on the wheel, she hung her head. After a few moments and several deep breaths, she'd calmed down enough to think rationally.

You need to call someone. Tell them what happened.

Jenna took her phone from her pocket, grateful the bastards didn't take off with it or her keys. Tapping on the green icon with the white phone, she opened her contacts with the intention of calling the first person on the alphabetical list. She froze mid-movement.

What the heck are you doing?

Heart racing for a different reason, she stared at the name of the man she'd almost reached out to.

The last time she saw Adrian Walker, the sexy, mysterious government agent had given Jenna his number and told her to call if she ever needed anything.

That was two months ago. After he'd kidnapped her, saved her from being sexually assaulted by some asshole thug he was pretending to work with, and damn near died while protecting her friend from a deranged killer.

Apparently, Adrian had been in the Marines, but ended up working as a super-secret agent for some underground CIA operation. For the past few years, he'd been playing the role of hitman for hire. In reality, he'd given up his life to help make the world a better place.

In the end, Ellena was saved. Gabe, Ellena's former SEAL husband, had been shot but thankfully survived. Adrian had vanished, leaving behind nothing more than his card and a promise to help if she needed him.

She didn't need him. She didn't need anyone. Except maybe the police.

With a mental slap to the face, Jenna closed her contact list and drove back around to the emergency room entrance. The hospital staffed off-duty officers to stand guard during each shift. That was who she needed.

An hour later—after reporting the incident to the police, her boss, and hospital security—she was still answering questions.

"Can you describe your assailant or the driver of the van?"

Anger toward the jerks who'd mugged her replaced the fear she'd initially felt. Biting the inside of her cheek, Jenna shook her head. "Not really. It was dark and everything happened so fast. I couldn't see the driver at all, and the other guy was hiding his face with a hood."

Standing in a quiet hallway adjacent to the emergency room waiting area, the officer taking her statement didn't bother looking up from his notes. Sounding almost bored, he asked her, "Any memorable features of the one you saw? Scars or tattoos of any kind?"

What part of it was dark and he was wearing a hood does this guy not understand?

"I already told you I didn't get a very good look at him."

She'd shared that with him and everyone else she'd spoken with. The morning's events had been playing on loop for the past hour, and she was more than ready to change the damn channel.

"Right." The young officer's thin lips curved into a placating smile. "Sorry. Okay, what about approximate height or weight of the man who came at you? Could you tell what race he was?"

"He was tall." Jenna stated with confidence. "Around six feet. And lean. Maybe two-ten, two-fifteen."

The asshole had towered over her. She remembered that one detail because, in the split second it took for the asshole to yank her purse from her shoulder and shove her to the ground, Jenna had noticed he was about the same height as—

Nope. Not going there.

With an unimpressed expression, the officer jotted down what she'd said. "Anything else?"

Closing her eyes, she willed her scattered mind to focus on her attacker. Conjuring up the infuriating scene, Jenna once again saw the man in question.

"Black jeans," she muttered softly. "Dark gray hoodie zipped all the way up." She couldn't see his face, but the guy's hands were coming toward her. Pushing against her chest as she yelled at him to give her back her purse. "He had olive skin. I think he may have been Hispanic, or maybe bi-racial."

Or maybe he had a tanning booth in his basement. Of course, if he could afford that, he probably wouldn't need to lurk around parking garages in hopes of stealing women's purses. Unless he was a sick freak who did it just for kicks. In that case, who knows why—

Jenna blinked, rubbing at her tired eyes. Jesus, she needed

to get some sleep. And then she was going to fix herself a very large, very stiff drink.

After I go to the bank to cancel my debit card, close my checking and savings accounts, and open all new ones.

On second thought, maybe she'd start with the drink. Or three.

"Okay, I think that's all I need for now." The officer slid his notebook and pen into his shirt pocket and handed her a small, rectangular card with his name, precinct address, and phone number printed on the front. "Here's my contact information. If you think of anything else, give that number a call."

In other words, he was going to file her report with the hundreds of other ones he's probably gotten this week, and that will be that. Not that she really expected any other outcome.

Although San Diego's crime rate had been decreasing slightly over the past few years, there were still plenty of other cases for the police force to worry about. Cases that were much more important than the petty thieves she'd encountered tonight.

"Thanks." Jenna shoved the card into her scrub top pocket. "I appreciate it."

She'd appreciate it even more if the cops could find the bastards and let her beat the hell out of them both…with the purse they stole. After she filled it with rocks.

"Do you have a way home, or do I need to find you a ride?"

Pulling her keys from her pants' pocket, Jenna held them up. "I'm good. But thanks."

"Okay, then. Be safe and don't forget to call if you think of anything else." With a nod, the officer turned and left her alone in the hallway.

With a sigh, she made her way to one of the employee

side-doors, opposite the E.R. waiting room. The last thing she wanted was to encounter more well-meaning co-workers anxious to hear the story of what happened.

Slipping out of the facility unnoticed, Jenna felt on-edge the entire way back to her car. She kept her head on a swivel, scanning her surroundings with a watchful eye.

Her heartrate increased while walking through the open parking lot. After being slammed with one patient after another for most of her shift, the place was relatively quiet, now.

Nearing her car, Jenna glanced at her keys. "At least they didn't get these," she mumbled the silver lining to herself as she unlocked the vehicle and got in.

By the time she got home, she wanted nothing more than to crawl into bed and block out everyone and everything. Instead, she put on a pot of coffee and changed clothes before heading back out to deal with the bank and that whole mess.

Three and a half hours later, Jenna was back inside her apartment with a new debit card, a new driver's license—something she'd thought of while she'd been waiting in line at the bank—and a headache the size of Texas. She'd just locked the door behind her and was heading to the kitchen for some ibuprofen when her phone dinged with an incoming text.

Taking it out of her pocket, she smiled when she saw the name on the screen. *Speaking of Texas...*

The message was from Ellena. After the whole kidnapping debacle—both hers and Ellena's—the sweet military psychologist had recently reunited with her estranged husband and Ellena moved from San Diego to Texas to be with him.

Naturally, Jenna understood her friend's need to be with

the man she loved, and she couldn't be happier for the two of them. Still, she missed Ellena like crazy.

The other woman was her person. Her confidant. Jenna told her almost everything, but right now, she was exhausted and more vulnerable than she cared to admit.

She shot Elle a quick text letting her know she'd had a really long day at work—not a lie—and was finally heading to bed. She ended the text with a promise to call her later this evening and hit 'send'.

Tears pricked the corners of Jenna's eyes, but she blinked them away. She wasn't normally one to cry, but recent events —and thoughts of a certain man she wished she could forget —had her on the verge of breaking down into a pathetic, watery mess.

Her phone dinged, the thumbs up and heart emojis Ellena responded with making her smile. Switching the device over to silent mode, Jenna shuffled down the hallway to the bathroom.

After washing away the hectic night shift and an even crazier morning, she crawled into bed and closed her eyes, wanting nothing more than to fall into a deep, dreamless sleep. Instead, the image of a faceless man wearing a hoodie flashed through her mind.

Her eyes flew open, and Jenna sucked in a quick breath. She gritted her teeth as the anger she'd felt before returned with a vengeance.

Damn it, she was stronger than this. Strong enough some purse-stealing punks shouldn't cause her to lose some much-needed sleep.

Throwing off the covers, she stormed out of bed and went in search of that drink she'd thought about earlier. Something to help her relax and forget this morning ever happened.

A glass of wine or two should do the trick.

A half a bottle of crisp, semi-sweet Moscato later, Jenna's anxiety had dulled, and her racing mind was starting to slow down. She went back to bed, and since she had that night off, she purposely didn't set her alarm.

Settling her head against her pillow, Jenna was falling into a peaceful, unconscious abyss when a sound woke her. She lay there, listening closely, but heard nothing. Chalking it up to the wine, she blew it off and closed her eyes once more.

It happened again. And this time, there was no mistaking the sound. Someone had just knocked on her door.

Seriously?

Thinking it might be the police with information—or if she was lucky, her purse—Jenna fought her desire to ignore whoever it was and went to her door. Looking through the peephole, she saw the back of a man's head as he began walking away.

It didn't matter that she hadn't seen *his* face. She knew exactly who it was.

A sudden onslaught of nerves left her fingers tingling and her heart beating hard against her chest. Releasing her locks, she opened the door and called for the man who'd apparently decided to leave.

"Adrian?" Her voice was rough with sleep.

The man who'd haunted her dreams for the past two months turned to face her. She looked up into his gray-blue eyes, and her heart stopped. Or skipped. Or *something.*

Truth be told, she wasn't sure what it did. She was too busy trying to convince herself he was real.

"What are you doing here?" she finally asked. Glancing over his shoulder, Jenna checked to see if Gabe or any of the other Bravo Team guys were with him. Her lower belly tensed when she saw that he was alone. "Is everything okay?"

The pair of tight fists at his sides told her something was

9

definitely bothering him. She was about to repeat the question when he opened his mouth and asked, "Can I come in?"

Without a word, Jenna moved to give him room and motioned for him to come inside.

≈

"We found it. Or more accurately, we found *her*."

The heart inside Matais Ortiz's chest beat with the force of a drum. Could it be? After all this time, had he finally found Adrian Walker's weakness?

Unable to contain his excitement, Matais asked the other man, "Who?"

"I.D. in her wallet says her name's Jenna Shaw. She's a nurse at a military hospital in San Diego."

"How did you manage to get your hands on her identification?"

"Grabbed her purse in the hospital parking garage a few minutes ago."

"You *mugged* her?" He closed his eyes and shook his head. "Christ, Sebastian. Someone could've seen you. She could *identify* you."

"Relax." His top lieutenant blew out a breath. "It was still dark, and I wore a hood. Garcia pulled up beside her. I jumped out and grabbed the purse, and we took off. No one saw us, and other than a few parked cars, the place was empty."

Ignoring the man's overabundance of confidence, Matias asked, "You're certain this the same woman Walker's been watching the last few weeks?"

"It's her," Sebastian confirmed. "At first we thought she might be his latest mark, but I'm thinking the rumors we've heard are true. That he really did quit."

Retired was the term most hired guns used when they got

out of the business, but he understood the point his man was trying to make. Word had it, the infamous Adrian Walker had decided to hang up his guns and walk away. Apparently, Sebastian believed what he'd heard.

You won't get away, my friend. Not this time.

"What makes you certain she isn't his target?"

"Because we're sitting across the street from her apartment. Bitch invited him inside."

Idiot. Sebastian's large build and brute force mentality made him the perfect bodyguard and enforcer. But the man didn't always see the finer details that made up the bigger picture.

"Walker didn't build his reputation by being sloppy. He could've used a guise to make her feel comfortable around him. Earned her trust before he did the hit."

It was the oldest trick in the book. The closer a person got to someone, the easier it was to take them out. A lesson Matias' father had taught him early on.

"He was there for four hours, Boss. Trust me. Walker didn't come here to kill her."

"Again, how can you be so sure?"

"For one, I can see her moving around through the window. Two, the look on the bastard's face when he left…" Sebastian chuckled. "Trust me. Those two did more than just talk."

"Sex doesn't necessarily mean—"

"She's the one, Matias," his man spoke with utter certainty. "We've been watching him for over a month now. There have been no other women. No other booty calls. The Shaw woman is the one you need."

Matias let the information sink in. Then he smiled. "Excellent."

"What's next? Should we grab the girl now, or…?"

He considered it for a moment but decided against it. "Not yet. There are still things I need to do to prepare."

This plan had been put into motion a long time ago, and Matias refused to rush it.

"When will you be ready?" Sebastian's impatience began to show.

"Soon, amigo." Matias promised his trusted lieutenant. "Very soon."

"You want me and Garcia to hang around until you give the green light?"

He nodded. "Si. Keep the woman in your sights, but don't let her know you're there."

"Understood, Boss."

"I'll be in touch."

Ending the call, Matias walked over to the floor-to-ceiling window in his home's private office. Looking out over his expansive property, he reminisced of simpler times. Times when he was just a child with no thoughts of drugs or money…or killing.

From the grass below, Matias' young daughter spotted him while playing with the family dog. Her face lit up as she waved up at him. His heart swelled, and he offered her his own smile and wave in return.

"I'm going to get him, Papa." Matias spoke aloud, the words meant for his deceased father. "I'm going to make Adrian Walker suffer in the worst ways imaginable. And then I am going to kill him. For you. For my children. And for this family's legacy."

CHAPTER 1

Three weeks later...

"You're doing *what*?"

"It's not a big deal, Elle." Jenna zipped her suitcase closed.

"Uh…you're moving. So, yeah…it is a big deal."

With her phone held between a shoulder and her ear, Jenna walked to her bathroom to grab the toiletries she planned to take with her. "It's a temporary move," she reminded her friend. "The contract's twelve weeks. I'll be doing the same thing there I do here but with a massive pay bump."

"And if you were only doing this for the money, I'd say go for it."

"Who says I'm not?"

Ellena's soft sigh hit her ear. "I know you, remember?"

"Meaning?"

"You're running."

Jenna frowned, her hand freezing as she was reaching for a bottle of lotion. "I am not."

"Yes, you are. And I'm pretty sure I know *who* you're running from."

Her muscles tensed. She yanked the lotion from the counter and threw it into her toiletry bag. "He has nothing to do with this."

Liar, liar.

"Come on, Jen. The guy shows up out of nowhere, spends a few hours giving you the best orgasms of your life…your words, not mine…and then splits while you're sleeping. He hasn't called or texted since. Of course, this is about Adrian."

Hastily grabbing the rest of her things, Jenna stormed back into her bedroom. "You shrinking me, now? Because I *thought* I was talking to my best friend, not my therapist."

"I *am* your best friend. I'm also a therapist. The two aren't always mutually exclusive." Ellena's voice softened. "It's obvious you're using this move as a way to avoid the real issue. An issue you're still going to have to deal with at some point."

"Thank you, Dr. Phil. I'll keep that in mind." Jenna cringed at her snarky retort. Placing the small bag onto the bed next to her suitcase, she blew out a breath and apologized. "Sorry. And…okay, fine. Maybe Adrian has a *little* bit to do with this. But he's not the entire issue."

"So what is?"

"I don't know." She plopped down onto her mattress. "I think I just need a change of scenery for a bit."

"A change of scenery does sometimes help to put things into perspective."

"Exactly. That's what I need. Some perspective."

There was a stretch of silence before Ellena asked, "How are you sleeping? Anymore nightmares?"

Jenna snorted. "Shouldn't I be asking you that question?"

"We're not talking about me."

"Now who's avoiding?"

Her friend chuckled. "I have the occasional bad dream, but not nearly as many as before. And when Gabe isn't out with his team, he's right there to remind me I'm safe. Plus, I've kept busy getting things ready for the baby."

A sudden jolt of jealousy left Jenna's insides clenching. Not because of the baby. Even at thirty, Jenna wasn't sure she was ready to take on that venture just yet.

No, her jealousy stemmed from the being alone part. When Jenna woke from a nightmare—which happened more often than she cared to admit—all she had were shadows and memories to comfort her.

Clearing her throat, she didn't dare let those thoughts show. "I'm so happy you two are back together. And the baby…I still can't believe you're pregnant."

"Me, either." Ellena's smile came through the phone. "Now, back to this move…"

"*Temporary* move."

"Temporary or not, if you're going to take a job in Texas, why not come to Dallas? I can talk to the medical director where I work. I'm sure they could use the help, too, and—"

"Who's taking a job in Texas?" Gabe's deep, rumbling voice joined the conversation.

"Jenna," Elle answered her husband, who'd apparently just entered whatever room she was in. "Here, I'll put her on speaker."

"Hey, Jen," Gabe greeted her. "How's it going?"

"I'm good. You?"

"Good. Busy."

Picking up on the man's tone, Jenna asked, "How many coats have you done so far?"

"Just got back from the store with color number four."

Jenna chuckled. Poor Gabe had been painting the small nursery for a week because Ellena kept changing her mind on which shade of pink she wanted.

"I know for a fact that Ellena appreciates all the hard work you're doing to make the nursery look perfect for when the baby comes."

"She'd better," the burly man grumbled. "But this is it. I don't care if it turns out looking like Madonna's kinky play-room, I'm not painting it again."

Jenna snorted. "Madonna's kinky playroom?"

"I'm sure it'll look fine, honey," Ellena assured her husband.

"It better 'cause I've inhaled enough paint fumes to make a damn tweaker feel jumpy." After both women laughed, Gabe said, "So, Jen…what's this about you coming to Texas?"

"She took a job with a nursing agency," Ellena answered for her.

"It's a travel nursing gig," Jenna added. "It's only for twelve weeks, and then I'll be back in San Diego."

"Sounds good. Where in Texas will you be working?"

"Gulfside Harbor."

Ellena spoke up again, her question directed at her husband. "Didn't you tell me once that Gulfside Harbor was dangerous?"

"Can be." Gabe's voice had turned serious. "It has some decent areas, but it's definitely not the safest city in Texas."

Great. Now *he* was going to be on her ass.

Almost afraid to hear the answer, Jenna asked the man, "What's wrong with Gulfside Harbor?"

The name sounded so calm. So peaceful. And the pictures she'd seen while Googling had looked quite pleasant.

"It's close to the border, which makes it vulnerable. There's a huge market for theft there, so you'll want to keep your purse close. I wouldn't take anything valuable with you, and if you go anywhere other than the hospital where you'll be working and the hotel where you'll be staying, you need to have someone else with you. Preferably a man."

The man's big-brother routine had one of her brows rising. Unable to resist, she challenged the alpha male by asking him, "Are you suggesting I can't take care of myself? Because I've been taking self-defense classes." She'd signed up for them the day after the mugging. "In fact, I could probably kick your ass."

She couldn't. The man was a giant. Still, it was fun to pretend she was strong enough to take the big guy down.

"You could try," Gabe chuckled. "And I didn't mean to imply—"

"I'm kidding, Gabe." Jenna let him off the hook too easily. "I know my limits, and I don't have a death wish. Trust me, I've experienced enough violence and crime to fill a lifetime." *And then some.* "I'm just going to go there, keep my head down, do my job, and come home."

"I still don't like it," Ellena piped back in. "Gabe, couldn't you assign one of the guys to go with her? You know, be her bodyguard or whatever?"

After leaving the Navy, Gabe had joined R.I.S.C., a private, black-ops security company. The acronym stood for Rescue, Intel, Security, and Capture, which pretty much summed up the types of services the company offered.

There were two teams: Alpha and Bravo. Gabe was the Bravo Team leader and had spearheaded the rescue mission that ultimately saved Ellena's life a few months back.

The guy and his teammates definitely knew their stuff, but Jenna wasn't about to ask any of them to tag along as her shadow while she took care of the sick and injured.

"I don't need a bodyguard, Elle," she told her friend firmly. "Seriously, you guys are making this out to be a much bigger deal than it is."

"But—"

"She's right, sweetheart," Gabe cut his wife's words off. "Jenna's a big girl. She can take care of herself."

"I can?" Jenna asked suspiciously.

"She can?" Ellena's surprised voice parroted her through the phone.

"Of course, she can," Gabe stood by his statement. Clearly speaking to Ellena, Jenna heard him say, "What? Don't give me that look. Aren't you two always telling me how women can do more than what we narrow-minded men want to admit? Well, this is me…admitting it."

That was way too easy.

"What's your angle?" she asked him.

"There's no angle, Jenna. I saw how you handled yourself when all that shit went down with Ellena. You're a strong woman…ahem, *person*. And you're an adult. You wanna to go to Gulfside Harbor, by all means, go."

Sitting on her bed with a narrowed gaze, Jenna suddenly wished she could see the man's face rather than simply hearing his voice. Ever since she'd known him, Gabe had always played the big-brother protective role with her.

Now, he was just giving up?

"So, the lecture's over? Just like that?"

"I can't win with you two, can I?" Gabe's question was clearly rhetorical. "I try to keep you safe, and I'm being over-protective. When I admit you're smart and independent, I'm acting suspicious. You know what? I take back what I said. I think I'll just hide away in the nursery, painting it over and over again until my daughter is born."

Both women laughed in unison, and Jenna tried not to listen as Ellena quietly comforted her husband with a few sweet words and soft kisses. When Gabe spoke again, his tone was loving and genuine.

"Good luck with your new job, Jen. I mean that. Be careful and, seriously…you need anything, don't hesitate to call us."

"Thanks, Gabe." Jenna smiled. "I'm sure I won't, but if I

run into trouble while I'm there, you'll be the first person I call."

"Good girl."

The corners of her mouth rose higher. For all the gruff she gave him, Gabe was the older brother she'd never had. Despite his tendency to overprotect—or maybe even because of it—Jenna loved him dearly.

"I'd better go, too. Make sure he *doesn't* turn our baby's nursery into something resembling a rock star's sex room."

Jenna barked out a laugh. "Yes. You should definitely do that."

The laughter dissipated into silence before Ellena asked, "You sure this is what you want to do?"

"I'm sure," Jenna answered confidently. "Now, go. It sounds like your husband is in desperate need of your interior decorating skills, and I need to finish packing."

"Okay. Call me when you land?"

"I will. I promise." After saying their goodbyes, Jenna ended the call and exhaled slowly.

With the phone held loosely in her lap, she looked around her bedroom. For what, she wasn't sure. A sign, maybe? Something to tell her she'd made the right decision.

She glanced at the armless accent chair in the corner of the room, her heart skipping half a beat from the memory that would forever be attached to it.

In her mind's eye, she saw Adrian standing in front of it. He was stripping off her clothes before ridding his incredible body of his own.

As clear as if it were happening in real time, Jenna watched as Adrian sat down in that chair, guiding her until she was straddling his lap. What happened after was nothing short of spectacular.

Jenna blinked the memory away.

Lordy, I'm a mess.

So there it was. The sign she'd been looking for. Leaving the memories this place held, even temporarily, was absolutely the *right* decision.

With renewed conviction, Jenna blocked out any further thoughts of Adrian Walker and stood. For the next hour, she moved about the apartment, packing and double-checking to make sure she hadn't forgotten anything important.

By the time she went to bed—with her bags by the front door and her ticket tucked safely inside her purse—she still believed taking this job was the right choice.

The next day, as the landing gear touched the runway at Gulfside Harbor International Airport, any remaining slivers of trepidation had all but vanished.

After checking into the hotel where she'd be staying over the next three months, Jenna found herself standing around a large conference room making small talk with some of the other nurses who'd signed up for the same gig.

"My husband was all for it," Shawna, one of the nurses, commented. Crossing her arms at her chest, the tall woman's blonde ponytail swished from side to side as she spoke to the small group. "With three kids under four, we couldn't pass up the extra money."

"Same." The woman next to Shawna—Amy, maybe?—nodded. "Except our kids are all teenagers and into every sport imaginable. That shit's expensive, y'all."

"Right?" Marie, a nurse from Kansas City, scoffed. "My two are in middle school. It costs an arm and a leg to keep them involved in all the crap they begged us to let them do. Baseball, soccer, dirt bike races…and that's on top of everything else like clothes and food. I mean, I love my kids and all, but I swear some days it feels they're like little parasites sucking my husband and I dry."

A collective laugh erupted amongst the three women. Jenna chuckled and nodded, feeling like a total fraud since she didn't have any kids, yet. Considering she didn't even have a boyfriend, her chances of popping one out anytime soon were slimmer than slim.

Not that she was ready for a kid. Truth was Jenna wasn't even sure she wanted kids. But it was awkward as hell standing around listening to the other women go on and on about theirs.

When they began pulling up pictures on their phones to pass around, Jenna opened her mouth to excuse herself but was interrupted when a short, middle-aged woman clapped her hands and addressed the entire room.

"Good afternoon," she spoke when the room quieted down. "I'm Taylore Wood, and on behalf of Saje Staffing, I want to thank you all for being here. As you know, hospitals around the country seem to get busier with each new year, yet quality nurses are harder and harder to come by. That's where Saje Staffing comes in. Each of you were chosen for this assignment because of your proven dedication for taking care of your patients, and we feel very lucky to have you on board. Now, if you'll take a seat, we'll go over the rules and policies you'll need to follow while you're in town."

Marie leaned toward Jenna as they followed Amy and Shawna to a row of empty chairs. "This is where she tells us we can't go anywhere or do anything outside the hotel."

"What?" Confused, Jenna swung her head around. "What do you mean, we can't go anywhere?"

"It's true," Amy whispered over her shoulder. "The agency enacted a lockdown policy after those two nurses went missing."

Jenna felt her eyes grow wide. "Lockdown? Wait. What are you talking about? Nurses are *missing*?"

Amy nodded but waited until they were seated to fill her in. With Shawna sitting between them, Amy leaned forward and spoke with a hushed tone from two seats down.

"It's not an official lockdown," she whispered. "Taylore won't say anything about it. No one around here will. That's why you haven't seen it on the news. The first one vanished two weeks ago after she left the hospital to come back here after her shift. Five days later, another nurse didn't show up for work. From what I heard, when Taylore went to the woman's room to look for her, she found it empty. The bed hadn't even been slept in."

Shawna met Jenna's blinking eyes. "I heard a group of men from Mexico had been kidnapping nurses and doctors from here and taking them back over the border."

"That's what I heard," Marie nodded.

Horrified, Jenna looked around at the other women. "Why would they risk sneaking into our country to kidnap a couple of nurses and then have to get *back* over the border with them?"

"Forced medical labor," Marie answered for the group. "At least, that's what I heard. But you never know."

Oh, my god. "Did they ever find the two missing nurses?"

The three women shared a look before Marie shrugged. "They found one. That's how my friend heard about the forced labor."

"Yeah, but the girl who was taken could be lying to cover up something she doesn't want us to know," Shawna pointed out.

Jenna glanced at the blonde. "Like what?"

"My guess? Sex trafficking."

Sweet Jesus. "Seriously, why haven't we heard about this before now?"

"Would you still be here if you knew ahead of time?" Amy directed the question to Jenna.

Jenna didn't hesitate. "Hell, no."

An agency that not only lost two women—one possibly

permanently—but then swept it under the rug? No, thank you.

"Exactly. Taylore and the others want to keep the incidents hush-hush so it doesn't hurt their business. But you didn't hear any of this from me." Shawna gave Jenna and the others a pointed look.

"Me, neither." Marie joined in. "I need this job."

"Same." Amy nodded. "As quiet as they've been about the whole thing, Taylore would probably ship our asses back home if she caught wind that we were even talking about it."

Stunned by the revelation, Jenna returned her focus back to the woman at the front of the room. Taylore looked nice enough but looks could be deceiving. Actions, too, for that matter.

Her thoughts turned to Adrian, and how his actions while serving as an undercover government agent greatly contrasted the man she knew existed deep inside. The world may not have seen it, but Jenna did.

He was a good man who'd done some not-so-good things. However, the not-so-good had been government sanctioned, and he'd single-handedly rid the world of many horrible, evil human beings.

As she always did when thinking of the frustratingly sexy man, Jenna felt conflicted.

On the one hand, Adrian was a killer. Something she—a nurse who'd taken an oath to do everything in her power to keep people alive—struggled with.

On the other hand, by taking the lives he had, Adrian had *saved* countless others. Innocent men, women, and children. He'd nearly died saving her best friend's life, so how could she not see the good in him?

I wonder if he sees it.

But that still didn't excuse the way things went down

between them. Leaving before she woke up? That wasn't cool. Not cool at all.

Clapping erupted around her as Taylore had finished her spiel. Jenna looked around, realizing she'd completely zoned out the rest of whatever the woman had said.

Damn it, Jenna. The man got what he wanted and moved on. Knock him off that freaking pedestal you put him on and do the same!

The annoying voice was right. She'd already spent way too long pining away for a man who didn't want her. And aside from his profession—one straight out of an action-adventure movie—Adrian Walker was no different than any of the other jerks she'd dated.

Keep telling yourself that.

Ready to smack her subconscious into next week, Jenna spared a quick glance to her right. Marie stared back at her with a knowing gaze.

"Don't worry." Marie smirked. "A friend of mine is part of the staff we're replacing. I'll fill you in on all the B.S. rules and policies over dinner."

Jenna frowned. "Dinner?"

The Kansas City native chuckled. "Did you hear *anything* Taylore said?"

"Not really," Jenna admitted.

Shaking her head, Marie chuckled. "We're all having dinner in the hotel restaurant in a couple of hours. I'll come down early and make sure the four of us get a table together."

Feeling chagrined, Jenna nodded. "Thanks."

"No sweat." The other woman stood. "In the meantime, I'm going to go take a hot shower and relax in my room for a bit. See y'all in a bit."

Following her lead, Jenna stood and bid the other two women goodbye before heading for the stairs. At the hospital back home, she always tried taking the stairs as much as possible. More convenient than a gym, and a hell of a lot cheaper.

As she exited the stairwell, she made her way down the third-floor hallway. When she got to her room, Jenna slid her keycard into the electronic reader, surprised when the pressure from her hand forced the door to open slightly.

What the hell?

Glancing back down the hall, the only sign of life Jenna found was a housekeeping cart parked outside a room several doors down. Her mind worked backward to earlier, when she'd left to go downstairs for the mandatory meeting.

Did I not pull it closed all the way? Jenna pressed a palm against the door and pushed. Still standing on the hallway side of the threshold, she peeked her head into the dark room.

"Hello?" She waited but got no response.

With another glance to each side, Jenna reached into her purse and pulled out the pepper spray she'd packed alongside her clothes. Taking a hesitant step forward, she thumbed the red tab to unlock the safety clip and held the compact cannister out in front of her.

"Is someone there?" She looked around the room as she moved.

The modest bathroom was on her left, and with the shower curtain pulled to one side, it was clear no one was hiding in there. On her right was a built-in closet with a sliding, mirrored door.

Heart in her throat, Jenna shifted the pepper spray into her left hand. Using her right, she slid the metal door away from her. Minus some hangers, an iron, and an ironing board, the tiny space was empty.

You're just being paranoid.

In a loud rush of air, her lungs released the breath she'd been holding. Stories about vanishing nurses had obviously left her spooked, but she decided to go ahead and check the balcony, anyway. Just to be safe.

Focusing on the closed, floor-to-ceiling curtains directly in front of her, Jenna started for the other side of the room. The second she cleared the corner of the wall where the closet was located—the one next to the nearest of the two beds—she realized her mistake.

A strong hand flew out from behind the wall, covering her mouth. Her attacker wrapped his other arm around her waist, the other hand muffling Jenna's screams as she fought and struggled to get free. The guy let out a few low grunts but didn't budge.

The spray! Use the damn pepper spray!

Mentally smacking herself for having momentarily forgotten it, Jenna spun the canister's opening around, nearly dropping it in the process.

With thoughts of those missing nurses swirling throughout her head, she pointed the nozzle toward the man behind her. Turning her head to the left and shutting her eyes to avoid accidentally hitting herself, Jenna squeezed the trigger and released the burning liquid.

The man behind her yelled. He immediately dropped his arms and stumbled away from her, his back hitting the wall behind him. Not taking any chances, Jenna ran forward a few steps before turning back around and pointing the spray at her attacker once more.

With his head down and his palms wiping at his eyes, the jerk growled against the pain. "Pepper spray? Really?"

What did you expect, dickwad?

Fear and anger poured through her as she stood her ground. "That's right, asshole! And there's more where that came from if you don't get out of my room right this second!"

"Holy hell, woman. To think I was worried about you."

The would-be kidnapper coughed and spit before releasing a low chuckle. "Christ, I forgot how much that shit hurts."

Even though the man's words were strained, and he was struggling to catch his breath, Jenna could've sworn she recognized his voice. With the dusk's light seeping in through a narrow break in the curtains, she took a few seconds to study the intruder more closely.

He was tall. Brunette. His black t-shirt stretched across muscles that seemed to go for days, and his denim jeans hugged his taut thighs like a second skin. If she didn't know any better, she'd almost think he looked a lot like…

No. No way.

Keeping the spray aimed at her target, Jenna slowly side-stepped to the lamp resting on the small table on her right. Not taking her eyes off the intruder, she fumbled a bit before finding the light switch and turning it on.

A sudden, dull glow illuminated the room—and the man standing before her.

With her heart thrumming wildly, Jenna said, "Show me your face."

Still grimacing in pain, the blinking man began to slowly raise his head. Sniffing, he used the back of his hand to wipe his red, watering eyes before bringing his pained gaze to hers.

His skin was beet red, and he could barely open his eyes. But there was no mistaking that handsome face.

Jenna released a breath she didn't realize she was holding. Her jaw dropped. *"Adrian?"*

"Hey, gorgeous." He smiled through the burn. "Miss me?"

CHAPTER 2

Adrian stood under the shower's pummeling spray, the cool water rinsing the soap from his face. He'd washed it four times, already, and the flames he'd felt with that first chemical splash had finally begun to diminish.

This is what you get for coming back to this hell hole.

The last time he was in Gulfside Harbor, he'd been searching for his sister. A sister he'd lost because he wasn't there to protect her.

This is also what you get for caring for a woman you barely know, asshole.

And he did care. More than he should. More than he had a *right* to.

That's why, when Gabriel Dawson had called to share his concerns about Jenna's new travel assignment and asked him to come down here and check on her, Adrian hadn't hesitated to agree.

Like Gabe, the idea of Jenna being anywhere near the Mexican border—especially in the same city his sister was taken from—scared the shit out of him.

And he wasn't a man who scared easily.

Except he'd damn near been terrified to see her again. Okay, maybe *terrified* was too strong a word. More like nervous as hell.

After leaving the way he had, Adrian was certain she'd yell and scream and tell him to go to hell. Or throat punch him.

It was a toss-up, really.

So, in an attempt to avoid starting a public spectacle, he'd decided to break into her room and wait for her there. In hindsight, hiding in the dark and grabbing her like he had probably wasn't the smartest move.

Occupational hazard and all that.

Adrian also wasn't sure which surprised him more—that Jenna had been carrying pepper spray or that she'd actually *used* it on his ass. Hell, he probably would've burst out laughing if his face hadn't felt as though it were melting off his damn skull.

One thing that didn't surprise him, however, was how fucking hot his fiery woman had looked. Especially when she was standing there, yelling and threatening to spray him again.

She's not yours, dipshit.

God, but he wished she was. He'd never had *anyone* to call his own. Not the women he used to occasionally hook up with for some mutual catch-and-release and sure as shit not Jenna Shaw.

A fact Adrian had been dumb enough to question.

His life had been going just fine until he'd kidnapped Jenna two months ago in order to help her friend out of a dangerous situation. One look, and he'd been knocked on his ass with lust.

After witnessing Jenna's spunky attitude and smart mouth that very first time, he knew he wanted her. But when he'd walked in on the fucknut he'd been working with trying to rape her, Adrian saw red.

He'd realized then that what he felt for her was more than mere physical attraction. But despite his newfound knowledge, he'd gone in, got the job done, and left.

Problem was, he kept *returning*.

Week after week, he'd go to her apartment. Adrian would stand outside, just until he saw Jenna and knew that she was okay. Then he'd leave again.

He thought that would be enough. That knowing he hadn't completely screwed her up would satisfy the gnawing hunger he felt deep inside.

But the pull he felt toward Jenna grew stronger and stronger. It *kept* growing until finally, he'd said fuck it and went back again.

Giving in to his incessant need to make sure Jenna really was okay after everything she'd been put through—what *he'd* put her through—Adrian had gone back to her apartment three weeks ago.

Only this time, he didn't watch her from afar like all the other times. He'd knocked on her door. To talk. Which they did.

Just not for long.

Honest to Christ, he hadn't planned on having sex with her that night. Truthfully, Adrian still wasn't even sure how it all started.

One minute he was asking her how she was, and the next, Jenna was in his arms and his mouth was on hers.

The hours that followed that first, blazing kiss were filled with raw, primal need. She gave and he took. He tasted, and she explored.

In that one night, the woman had given Adrian more pleasure than he'd ever felt in his thirty-two years combined.

So, he'd left.

Not that he'd wanted to. It was just how things had to be.

No matter how many nights he lay awake wishing things were different, wishing she *belonged* to him, Adrian knew the status quo would never change. Not for a guy like him.

It was that knowledge that drove him away that next morning. From her bed and out of her life.

Memories from that night would be forever burned in the deepest parts of his brain. But unfortunately for him, that's all he could afford to keep. Sweet, hot-as-fuck memories that left him wanting something he'd never have.

Life really sucked big, hairy balls, sometimes.

Adrian scrubbed hard against his raw face to clear his thoughts before glancing down at his raging hard-on. For half a second, he considered dealing with it himself, but quickly decided against it.

The idea of jerking off with her waiting for him in the other room ranked too damn high on his creep-o-meter.

Ignoring his greedy cock, he rushed to wash the soap from the rest of his body. While he rinsed off, he silently cursed the unfairness of it all.

After the shit he'd done and seen over the years, he'd finally met a woman he could see himself with long-term, yet he'd been forced to walk away. Why?

Because I don't deserve her.

Any semblance of a normal life with a normal relationship went out the window the second he signed on Uncle Sam's dotted fucking line. Adrian knew that. Had always known that.

So why did you think this time...or this woman...could possibly be any different?

"Fuck if I know," he muttered to himself before turning off the water.

Not one to normally let his emotions run wild...or at all...Adrian used the time he spent drying off to regroup. He was here as a favor to Gabe and his wife. Nothing more, nothing less.

Keep piling up the lies up, Walker. It's what you do best.

With more force than necessary, he tossed the towel onto the floor beneath the floating sink. Ignoring the annoying voice in his head, he threw on his boxer briefs and jeans but decided against the shirt.

The pepper spray had dripped all over the front of it—probably ruined the fucking thing—but at least his other clothes had been spared.

At least I'm here, with her.

Shutting his subconscious out, Adrian ran a hand through his wet hair, drew in a breath, and opened the bathroom door.

Jenna had pulled the curtains back and was standing with her arms crossed at her chest, staring out the balcony window. Though he knew she could see him through the window's reflection, she didn't bother turning around.

For some reason, he found her willingness to ignore him hot as shit. Probably because he was one sick bastard.

Tell me something I don't already know, asshole.

"Thought maybe you'd join me," he teased, keeping his voice low and steady. "Offer to kiss the boo-boo you inflicted."

"Well, I wouldn't have had to inflict *anything* if you hadn't snuck in here and grabbed me like a damn kidnapper. Oh, wait." She did turn around then, her kissable mouth curling into a snarky smirk. "You *are* a kidnapper."

"Touché."

God, he loved her sass.

Her eyes slid to his bare chest, their focus landing on the Marines tattoo on his right pec. Adrian watched as her pupils dilated from an arousal, even though she was doing every-thing to hide it.

"Really?" She *rolled* those gorgeous eyes of hers. "You couldn't be bothered to put your shirt back on?"

"It's covered in pepper spray."

Jenna looked as if she were about to smart off again. Instead, she bit her bottom lip and looked away. "Oh."

Shit. He hadn't meant to make her feel bad. It was his fault for sneaking up on her the way he had. Not that he was about to admit that to her.

"You know." He laid it on thick. "If it bothers you that much, you could take off your shirt, too. Just so we're even."

"Cut the crap, Adrian." Jenna planted her hands on her hips. "What the hell are you doing here?"

The angry woman was dressed in a pair of purposely ripped jeans that hugged her toned legs just right, and a white, long sleeved t-shirt that both hid and showcased her perky breasts. With her wavy, red hair gathered over one shoulder in a thick braid, she looked even more tempting than he remembered.

Smartass that he was, Adrian licked his lips and smiled. "I get it. First, we talk, and *then* we…" He slid his eyes to the bed and back to her before waggling his brows.

Jaw dropping—which was the exact reaction he was going for—Jenna fumed as she dropped her arms and stormed toward him. "If you think you can just show up here for another drive-by, you're out of your damn mind."

"Drive-by?" he snorted.

Moving her hands back to the narrow hips he remembered so fondly, Jenna glared up at him. "You showed up at my place, somehow managed to finagle your way into my bed, and then poof. You were gone."

Christ, she's something.

"One, when it comes to women, I make it a point not to *finagle* anything. Too messy. Two, you invited me into your bed, and three, there were hours of pleasure between us."

Taking a chance, he slowly began closing the distance between them as he spoke. "As a matter of fact, I recall you enjoying multiple…*interactions* between my arrival and departure."

Jenna's delicate throat worked as she swallowed hard. Almost as if she'd just noticed her reaction to his descriptive words, she narrowed her eyes and jutted her chin. "You vanished as quickly as you came. And yes, jackass. The pun was intended."

Ouch.

Despite the harsh—and very much *not* true comment—Adrian's dick began throbbing behind his zipper. Damn, she really was pissed.

Good thing she had no idea how much that shit turned him on.

"Admit it, sweetheart." He grinned. "You're happy to see me."

"Right." She pointed to her gorgeous face. "Because *this* is the face of someone who's happy."

"Oh, come on, Jen. I only put my hand over your mouth so you wouldn't scream."

Her eyebrows shot up and her voice rose an octave. "I wouldn't have screamed at all if you'd waited for me in the hallway like a normal person!"

Adrian shrugged. "Normal's overrated. Don't you think?"

Jenna opened her mouth and closed it again. She repeated the move, looking like a fish out of water while she tried to decide what to throw back at him next. As usual, the woman surprised him.

"How are your eyes?"

"I'll live." He tipped his head. "Thanks again for letting me use the shower."

Shifting her weight, she looked away and shrugged. "Didn't want to risk you having any permanent damage."

"So, she does care."

Rather than come back with another witty remark, as he'd expected, Jenna sat down on the bed closest to her and sighed. "Unbelievable."

"What?"

"I came here to get away from...never mind." Her emerald eyes lifted. "How did you even find me?"

Came here to get away from what, sweetheart?

"I was in the neighborhood," Adrian spoke the lie with ease. "Thought I'd stop by for a chat."

The quipped response was his automatic go-to. Bullshit had been his native language for years, and he didn't know any other way.

The lying. The smartassed, I-don't-give-a-shit attitude. That was who he was, and up until the moment he met the sexy nurse from San Diego, Adrian was perfectly fine with that.

But now, with Jenna, he found himself wanting to be something different. Something *more.*

"Adrian..." she warned with an arched brow.

His dick stood at attention. Or it would have, if he'd let the greedy fucker loose.

It happened every time his name fell from this woman's lips. Knowing she was calling him on his shit? That made him want to push her back onto that bed and lose himself in her forever.

It also made him want to be honest with her.

"Dawson called me late last night. Asked me to come down here and keep an eye on you."

"He did *what?*" Jenna shot off the bed. Fire burned behind her emerald eyes as she stared back at him. "You have got to be kidding me."

"Calm down, gorgeous. He's just worried about you. Ellena is, too."

"Don't tell me to calm down." She crossed her arms like before, the move inadvertently pushing her breasts higher. "Um, hellooo…" Jenna snapped her fingers in front of his distracted face. "I'm up here, remember?"

Not embarrassed in the least that he'd been caught staring at the luscious swells of her breasts, Adrian slowly brought his gaze back up to hers. "Trust me. I remember."

"Don't." Jenna moved past him in a huff.

"Don't what?"

She turned, backing up a step when she realized he was closing in on her. "You know what. You're trying to use sex to get what you want."

"And what is it you think I want?" He kept moving toward her.

"To babysit me while I'm here."

"That's not what I want."

"No? Then why go through the trouble of breaking into my hotel room and scaring the bejeezus out of me?"

"Didn't mean to scare you."

He continued his advance. She kept retreating.

"Well, you did."

"My apologies."

Jenna was forced to stop when her back hit the wall behind her, but Adrian kept on until his booted toes met hers.

"Adrian…"

He could hear her throat working. Could feel the heat radiating from her body. Her breasts brushed against his chest with every heavy breath she took, and his cock pressed so hard against his zipper, the damn thing was probably going to be scarred before the night was over.

Adrian leaned in. He cupped her cheek with his hand. "I don't want to babysit you, gorgeous."

She lowered her gaze to his mouth before finding his eyes once more. "What do you want to do?"

"This."

He brought his lips to hers in a kiss that stole his breath and filled his soul. Beneath him, Jenna hesitated only slightly before responding in a way he'd spent weeks dreaming about.

With both of her hands clutching his bare shoulders, Jenna rose to her tiptoes and pulled herself closer. Her covered breasts pressed against his chest, flooding his mind with memories of making love to her.

No, not *love*. Sex. They'd had hot, sweaty, incredible sex. And he couldn't wait to do it again.

Bending down just enough, Adrian grabbed the backs of Jenna's thighs and hoisted her into his arms. Without pause, she wrapped her petite legs around his waist as they continued feasting hungrily on each other's need.

Walking backward, he carefully moved them to the bed she'd been sitting on. When he felt the back of his knees hit the mattress, he spun them around and carefully lowered Jenna onto the bed.

He followed her down.

"God, I've missed your taste," he growled. Using his lips and teeth and tongue, he ate at her like the starved man he was.

A tiny whimper escaped the back of her throat, but she said nothing. Instead, Adrian felt her warm hands sliding between them as they began working the button on his jeans.

He'd been waiting for this moment. Had lived night and day fantasizing about seeing her again. Feeling her wet heat sucking his hard body dry. But now that he was here, Adrian found himself pulling away.

"What's wrong?" She nibbled his chin. "Do you need a condom?"

"What? No." He frowned. "Why? Do you have one?"

If she did, that meant she'd packed it. If she packed it, that meant she'd planned on having sex.

Given her reaction to seeing him here, Adrian was confident he wasn't even a blip on her radar, which meant she'd thought about having sex with someone *other* than him.

A powerful surge of jealousy rolled through him, followed by a sudden and intense feeling of nausea. The reaction took him off guard.

He'd never been possessive of anyone before, but the idea of Jenna sleeping with another man made him physically sick.

"No, I don't have one." She chuckled but a second later, her smile faltered as she stared at him a little too closely. "Would it be a problem if I did?"

Lie, dickhead. Lie your ass off right fucking now!

"Someone even thinks about touching you, I'll kill them."

So much for lying.

Jenna sucked in a breath. Her green eyes darkened.

Adrian had seen a lot of women drop their panties for big, tough, alpha assholes. He'd never understood it, and frankly, Jenna didn't strike him as the type.

So he shouldn't have been surprised when she began glaring at him and pushing against his chest. Yet, he was.

"Get off of me," she growled.

He blinked. "What?"

"You heard me." She shoved at him again. "I said... get...off!"

Pushing himself from the mattress, Adrian lifted his weight from her and stood. "You gonna tell me what's wrong?"

"This." Jenna motioned toward his face as she scooted herself off the bed. "This is what's wrong."

"My face?"

"The *look* on your face when you thought I'd packed condoms. And threatening to kill anyone who dares to touch me? How dare you!" Daggers flew from her eyes as Jenna poked him in the chest. "Let me tell you something, buddy. I get that you saved my friend's life. And yes, you pulled that jerk off of me when all that shit with Elle went down, but you gave up *any* right to have a say in what or *who* I do the second you snuck out of my bed like a freaking coward."

Jesus. The more pissed off she got, the more turned on *he* got.

"I didn't sneak out," Adrian stated calmly. "I left. There's a difference."

Jenna dropped her hand. "You're unbelievable, you know that?"

"Actually, I think the word you're looking for is 'unforgettable.'"

For fuck's sake, shut the hell up.

"Get out."

Shit. She was serious, and he'd clearly taken things a step too far. Time to retreat and recover.

"I'm sorry, okay?" That's what women wanted to hear when they were mad, right?

A narrowed, suspicious gaze landed on his just before she asked him, "For what, exactly?"

Damn. The question was simple enough. So why did it feel like some sort of test?

"For...upsetting you?"

Jenna's dark brows turned inward. "Are you asking me?"

"No. I mean, that's why you're mad, isn't it?"

"I'm mad because *you* were mad."

"No, I wasn't."

I was jealous. There's a difference.

"Bullshit." Jenna didn't hesitate to call him on his crap. "You were pissed because you thought I might want to sleep with someone else while I'm here. Which, if you and I were actually dating, I could understand. But we're not dating, Adrian. We're not anything. You wanna know why?"

Shoving his hands into his pockets, Adrian casually adjusting his painful erection as he did. "I'm guessing you're about to tell me."

"Damn right, I'll tell you. Drive-by, remember?" She put her hands on her hips again. "You showed up, we had sex, and you left. No note, no 'thanks for the nice fuck'…nothing."

Her choice of words made him flinch. For his entire adult life, when it came to women and sex, fucking was all he knew. But with Jenna, it had been different. It *felt* different.

"You're right," he admitted quietly. "I shouldn't have left without saying goodbye."

For some reason, his comment saddened her. "It was a one-night stand, Adrian. Or one-morning stand. Whatever. It doesn't matter." She waved her hand in the air. "The point is, you can't leave the way you did and then expect me to be celibate the rest of my life. And you sure as hell can't just show up here and expect me to just fall right back into bed with you."

"I told you. I'm here because Gabe and Ellena—"

"Need to mind their own business," Jenna finished the sentence for him. "Look, Adrian…I appreciate the thought, but I'm a big girl, and I've been taking care of myself for a long damn time. So, you're off the hook."

His brows rose. "The hook?"

"You're here out of some sort of misplaced obligation to keep me safe. But you don't owe me anything."

"You think I came because I feel obligated?"

Jenna's eyes softened a tiny bit. "I know you do. And as sweet as it is, I'm doing just fine without you." She glanced at her watch. "Now, if you don't mind, I'm supposed to be meeting some of the other nurses downstairs for dinner."

"You're kicking me out?"

"No." She jutted her adorable chin. "I'm asking you to leave."

CHAPTER 3

Jenna submitted her final chart of the day, and it couldn't come soon enough. To say her first week working at Gulfside Regional Medical Center had been eventful would be a major freaking understatement.

Over the course of the six-day stretch, she'd treated six gunshot wounds, seven stab wounds, a broken arm, broken wrist, and a multitude of other bumps, bruises, and abrasions. And all had resulted from some sort of criminal activity.

It wasn't like she was new to the chaotic rush of a busy emergency room. Jenna kept busy in her ER back home, and she'd seen her fair share of violent crime victims... Just never so many in such a short period of time.

Adding to Jenna's frustrations, her boss had done a complete one-eighty since her heartwarming welcome speech the day she'd first arrived.

At first, Taylore—Saje Staffing's nurse manager—had come off as this sweet woman who cared about her nurses. It didn't take long for Jenna and the others to realize that wasn't always the case.

Taylore *could* be sweet and caring. She could also be a real bitch, which was the nucleus of problem. With the dawn of each new day, Jenna was never sure which Taylore she was going to get. That meant she and the other nurses continually found themselves walking on eggshells while also navigating throughout their shifts.

Gabe and Ellena were right. I never should've come here.

Not that Jenna would ever admit that to either of them. But, hey... at least she'd been too busy to think about Adrian.

After his surprise visit to her hotel room almost a week ago, the chaos of the unfamiliar hospital—and even Taylore's unreliable personality—had been a welcomed distraction.

Deep down, Jenna knew Gabe and Ellena only wanted her to be safe, but for them to go behind her back and ask Adrian to come down here to watch over her had felt like a slap in the face.

Elle was like a sister to her, and Jenna loved Gabe like a brother. But damn it, she was an adult and could take care of herself. Something she'd promptly called and told them both the minute Adrian had left her room that night.

Gabe admitting he should've spoken to her about it, first. But Elle's only response had been an unapologetic reminder that payback was a bitch. It took all of two seconds for Jenna to understand what her friend meant by that.

Back when Elle's life was in danger, Jenna had arranged for Gabe to return to San Diego to help keep her friend safe...without Elle's knowledge. Even though it all worked out in the end, Elle had used this opportunity to return the unwanted favor.

Jenna had tried explaining that the previous situation had been completely different from hers. Someone had actually been trying to *kill* Ellena back then. Not to mention, Gabe had been living states away and needed to get his head out of his ass and reconcile with his wife.

So Jenna had done what any good friend would do. She'd done what was necessary to keep her friend safe and helped get the stubborn couple back together.

Two birds, one stone, and a happy couple later, the two of them should've been *thanking* her. Not conspiring against her.

Not that any of it really mattered now, anyway. Gabe and Ellena understood they needed to respect her independent nature. Jenna understood her friends had meant well by sending Adrian here. And Adrian had left, just like she'd asked him to.

She'd gotten exactly what she wanted, so why did she have a nagging feeling in the pit of her stomach that she'd made a terrible mistake by sending him away?

Brushing it off, and more than ready to have a *day* off, Jenna went to the ER staff locker room to change.

Part of their travel contract included scrubs provided by the hospital. The extra perk was great and saved on her laundry expenses. The only downside was, it meant wearing her regular clothes to and from work.

Finally back in her denim capris, sandals, and a blue, loose-fitting blouse, Jenna grabbed her purse and closed her locker.

"Hey, lady," Marie greeted her as she and another nurse who'd been assigned to a different department walked into the room. "You off or just coming on?"

"Off. You?"

"Same. A few of us were going to check out a club we heard about. It's not too far from the hotel. Wanna come with?"

"Now?"

"Why not?" Maria shrugged. "You got something better to do?"

I would if I hadn't made Adrian leave.

The guy hadn't even put up a fight. She'd told him she didn't need a babysitter, asked him to leave, and he had. Guess the jerk wasn't as into her as he'd lead on.

Can't get mad at him for doing what you asked.

The voice in her head was right, which only angered Jenna that much more. Pushing all thoughts of Adrian aside, she asked her new friend, "Are we even allowed to go to bars?"

There had been so many rules and policies during that first welcome meeting, she couldn't remember them all.

"Technically, no." Maria's rosy lips curled. "But hellooo… we're responsible adults who've more than earned the right to blow off some steam. Besides, what Taylore doesn't know won't hurt her, right?"

Jenna mulled the idea over. Despite not having experienced any trouble in the slightest, Gabe's concerns about the dangers of this area floated around in the back of her mind. So did the risk she knew she was taking by going against the rules.

I bet Adrian would go if he were here.

Gah! Why did every single conversation make her think of him?

Screw it.

Jenna's desire to forget all about Adrian Walker trumping everything else, she smiled back at Marie and said, "I'm in. Although"—she looked down at herself—"I should probably wear something a little more club-ish, though. Don't you think?"

Maria waved a hand toward her own twill pants and white t-shirt. "Girl, you think I'd wear this out dancing? We're all going to back to the hotel to shower and change, first. Besides, that way we'll be telling the truth when we check in with Taylore to say we made it back to the hotel safe and sound."

One of the many rules she'd been informed of *after* she arrived last week.

On the days they worked, the nurses were allowed to go from the hotel, to the hospital, and back to the hotel. Period. They also had to check in with Taylore or one of the other Saje admins when they got back to their rooms every night after their shift ended.

If they needed food, they could order room service or have something delivered. If they needed a necessity of some sort, they were to call Taylore, and she'd arrange for a Saje escort to and from the store.

They also weren't allowed to go *anywhere* on their own during their days off. If they wanted to go sight-seeing or shopping, they had to take a buddy.

Jenna still found it odd that her new boss had never mentioned the nurses who'd gone missing. Taylore had only explained the rules as 'precautionary'.

Either way, Jenna hadn't been kidding when she'd told Adrian—and Ellena and Gabe—that she didn't need someone watching over her.

This was further proven when, two hours later, after arriving at their destination safely, Jenna was sipping on a delicious fruity drink while watching Maria and two other girls dance the night away. They were having a good time and were perfectly safe doing so.

The club they'd found wasn't very big—the entire place was about the same size as her apartment. But it was packed.

"You ready for another one?" The bartender spoke loudly over the thumping music.

"Sure," she offered him a smile.

Sucking up the remainder of her first drink of the night, Jenna turned and sat the empty glass on the bar behind her. She couldn't remember the name of the drink, but whatever the concoction was, it was yummy.

A subtle warmth spread through her veins as the alcohol she'd already consumed took effect. Enjoying the pleasant buzz, Jenna looked back over the crowd. Feeling more relaxed than she had in months, she began swaying her hips back and forth to the beat of the music.

"Here ya go." The bartender sat the filled-to-the-rim glass in front of her.

Feeling generous, Jenna held out a ten and a five. Leaning over the bar so he could hear her, she said, "Keep the change."

"Keep it." The young man smiled but waved her off. "It's already taken care of."

She frowned. "What?"

He pointed to a guy sitting alone at the end of the bar. A dark-haired, olive-skinned guy who looked like he stepped off a freaking Gorgio Armani runway. "My friend thinks you're pretty. Wanted to buy you a drink."

Jenna blinked. "Oh. Um…thanks."

"Don't thank me." He winked and was off to take another customer's order.

Feeling more than a little awkward, she glanced back down at the man who'd bought her a drink, but he was gone.

That's odd.

Jenna pulled the cool, blue liquid into the straw, savoring each drop as it made its way down her throat. She licked her lips, the slightly bitter aftertaste something she hadn't noticed before, but shrugged it off, assuming the bartender had made this one a little stronger than the first.

"Enjoying your drink?"

Startled by the deep, thickly accented voice in her ear, she turned quickly, nearly tipping her drink in the process.

"Oh!" She offered the man who'd bought it a smile. "Yes. Thank you."

Damn. She hadn't even noticed him walk up to her.

Pay attention to your surroundings, gorgeous.

47

Jenna's heart gave a hard thump at the sound of Adrian's voice in her head.

"You're most welcome," the stranger grinned. "I'm Amanté. I couldn't help but notice you're standing here, alone, while your friends are out there." He motioned toward the dance floor.

"Yeah, I'm not really much of a dancer." She wasn't horrible by any means, but the fast-pumping music the DJ had been spinning wasn't really her jam.

"Everyone can dance with the right partner, hermosa." The man held out his hand and waited for her to take it.

Don't trust him.

There it was again and, Christ on a cracker. Even her subconscious was on Adrian's side.

Jenna hesitated a moment, but soon realized she had no valid reason not to dance with the nice man. After all, she was a single woman out with some friends.

Come on, Jen. The whole point of coming here was to forget about Adrian and have a good time.

With her subconscious back on *her* side, where it belonged, Jenna started to set her drink down onto the bar but the mysterious stranger stopped her.

"Bring it with you."

She stared questioningly into his dark eyes.

"You can drink and dance at the same time, no?" He waved his hand to several others who were doing just that.

Whatever, dude.

If he wanted to end up covered in blue coconutty goodness, so be it.

With her free hand in his, Jenna allowed him to lead her through the crowd and onto the dance floor. Taking another long sip, she threw caution to the wind and began moving to the music's fast, even beats.

By their third dance, the only thing left in her glass were ice cubes, and the song had changed to a slow, sexy ballad.

"Allow me." The man took her glass and set it on a nearby table. When he returned, he put his hands on her hips and began moving their bodies side to side. "Better, yes?"

Not really. The familiar song was more her vibe, but for some reason Jenna's movements still felt jerky and awkward.

Because you don't have the right partner.

Adrian's face instantly filled her mind's eye, and Jenna mentally cursed herself for still thinking about him. Seriously, of all the men in the world, *he's* the one she was hung up on?

They'd shared one magical day together. *One.* And he hadn't even bothered to stick around after.

The music's volume hid her loud sigh. For her entire adult life, all Jenna had ever wanted was to be successful with her nursing career and to find a nice guy to settle down with. Adrian Walker was a lot of things, but she wasn't sure nice was one of them.

Jenna stole a glance at the man who was holding her a little too closely. Tall, dark, and model-worthy, Amanté was every woman's dream. He'd also been very nice to her so far. So why didn't she feel the least bit attracted to him?

Maybe nice was overrated.

Or maybe it's because he's not Adrian.

Wanting to scream at her inner self, Jenna attempted to shake her frustration away. Almost immediately, she closed her eyes and waited for the sudden wave of dizziness to subside.

Damn. Those drinks must have been stronger than she'd originally thought.

Deciding she'd better go back to the hotel before she lost all ability to think clearly, Jenna stopped dancing. "I need to call it a night." She smiled politely. "Thanks for the drink and the dancing."

"But the night is so young." He pouted as he reached an arm around her waist and pulled her to him. His obvious erection poked against her lower belly.

Yeah, that's not happening, buddy.

Doing her best not to react, Jenna gently freed herself from his hold once more. "I've been working all day, and I'm really tired."

"Your friends are still having a good time." Amanté tipped his head in Marie's direction. "At least let me drive you to the hotel."

His words gave her pause. Had she told him she was staying in a hotel? No, she was almost positive she hadn't. Maybe he'd just assumed she wasn't a Gulfside Harbor native.

Or maybe he's some creep who's trying to get into your pants.

Jenna blinked slowly, noticing how the music's steady beat had become oddly soothing. Feeling even more light-headed than before, she once again thanked the man—Amanté—and made her way over to Marie and the others.

"I'm heading out."

"Already?" Marie looked at her watch. "It's barely eleven."

"I know, but I'm not feeling very well. I don't think the alcohol is settling right."

Marie chuckled. "Too many drinks, huh?"

"Actually, I only had two, but damn. They must've been strong."

"I'd say so." One of the other women laughed. "You look like you can hardly stand up straight."

Marie chuckled as she linked her arm with Jenna's. "Okay, Lightweight. Let's go."

"No." Jenna slid her arm free. "Stay. You're having too much fun for me to ruin it."

Woah. She'd definitely slurred the last few words of that sentence.

"You know the rule," Marie locked elbows with her again. "No one goes anywhere alone."

Rules, shmules.

Jenna's shoulders shook with a silent giggle, but she immediately cleared her throat...and tried clearing her head.

"Really, I'm good." *Liar.* "There's no sense in you guys ending your night early because of me."

"Fine. How about this?" Marie got on her phone and began typing on her screen. "I'll order us a cab back to the hotel. I'll go with to make sure you get inside okay, and then have the driver bring me back here."

"But...you'll be alone on the ride back."

Marie thought about this for a moment. "I'll Facetime with these two on the way back."

"Are you sure?" It wasn't the greatest of plans, but Jenna didn't have the energy to keep arguing.

"Trust me. You can never underestimate the buddy system in a place like this."

"Fine." Jenna swayed a bit before righting herself. She licked her lips, which felt much fuller than normal. "But I'll pay for the...ride."

"Deal." Marie looked at the other two nurses. "You two stay here and stay together, okay? I'll be back in a flash."

"You got it," one responded while the other nodded.

"Come on."

Following Marie's lead, Jenna stumbled toward the club's entrance. With her head on a swivel, she glanced around the crowd in search of the man she'd been dancing with. She found him back at the end of the bar, and he was staring at her intently.

Welp, he looks pissed.

Just as well. It wasn't like she'd planned to do anything

with him, anyway. There was only one man she wanted...and she'd sent him away.

God, what is it about him?

Hard as she tried—and she'd been trying like hell all week —her mind refused to depart the Adrian train. Her heart was even worse, constantly aching with regret she shouldn't feel.

Jenna didn't understand the pull she felt toward the frustrating man. It wasn't like he was looking for anything more than a quick lay. Hell, the only reason he'd come here at all was because Gabe had asked him to.

"I can't believe you wanted to leave." Marie's low whistle from the passenger side of the back seat was a welcome distraction. "That guy you were dancing with was smokin' hot."

"He was...s'kay, I guess."

Jenna's slurring had gotten drastically worse in the last few minutes. Not only that, her lips and fingertips had begun to feel tingly, and she had to fight the urge to close her eyes.

Why do I feel so sleepy?

"*Okay?*" Marie looked over at her like she was crazy. "Girl, you would've had to peel me off of him if I'd been the one dancing with him. If I wasn't already happily married, that is."

Marie continued talking, some story about her husband who was back home in Missouri with the kids, but Jenna could barely make out what she was saying. Leaning her head against the cool glass of her window, she let her eyelids close and tried to ease the spinning in her head.

"Jenna?" Maire nudged her. "Hey, are you okay?"

"Hmm?" She peeled her eyes open and faced her friend. Marie's concerned face blurred in and out of focus.

"How much did you say drank tonight?"

"Jus...two."

Why couldn't she speak clearly? And why did she

suddenly feel as if she was going to either pass out or throw up?

Something's off. You shouldn't feel this out of it from two drinks.

"Look at me."

She did.

"Shit, Jenna." Marie's brows scrunched closer together. "Your pupils are the size of saucers. Did you take something?"

"Did I...what?"

"Drugs." The other woman cupped Jenna's face to hold her head still. Staring into her eyes with a nurse's assessing glance, Marie spoke more sternly. "I'm asking if you took drugs."

"No." She shook her head vehemently before closing her eyes to stave off another wave of dizziness. "No way."

The other woman let out a low curse. "That's it. You're going to the hospital."

Jenna half-listened as Marie gave their driver instructions to take them to Gulfside Regional instead of the hotel. Panic began to set in.

She'd never done recreational drugs in her life, so the only way something could've gotten into her system would've been if she'd accidentally ingested it. Which made no sense.

All three nurses had eaten the same food from the same restaurant, so it couldn't have been from their dinner. And she'd gotten her drinks straight from the bartender, so it couldn't have been him.

Jenna willed her mind to focus as she thought back to earlier. Through the thick fog, she remembered that she'd ordered the first drink.

My friend thinks you're pretty.

The bartender's words echoed through her ears. At least

that's what she *thought* he'd said. For some reason, it was getting harder and harder to recall the night's events.

Blinking to regain a sense of focus, she went back over the moments just before she'd been given the second drink. The bartender had walked over to the other side of the bar before coming back over to mix it. Which he'd done on the lower section of the bar—out of her line of sight—before handing it to her.

Another alarming thought struck. She'd tried putting the drink down, but the one guy had insisted she bring it with her onto the dance floor.

A gnawing feeling grew in her already churning gut. He wanted her to finish that drink. Had encouraged her while they'd danced to 'drink up'.

There was only one reason she could think of for him to be that interested in her consumption.

Nausea rolled through her from the realization that the attractive man with the nice smile had most likely drugged her.

Oh, god. How could I be so stupid?

On the verge of passing out, Jenna knew she needed to tell Marie her suspicions about the guy, but her tongue felt too thick and heavy to get the words out.

Licking her numbing lips, she was about to try again when the cab's interior became illuminated by a set of blinding beams. They were coming from Marie's side of the cab...and they were getting closer.

"What the..." Marie started to turn toward her window.

A fraction of a second later, Jenna was thrown against her door. Her head hit the window with a hard thud as another vehicle rammed into the side of the cab—right where Marie was sitting.

The car they were in spun, the entire vehicle lifting from

the ground a fraction of a second before landing back down with a thundering jolt.

Holy shit.

Holding the side of her head—because damn, that had hurt—Jenna did her best to bring Marie's slumped figure into focus.

She wasn't moving, and even in her altered state, Jenna could make out the blood running down the other woman's face. The passenger window was broken, the fissures in the glass creating a spiderweb pattern from where Marie's head had likely hit.

Ohmygod!

"Marie?" Jenna fumbled with her seatbelt. "Talk to…me. Are you…okay?"

Crap. If she felt nauseated before, it was nothing to the way she felt now.

Ignoring the incessant pounding in her head, Jenna fumbled to work the buckle holding her in place. Her fingers felt heavy. Numb. But she refused to give up. *Finally*, she heard the blessed click of its release.

With her medical training kicking in, she moved sluggishly across the seat to her friend. Lifting her weighted arm, Jenna pressed her fingertips to the side of Marie's neck.

She found a pulse.

Thank God.

A low, muffled moan reached her ears, and at first, Jenna thought Marie was coming to. It didn't take long for her to realize the sound had actually originated from the man behind the wheel.

Shit. She'd forgotten about the driver.

"Sir?" Jenna tapped on the plexiglass partition separating the front seat from the back. "Are you okay?"

Cursing up a storm in a language she assumed was Spanish, the cab driver ignored the question and got out. When he spotted another man approaching the cab—Jenna assumed he was the driver of the other car—their driver began spewing English curse words.

"Dumbass!" the cab driver yelled. "Don't you know how to fucking drive?"

Jenna looked away, uninterested in watching the two men bicker about who's fault the accident was. She needed to tend to Marie.

You need to call for an ambulance.

Crap. She really was out of it.

Leaning back against the seat, Jenna shoved her hand into her pocket and pulled out her cell phone. She dialed 9-1-1 and did her best to tell the operator what had happened.

Through her blurred vision, she spotted the nearest road sign. Doing her damnedest to enunciate each word clearly, she was relaying the name of the street when a loud pop filled the night air.

Jenna's entire body jerked from the unexpected sound, but when she saw a shower of blood spray from the back of the cab driver's head, she screamed.

"Was that a gunshot?" the operator asked.

Jenna nodded before remembering the woman on the other end of the phone couldn't see her. "Yes. He…"—*Oh, God*— "H-he shot…him."

"I'm having a hard time understanding you. Did you say someone was shot?"

"Yes!" Jenna yelled. "Please…h-hurry!"

"Help is on the way, Miss. Are you in a safe place?"

The man with the gun turned toward her, his cold eyes meeting hers through the cab's window.

"No."

He walked around the front of the car and headed for her door. Jenna's heart thumped hard against her ribs, the dizziness and need to vomit increasing with every beat.

"Coming...for...me." She felt even weaker than before.

Damn it, Jenna. Fight against the drugs. Fight against him!

Blinking the fuzziness away, she looked around the back seat for something—anything—to use as a weapon. She found nothing.

The man opened her car door. He leaned in and reached for her. Jenna screamed as she scrambled clumsily toward Marie.

Not that it would do any good. Marie was still unconscious, and that side of the car was so smashed in, there was no way the door would open. Still, Jenna refused to end up a statistic like those other missing nurses.

Using the massive shot of adrenaline her shock and fear had created, Jenna kicked against the man as hard as she could. He cursed and growled but didn't give up.

Neither will I, asshole.

Unfortunately, she had nowhere to go and no way to escape. She was also starting to fade as whatever drugs were in her system began hitting their peak.

Adrian!

Without conscious effort, Jenna screamed for him in her mind. But she knew he wouldn't come. And for that, she had no one to blame but herself.

A low rumbling sound appeared from somewhere in the distance. It almost sounded like a motor of some sort. Someone coming to their rescue, perhaps?

Knowing she couldn't count on anyone else to save her and her friend, Jenna kicked the asshole again, as hard as she could. Her booted foot hit the jerk square in the nose, the sickening crunch of bone more satisfying than it probably should've been.

"Fucking bitch!"

Murdering bastard!

Blood gushed from the man's broken nose, but that didn't

deter the asshole as much as she'd hoped. Instead, it seemed to motivate him even more.

Despite the fact that he was still holding a gun, the man chose to shove the weapon into his waistband and grab both of her ankles. He yanked her roughly toward him, and Jenna screamed again.

For help.

For Marie to wake up.

For a man who wasn't coming.

The drugs made her thoughts and movements jumbled and uncoordinated as she clawed at the leather seat beneath her. Within seconds, the man had her out of the car and was dragging her toward the back of the cab.

The rumbling she'd heard before grew louder. Closer.

Please let someone come before they take me. Please!

Refusing to give up, Jenna continued fighting. She dug her nails into the man's hand, raking them across his skin as her fingers flailed against him. She screamed until her voice was nearly gone, and when that didn't work, she made her already waning body as limp as possible.

He may win, but I'll be damned if I make it easy for him.

"Stupid bitch." He struggled to bring her to her feet. "Stand. Up!"

"Fuck…you."

Jenna was fading fast. She knew it, and her attacker knew it, too.

With two hands below her armpits, he lifted her up just enough to reach around her waist and haul her over his broad shoulder. Pushing against him, Jenna did what she could to get free, but it was no use.

This man was too strong, and she was way too out of it to even try anymore. Tears fell from her sleepy eyes.

I don't want to disappear.

They were almost to the other car when the distinct roar

of motorcycle engine approached them. Tires squealed, the smell of burning rubber filling Jenna's nostrils as the rider skidded to a halt nearby.

"Let her go!" A man yelled. His growl was deep and animalistic.

The jerk holding her opened fire.

The good Samaritan fired back, and Jenna felt her attacker jerk beneath her as a bullet entered his body somewhere she couldn't see.

Crying out in pain, the man holding her stumbled, his hold on her loosening to the point she began to slide down his arm.

"Forget it!" A third man hollered from behind the wheel of the other car. "We'll get her another time!"

Taking his partner's advice, the guy threw her off his shoulder and ran-limped to the car. Jenna's limp body smacked against the road's unforgiving asphalt, pain radiating throughout her body as she hit.

Firing toward the man who'd come to her rescue, her would-be abductor pulled the trigger on his gun again. Jenna squeezed her eyes shut, refusing to watch another innocent man get murdered.

Once.

Twice.

Over and over again, the bastard shot blindly as he ran, not stopping until he and his getaway driver sped away from the scene.

"Jenna!"

With her eyes still closed, Jenna felt herself being rolled over onto her back. Unable to control her movements, she had no choice but to allow it.

Wait. Did he just call me by my name?

"Jesus. Are you okay?" Her hero's voice shook. "Stay with me, baby. The ambulance is almost here."

Baby?

Jenna's eyes fluttered open and she got her first real look at the man who'd just saved her life. The drugs in her system must be some sort of hallucinogen, because he looked and sounded just like…

Adrian.

She let her lids fall shut, unable to allow herself to keep imagining a man who wasn't here.

"Nope. You've gotta open your eyes, sweetheart," the stranger ordered sharply. "Goddamn it, Jenna. Open your eyes and look at me!"

Peeling her lids apart, Jenna sucked in a breath when she realized…

Oh, shit.

"Real-ly…y-you." She tried reaching for him, but her hand only made it a few inches off the ground before dropping back down toward the ground beside her.

"Yeah, gorgeous." His eyes softened as he caught her falling hand and held it in his. "It's really me."

"Thought you…left."

Sirens that had been blaring in the distance got closer.

Adrian shook his head, giving her hand a gentle squeeze as he leaned in closer and whispered, "Never again."

CHAPTER 4

Adrian sat in the uncomfortable-as-fuck chair, staring at the most beautiful woman he'd ever met. Still sleeping, her long lashes rested on her cheeks as the slow drip of the IV solution pushed the drugs that fucker had given her out of her system.

For the past few hours, he'd replayed the scene over and over in his head.

Seeing her on the dance floor with that smooth-talking prick. Watching her stumble as she and the other nurse left the club.

I should've gone to her, then. Should've let her know I was still here, and I should've been the one to escort her to the hotel.

Instead, he'd been afraid of how Jenna would react if she found out he was still in town. So, he'd kept his distance. Keeping an eye on her—protecting her—but doing it from afar.

Right. Some protector you are.

Adrian spent the night watching from the shadows—like he had every night since she'd thrown his ass out of her hotel room.

Just because she didn't want his protection didn't mean she didn't need it. Tonight was the perfect example.

He'd waited until her cab pulled away to exit the club and jogged down the block to the bike he'd borrowed from a local acquaintance. He'd even taken the road running parallel to the one she was on in order to avoid her or the driver becoming suspicious.

For a minute, he'd convinced himself he was overreacting. That she'd gotten a little too tipsy while hanging out with her friends.

She'd go back to her hotel, he'd make sure she was locked away in her room safe and sound, and that would be that.

But when he was on the bike and saw the car cross the road ahead of him, Adrian had known something was off. The biggest red flag? It had sped up as it headed for the intersection Jenna's cab had been approaching, rather than slowing down.

His suspicions were confirmed seconds later.

Even with a helmet on and the low rumbling of his bike's motor, Adrian had heard the crunch of metal against metal.

I can still hear it.

A nagging feeling in his gut had sent him doubling back around to a side road he'd already passed to try to approach without suspicion. The plan was to come up on the scene as nothing more than a bystander offering to help. In case it was just a stupid accident.

For all he knew, the driver of the car could've been drunk or high, but something had told him that wasn't the case. Unfortunately, he'd been right.

Adrian closed his eyes and hung his head. He could still see the wreckage. Could still *feel* the way his heart had damn near stopped, knowing Jenna was inside the mangled car when it'd been struck.

Then his heart *did* stop when he saw the passenger of the

other car execute the cab driver and then go after the women.

No, not women. Woman.

There was only one person those assholes had been interested in.

Jenna.

Fearing he wouldn't get to her in time, Adrian had pushed his bike to the limit, expertly laying it down and running as fast as his legs would move. Determined to save her from whatever the two men had planned.

He'd never wanted to go for a kill shot more than he had in that moment, but the bastard had been holding onto Jenna in a way that made it too risky. He couldn't risk her. Never her.

So he'd gone for the guy's exposed leg, instead.

If this were a job, he would've called for help for the woman and then gone after the two men. But this wasn't a job. Jenna wasn't a random woman, and he'd almost lost her.

Just like he lost his sister.

Adrian's gaze lifted, sweeping back over his sleeping beauty. She'd passed out at the scene and, other than vomiting on the ambulance ride here, she hadn't regained consciousness since.

That shit worried the hell out of him, but the doctor and nurse assigned to her both assured him it was to be expected. They'd also informed Adrian that Jenna's bloodwork showed a high dose of ketamine, and she had a mild concussion from the wreck.

His eyes fell on the bruise near her left temple. His fists clenched and released as he fought against the murderous rage bubbling just beneath the surface.

It wasn't a coincidence someone slipped her one of the most commonly used date rape drugs right before two men slammed into her cab and attempted to abduct her.

The dead cabbie was proof enough for him.

Leaning forward, he rested his elbows on his thighs. With his fingers linked loosely between his knees, he rubbed his thumbs together as he went back over the night's events for what felt like the millionth time.

The attack had been planned. Calculated. She'd been drugged and followed. And damn near been kidnapped. Given the men's disinterest in the nurse named Marie, Jenna had definitely been targeted.

Question was by whom. And why?

The job seemed professional, even if the players were sloppy. Adrian had no idea why they'd chosen Jenna, but one thing was certain…When he found the fuckers responsible, there was going to be hell to pay.

I'll fucking kill them all.

A soft moan tore him away from his murderous thoughts.

Scooting as close to the bed as he could, Adrian reached over the metal railing and carefully slid his hand beneath hers.

"Jenna?" He waited a beat. "Can you hear me?"

Her brows scrunched together, a soft swishing sound filling the quiet room as her head moved back and forth against the stark white pillow.

"Look at me, Jenna," Adrian ordered softly. "That's it, sweetheart. Let me see those gorgeous green eyes of yours."

He waited and watched as her lashes fluttered against her skin. Her weakened fingers curled around his hand in a barely-there grasp, and a second later, her unfocused gaze was rising to meet his.

"Hey." Her voice was rough with sleep.

For the first time in hours, Adrian felt as if he could breathe again. "Hey, yourself."

As if just realizing his presence was abnormal, Jenna

frowned. Struggling to bring everything into focus, she blinked quickly and took in her surroundings.

"I'm in the hospital?"

She glanced down at the IV in her arm. The rhythm of steady beeps coming from the machines increased as her chest began to rise and fall at a faster rate.

Her eyes grew wide as they searched his for an explanation. "What...?"

"It's okay," he told her softly. "You're safe."

"Safe?" Swallowing against her dry throat, her widened eyes swung back to his. "I don't understand." She licked her dry lips. "What happened?"

"You don't remember?"

Jenna shook her head, the panic in her eyes ripping into a heart he could've sworn he'd never had.

Her loss of memory didn't come as a huge shock to him. Ketamine was known to cause amnesia. One of the main reasons ball-less pricks use it as a date rape drug.

No memory of the crime, no conviction.

Still fighting an unprecedented rage at the thought of what could've happened to her, Adrian somehow managed to keep his hold on Jenna's hand a gentle one.

"Tell me what you *do* remember."

"Working." She slid her hand free in order to push herself up higher in the bed.

"Here. Let me help." He pressed the control on the bed to raise her head. Waiting for her to get situated, he asked, "Better?"

Jenna nodded. With another lick of her lips, she cleared her throat. "I-I was here. Working. I'd just finished my shift..." She trailed off for a moment, her emerald eyes growing wide with worry. "H-how long have I been here?"

"Easy." Adrian patted her covered leg for comfort. "It's only been a few hours."

Bringing her breathing back to a healthy pace, she glanced at the clock on the wall facing the bed. He could see more questions brewing.

"How about we start with the last thing you remember?"

"O-okay." Jenna gave him a jerky nod. She thought for a moment. "I remember being in the nurse's locker room. I was talking to Marie and a couple of the other nurses. They invited me to go out, I think."

Confusion and fear filled her eyes. Running a hand through her mussed hair, Jenna winced when her fingertips found her bruised skin. The fear in her eyes gutted him. "Adrian, what happened to me?"

"You were drugged," he answered bluntly. "At the club you went to with Marie and the others."

Unable to sit still with so much rage still coursing through him, Adrian stood and walked to the foot of the bed. From there, he went on to tell her the rest.

He told her how she and Marie had left the club together. That two men had purposely smashed their car into the side of their cab. And the worst of all, that their driver had been murdered in cold blood before the men tried to *kidnap* her and kill Adrian in the process.

Through it all, Jenna didn't say a word. She just sat there, listening as new tears formed with each new detail he shared.

The longer he spoke, the more Adrian's heart ached to the point of physical pain. At one point, he actually rubbed his chest, hoping it would help. He couldn't understand why it didn't.

You know why, asshole. You're just scared to admit it.

Tears had never bothered him before, but the mere sight of this woman crying made him want to howl like a rabid fucking wolf.

I'll find them all. Every. Last. One. And God help them when I do.

"I can't believe this." Jenna sniffed and swiped at her damp cheeks. "God, that poor driver. Did the police catch the man who killed him? And Marie. Have you seen her? Is she okay?"

She'd been drugged and damn near abducted, and her first thought after learning this was to ask about her injured co-worker. A woman she'd known less than a week.

Damn, she's amazing.

"Marie's going to be fine," Adrian assured her. "She has a concussion, but the doctor said she'll recover fully. She's in a room a few doors down."

He'd already questioned Marie about what happened. She hadn't told him anything he didn't already know, other than how out of it Jenna had been during their time in the cab.

Jesus. She'd been so damn vulnerable. If I hadn't made it to her when I did...

"Thank God." Jenna's soft exhale filled his ears. But then her shoulders fell with worry as she thought of something else. "What about the police? Do they know anything about the men who did this?"

"Cops came by while you were still out. Said they'd come back later to get your statement."

Jenna huffed a frustrated breath. "Won't be much of a statement since I can't remember anything that happened."

Thank fuck for that.

"Shit. Has Taylore been by yet? She's my boss. About five-six, round with short, dark hair."

"Taylore Wood?"

Jenna blinked. "You know my boss's name?"

Oh, he knew all about Ms. Wood. The important parts, anyway.

During the early hours of Jenna's recovery—while she was still unconscious, and he thought he'd go nuts with worry—Adrian had been in desperate need of a distraction.

So, he'd contacted Gabe and told him what had happened.

After reassuring both him and a very worried Ellena that Jenna was going to be okay, he'd asked Gabe to find out all he could about Saje Staffing...and the woman in charge. It took Nathan Carter—Gabe's tech genius teammate—less than ten minutes to email him a virtual file on the company and Taylore Wood.

On paper, Taylore was all that she seemed. A selfless, hard-working nurse whose entire life goal was to help others in need. However, Adrian knew better than most how easy it was to hide one's true colors... and the truth.

"I did a little digging while you napped." He gave Jenna a wink.

Actually, Gabe had enlisted the help of his team. They did the digging, then passed the information on to Adrian via text.

"Please tell me you're kidding."

"Interesting reading, actually." He shoved his hands into his pockets. "I found out quite a bit about your boss."

"You can't just invade people's private lives like that, Adrian. God, this is a nightmare." Jenna closed her eyes, her head falling back against her pillow. "If she finds out..."

"You lost an entire night." Adrian scowled. "You were almost *kidnapped*, and you're worried about losing this shit job?"

"It's not a shit job." She glared back at him. "This hospital is severely understaffed, even with us here to help. The ER has been non-stop since I got here, and with Marie out of commission, they'll need me more than ever. And yes, as selfish as it may seem right now, my professional reputation *is* important to me. It's...it's all I have."

Those last four words broke his heart because, fuck. She actually believed that shit. It was there, in those spellbinding eyes of hers.

Not true, gorgeous. You've got me.

It was Adrian's turn to blink. That line of thinking was damn dangerous. Especially for a guy like him.

Especially for her.

"I'm not like you, Adrian," Jenna continued on. "I can't just pick up and leave everything behind without any regard to anything or anyone else."

"Yet here you are."

It was an asshole thing to say, but he needed her to see what she was doing. He needed the spirited, ballsy woman he knew and lo—

Adrian sucked in a silent breath. Nope, he was not going there.

Not. Fucking. Doing. It.

It was one thing to like this woman. To want to spend time with her and get to know her better. But the path he'd just about let himself go down... Guys like him weren't welcome on it.

You sure about that?

Jenna opened her pretty mouth but almost immediately closed it. He watched as the delicate muscles in her jaw worked as she thought about what to say. "Why are you here? Why did you come back to Gulfside Harbor?"

Confession time. "I never left."

New wrinkles formed on her forehead. "What do you mean you never left?"

"Just what I said." Adrian slid his hands into his pockets. "I was going to leave after you kicked me out of your room last week, but I decided to stick around for a while."

He kept his gaze laser focused on her. Knew the exact moment it clicked for her.

"Ohmygod." She put a hand to her mouth. "You've been watching me this whole time, haven't you?"

The trepidation in her eyes bothered him. A. Lot.

"Yes."

"Why?" Jenna's voice rose, an appalled expression washing over her. "Is Gabe paying you to watch over me or something?"

"No, he's not fucking paying me."

Christ, is that what she thought? That *money* was his reason for being here?

What the hell else would *she think, dumbass? Not like you've shown her you actually give a damn.*

"If you're not being paid, then why are you still here?"

Adrian stared back at her but remained silent. He didn't have a quippy comeback. Wasn't trying to smooth-talk her into submission like he normally would. Mainly because he had no idea what to say.

He'd steered clear of this very thing his entire adult life, and for good reason. Getting close to someone…allowing himself to care…Those were life luxuries Adrian could never afford.

It was always too damn risky. His job—his life—was too dangerous. Yet here he was, at a fork in the same damn road he'd done everything he could to avoid. And now that he was here, Adrian was confused as fuck with no clue what he should do.

Tell her the truth or lie?

It would be *so* easy to lie. To convince her that there was some other reason for his being here. Something other than the fact that his days were filled with thoughts of her, and his nights were consumed with memories of the incredible afternoon they'd shared.

But he didn't want to lie. Not anymore. Not to *her*.

Fuck it.

Before he could talk himself out of it, Adrian went to Jenna. He raised a palm to one of her silken cheeks, and he whispered, "I stayed because I was worried about you."

The greens in her eyes darkened. Her lips parted, and she whispered his name. "Adrian?"

He started to lean in. To taste his new favorite flavor in the whole world. He wanted to hold her in his arms, and he needed to—

Jenna's doctor chose that moment to barge into the room. "I thought I heard voices coming from in here."

Sonofabitch.

Despite their unwanted guest, neither Adrian nor Jenna pulled away immediately. Instead, they kept their gazes locked with one another's. Her staring deep into the depths of his soul. Him wishing like hell he knew what she was thinking.

The man behind him cleared his throat. "I'm Dr. Evans. How are you feeling, Ms. Shaw?"

"Okay." Jenna broke eye contact to look at the doctor. "Considering."

Mid-fifties, the balding doctor offered her a warm smile. "You're a very lucky lady. I assume your fiancé explained what happened?"

Stunned by the man's comment, Jenna's round gaze shot back to his. Removing his hand and standing tall, Adrian simply shrugged it off with a look that said *just go with it.*

"Uh…y-yes," Jenna returned her focus to the doctor. "He said I was drugged."

"Ketamine." The doctor confirmed. "Good for some things, but when used improperly, it can be very dangerous. Unfortunately, we're seeing more and more instances like yours every year."

After sliding a sideways glance in Adrian's direction, Dr. Evans made his way to the opposite side of the bed.

Smart move, Doc.

Pressing a button on the control panel there, he lifted the top half of the bed even more. Removing his stethoscope from his neck, he said, "Let's see how things sound, shall we? Can you lean forward a little more for me?"

Without asking if she needed the help, Adrian slid a hand behind Jenna's back. Ignoring the electric pulse radiating from her warm, bare skin where her gown had become separated, he kept her steady while she moved.

"Thanks," she mumbled softly.

After five minutes of poking and prodding, followed by another five minutes of questions and instructions, Dr. Evans told them Jenna could go home.

"I'll have the nurse print off your discharge papers." The older man made his way to the door. "It shouldn't be long."

Adrian tipped his head. "Thanks, Doc."

"Take care of yourself, Miss Shaw. And be careful going out in the city at night. Especially if your fiancé isn't with you." He added quickly, "That's not a sexist remark. Just thirty-two years of experience living and working here."

With that, the other man waved his hand and left. Jenna looked up at him, an auburn brow arched high.

"Fiancé?"

"It was the only way they'd let me—"

The door opened again.

For the love of...

"Taylore," Jenna greeted her temporary boss. "I wasn't sure if you'd come by."

"Two of my nurses were in an accident while leaving a night club after one of whom—*you*—was slipped a roofie. Of course, I'm going to come by."

"That's kind of you, but I'm fine. Really. And Adrian said Marie's going to be okay, too."

"I didn't come by to check on you, Jenna." Taylore jutted her chubby chin. "I'm here to inform you that your services with us are no longer needed."

"You're *firing* me?" Jenna's voice rose an octave. "On what grounds?"

"You knowingly went against company policy. It very clearly states there is to be no alcohol consumption during your three weeks with us."

"No, it doesn't," Jenna spoke with confidence. "It says we're not supposed to drink while we're *working*. We were off the clock."

Taylore's thin lips curled into a spiteful smirk. "Even so, you four ladies failed to inform me that you were leaving the hotel. A clear violation of the rules. And as you know, a breach of contract is grounds for termination."

"You've got to be kidding me." Jenna's face twisted with a disbelieving scowl. "You've seen how busy this place is. Patients were literally lying on beds in the hallways this week because the staff couldn't keep up."

As if she hadn't spoken a word, Taylore—the bitch—said, "Effective immediately, you are no longer employed by Saje Staffing. I suggest you pack your bags and head back to California."

She started for the door, but Adrian waited until she was reaching for the handle to make his move.

"I'm curious," he began. "What's Saje's policy about hiring convicted felons?"

The hateful woman turned back to him. "Excuse me?"

"You seem well-versed in your company's dos and don'ts. I'm assuming your knowledge of its hiring polices is just as extensive."

"Adrian, what are you—"

Taylore cut Jenna's question off short. "And you are…"

Someone you don't want to mess with, lady.

"Name's Walker." He glanced at the woman lying on the bed, the corner of his mouth twitching with a slight grin. "Jenna's fiancé."

The smile tugging at Jenna's lips sent his heart racing and his dick twitching.

"Well, Mr. Walker. To answer your question, yes. It is my job to be familiar with *all* Saje Staffing employee policies."

"Glad to hear it." Adrian turned back to her, the woman's annoying voice and condescending tone instantly dousing every drop of arousal he'd just been feeling. "Then you know about the fraudulent information clause."

"The what?"

"You know, the one stating that any Saje employee found to have falsified any portion of their application and/or verification paperwork will be terminated immediately."

Taylore frowned, the wrinkles on her forehead deepening with the move. "Of course, but that clause has absolutely nothing to do with Jenna's situation."

"Sure doesn't. However, it *does* have something to do with you." He took a step toward the troll.

"Me?" She gasped. "What on earth are you—"

"I did a little light reading while my fiancée was still unconscious." Damn, he liked the sound of that. *Fucking sue me.* "I discovered quite a few things about you." To Jenna, Adrian asked, "Did you know Taylore's uncle works for Saje?"

Jenna shook her head back and forth.

"Well, he does." Adrian offered Taylore a sugary-sweet smile. "In fact, he's the man in charge of running all employee background checks. At first, I thought it was just a coincidence, but then I came across this." He pulled his phone from his pocket and swiped at the screen a couple of times before holding the phone up for Taylore to see. "I believe that's you."

Adrian watched with satisfaction as a slack jawed Taylore stared back at her own mugshot.

All the color drained from the woman's face. "H-how

did...w-where did you..." She was so shocked she couldn't even formulate a whole sentence.

Damn, this is fun.

"Five years ago, before you started working for Saje, you and your sister spent an evening out on the town. I believe the police report said you'd been celebrating a friend's birthday? That's not really important." He waved it away casually. "The point is, you had a few too many drinks that night but decided to drive home, anyway. That was your first DUI. Your second came six months later, costing you a pretty hefty fine and a handful of days in jail. And your third, well, that one cost you your nursing license."

"You lied about being a nurse?" Jenna spoke up from her place in the bed.

"Just because I don't have a piece of paper behind my name doesn't mean I'm no longer a nurse."

Jenna looked at the other woman as if she'd lost her damn mind. "Um...actually, that's exactly what it means. I can't believe you had the nerve to come in here and lecture me about policies after what you've done. Getting your uncle to cover up your arrest record and then posing as a licensed medical professional?"

"The only thing I've done is help hospital patients get the care and treatment they deserve."

Jenna snorted. "Because you can't give it to them yourself."

Taylore narrowed her gaze at Jenna then immediately swung her attention back to him. "So, what is this? Are you trying to blackmail me into giving Jenna her job back?"

"Actually, I don't I want my job back." Jenna spoke up from the bed. "I'd rather just go home and forget I ever agreed to work for someone like you."

That's my girl.

"You are right about one thing, though," Adrian told Taylore. "I am blackmailing you."

"For what?" She appeared thoroughly confused. "If you think I'm going to pay you to keep quiet, you're sorely mistaken."

He threw his head back and laughed. "Trust me, lady. I've seen your financials. Trying to squeeze money outta you would be like trying to get gold from a turd."

Taylore's round cheeks blazed with embarrassment. "Then what is it you want?"

"I want you to pull in every member of the staff you still have here—today—explain to them why they need to be so careful when they're out in this city."

"I already told them—"

"You didn't tell us anything," Jenna chimed in again. "You went over the rules with us, but you never *once* mentioned anything about the two nurses who went missing less than two weeks before we arrived here. Nurses who worked for *you*. Instead, you swept it all under the rug. Just like the fact that you're not actually a nurse anymore."

Adrian was relieved to see Jenna's fire return. Taylore, on the other hand, was getting more nervous by the minute.

She licked her lips nervously as she tried weaseling her way out of the situation. "If word gets out about those nurses, the media will pick it up. Saje will most likely go out of business, and all those good nurses and other staff members will be left without jobs. Do you really want to be responsible for taking away a steady paycheck from those people, Jenna?"

"Oh, cut the crap, lady." Adrian crossed his arms at his chest. "I've seen you around. How you treat everyone here. You don't give a shit about your staff. All you care about is keeping up appearances. That and making sure your dirty little secret stays hidden."

"That's not true."

"But you're right about the media." He ignored her denial and continued on. "If they catch wind about what happened to those two women...and Jenna and Marie...they'll dig into your company until they find something juicy to report. Something like, say, a boss with a felony record who lied to get the job and the uncle who helped cover it up. Can't really blame them." Adrian shrugged. "It's what they do."

"Please," Taylore begged. "There has to be something we can work out."

Got ya.

"Jenna gets to resign with absolutely no ramification from you or Saje Staffing. As of this second, her contract with you is null and void, and Saje Staffing cannot come after her in any way."

"Fine," the begrudging woman agreed. "Whatever."

"That's not all." Adrian kept going. "Jenna will also get a glowing letter of recommendation written by you. It will be certified and mailed to her home address. Anyone ever calls you for a reference, you'll tell them what an outstanding nurse Jenna is. Period."

Having been watching over her this past week, he'd seen Jenna in action enough times to know she was an incredible nurse. Adrian had loved how focused and dedicated she was. To both her patients and the job in general.

"Is that all?" Taylore asked, chomping at the bit to leave.

"No." Adrian shook his head curtly. With a sliding glance in Jenna's direction, he told Taylore, "Be nicer to your staff. And be consistent. No more of this Jekyll and Hyde bullshit."

Jenna's tiny cough left his lips twitching.

"Fine." Taylore exhaled loudly. Straightening her spine, she looked at Jenna and nodded. "I'll type up the letter of recommendation and have it in the mail today. Now, if you'll excuse me, I have a staff meeting to arrange."

And with that, the pathetic woman left the room.

"I can't believe you just did that." Jenna stared up at him.

"It needed to be done." He slowly sauntered back over to where she lay, his eyes remaining locked with hers the entire time. When he made it to the head of the bed, he leaned down, caging her in with a hand on each side of her head and whispered, "So does this."

"What are y—"

Pressing his mouth to hers, the kiss he gave Jenna was soft and deep. His selfish need to feel her again...to taste her and remind himself that she really was okay...taking precedence over anything and everything else.

And *hallafreakinglueah,* she actually kissed him back.

CHAPTER 5

Jenna swiped her palm across the bathroom mirror, watching as tiny droplets of condensation fell.

Her gaze lifted to the sad, green eyes staring back at her. Studying her reflection, Jenna took a good, long look at herself for the first time in a while.

She didn't like what she saw.

"What are you doing?" she whispered. Desperately wishing the woman in the mirror would tell her.

Because she had no freaking idea, anymore.

Jenna *thought* she did. Thought she was happy with her life. Thought her friends had been wrong to worry. And being her usual, stubborn self, she'd been convinced that coming here was the absolute *right* choice.

You couldn't have been more wrong.

The change of scenery was supposed to give her a chance to reset. To mix things up a bit while also evaluating what she really wanted from life. Instead, she'd walked into a nightmare...and right back into Adrian Walker's arms.

He was still out there, waiting for her on the other side of the bathroom door. So, she was in *here*, hiding like the coward she was.

Jenna glanced at her reflection once more. Again, she wondered…

What. Are. You. Doing?

She was no closer to finding the answer to that question than she was ten seconds ago. Nor was she any closer to discovering who the *real* Adrian Walker was.

You know.

Did she? Jenna wasn't so sure. She wasn't sure of anything, anymore.

Her phone—the phone she still had because Adrian had thought to grab it and her purse from the back of the cab before heading to the hospital—began to ring.

Glancing at the screen, she saw Elle's name. Her gut tightened. Did she know what happened to her? Had Adrian snitched to Gabe?

Only one way to find out.

Jenna picked up the phone and answered it. "Hey."

"Hey yourself. How's it going?"

She sounded cheery. Cheery was good.

"Good." Jenna lied. "I'm good. What about you?"

"I'm going crazy. Certifiable, actually. And I'm a psychologist, so I know what that looks like."

Jenna chuckled. "Gabe driving you nuts?"

"You have *no* idea. We've still been trying to agree on the color for the nursery. I was good with the last attempt, but now he's changed *his* mind. Instead of pink, he wants to do the room in camouflage with pink accents. Can you believe that?"

Yes. She could absolutely believe that.

"Between that and him hovering over me like a badass papa bear… Jenna, I swear, I love that man to pieces, but if he doesn't stop treating me like I'm spun from glass, I'm going to have to take the big guy out."

Elle obviously didn't know anything about what happened. If she did, she wouldn't be talking paint colors or bitching about the husband she loved more than life itself.

"Enough about me." Her friend's smile reached her through the phone. "I want to hear about *you*. How's the job? This is your day off, isn't it? I thought that's what I had written down."

"Yep, I'm off today." *Not a total lie.* "And the job's...fine."

Okay, that *was* a lie. One Jenna felt bad about. But she didn't want to get into that whole sordid mess. If she told Elle she'd been fired, she'd have to explain why.

And that was the exact conversation she was trying to avoid.

"You, uh...hear anything from Adrian?" Elle tried—and failed—to sound casual.

Ah...the real reason for this little chat.

"He's with me right now, in fact. Well, I'm in the bathroom. He's waiting for me. We're actually about to have dinner."

Jenna smirked. *Let's see what she thinks about that.*

"He's there? I mean...I-I thought you told him to leave town?"

"I did. He didn't listen." Shocker. "But something tells me you already knew that."

The pause that followed was priceless.

"Okay, fine." Elle broke like Jenna knew she would. "Gabe told me Adrian was sticking around town." There was another pause and then, "Are you mad at me?"

"No." Jenna lowered the toilet seat lid and plopped down with a sigh. "I know Gabe sent him out of love."

"He does love you," her friend stated sincerely. "So do I."

"I know. I love you guys, too."

"So…dinner, huh?"

"What?"

"You said you and Adrian were about to have dinner."

Jenna knew that tone. "It's not like that."

Really? Because that kiss he gave you earlier suggests otherwise.

Question was, did she even want to risk letting her guard down with him a second time?

That's the problem. I don't know.

"So what *is* it like?" Elle's prodding voice tore through her inner thoughts.

Shit. What should she say? That Adrian brought her here from the hospital after he gunned down a guy while saving her life mere hours ago?

No, she wouldn't—*couldn't*—tell her everything. It would only upset her, and Elle needed to stay calm for the baby.

Plus, Jenna would never hear the end of how right she and Gabe were about her not coming here.

She did have to give her *something*, though…

"I was in an accident."

Truth.

"*What?*"

"I'm fine," Jenna rushed to assure her friend. "It was no big deal. Some guy ran a stop sign and hit the cab I was riding in. Adrian was nearby, so he gave me a ride here."

Only a partial lie, that time.

"Jesus, Jen." Concern mixed with the relief in Elle's voice. "I'm so glad you're okay. And thank goodness Adrian was there!"

"Yeah." Jenna nodded. "I was pretty lucky."

Elle waited a beat and then, "So…you're not mad at him, anymore?"

"Honestly?" She blew out a breath. "I don't know what I am."

Another truth.

"Adrian's just there to keep you safe until you go back home, Jen."

Is that really all he's doing?

Jenna glanced at the closed door. She thought about the man on the other side. "His wanting to keep me safe isn't the issue."

"Then what is?" Elle pushed. "Wait, is he being a jerk to you? Because Gabe and I are more than happy to come down there and—"

"He's not being a jerk." Jenna blew out a breath. "He's actually been pretty...sweet."

"Oh. So what's the problem? He too handsome for you? Too built? Too—"

"The man's spent his entire life pretending to be someone else, Elle," she cut her friend off. "Hell, half the world probably still thinks he's a traitor."

For years, Adrian had lived with one goal in mind. Making people think he was a dangerous killer.

He is a killer.

It was the one truth Jenna *did* know. And God help her, she still wanted him

The potent attraction she felt toward the man was what had her so uncharacteristically flustered. Mainly because it made absolutely no sense.

"He's not even my type."

"Because your type is boring."

Jenna scowled. "It is not. And sketchy past aside"—she continued—"Adrian's one of the cockiest, most arrogant men I've ever met. He's even more stubborn than I am, Elle. And you know that's saying a lot."

"Yeah, it is." Elle chuckled. "Cocky, huh?"

"Please. You've spent more time with him than I have. You know how he is."

The second the words were out, Jenna wanted to take

them back. Elle *had* spent some quality time with Adrian—while the two of them were being held captive by the man wanting Elle dead.

Not a time either one of them wanted to remember.

Jenna quickly moved on. "Besides. The one and only time Adrian and I did sleep together, he totally ghosted me. The jerk probably wouldn't know a real relationship if it smacked him in his gorgeous face."

He may be an unsung hero, but Adrian Walker was definitely *not* the kind of man Jenna wanted to get involved with.

He. Was. Not.

Except...

He'd risked his life to save her from those men. Would a heartless bastard who didn't give a crap about anyone else do something like that?

You know the answer to that one.

"So you admit the guy's gorgeous."

Jenna huffed a breath. "That's it. I'm hanging up now..."

"Wait!" Elle stopped her from ending the call. "Promise you're really okay? After the accident, I mean?"

"Yeah, Elle. I'm fine." Physically, anyway.

"Good. Now go have your non-romantic dinner with the gorgeous, cocky man in your hotel room. And...don't do anything I wouldn't do." Ellena quickly added, "With my husband, I mean. Not Adrian."

Jenna laughed. "Bye, sweetie."

"Bye, Jen. Love you."

"Love you, too."

For the next few minutes, Jenna sat on the closed toilet collecting her thoughts. Or trying to, at least.

Instead of focusing on Adrian, she put her energy into trying to remember what happened before the wreck. But the ketamine seemed to have permanently erased those several minutes from her memory forever.

Now all she had to go on was what Adrian had told her… and the detectives who had come by her hospital room earlier.

After Taylore had left—in a huge-ass hurry that still made Jenna want to smile—two Gulfside Harbor cops had shown up.

Apparently, Adrian knew some GHPD bigwig—because of course, the man had powerful friends. Why wouldn't he? He'd used that connection to get the cops in charge of the case to hang around and get their statement once the drugs were out of her system.

When Adrian finally allowed the two detectives to enter her room, Jenna sat in her hospital bed, listening to every incredible word pouring off his tongue.

First, Adrian dropped Gabe's name, which didn't impress either detective. But then he mentioned R.I.S.C., and the men's ears immediately perked up. Not that she could blame them. She'd witnessed first-hand how badass the black ops security company was.

Adrian told the two detectives that he'd come to Gulfside Harbor to protect her. That he'd watched over her from the shadows this past week. How he'd seen her dancing with some guy they suspected slipped the drugs into her drink, and how he'd left the bar when she did and followed her cab on a motorcycle.

Jenna had no idea where the bike even was at this point. Just that, according to Adrian, it had been 'taken care of'.

The most shocking part wasn't when he'd admitted to the cops that he'd *shot* the man who'd murdered the cab driver in order to prevent her from being kidnapped. Adrian had already told her those details. What had thrown her off balance was the *way* he'd said it this time.

I knew if the bastard got her in that car I'd never see her again. So I shot him.

So confident. So unapologetic. So…alpha protector.

Jenna wasn't sure how she felt about that.

Yes, you are. The guy turns you on with a wink and a smile. And if he hadn't shot that man, who knows what would've happened to you.

The voice in her head was right…about that last part, anyway. Adrian had saved her from…God, she didn't even want to *think* about the horrors that awaited her had the man actually gotten her inside that car.

So, no. She shouldn't be mad that he'd stayed. Or that he'd purposely shot someone. Especially since he'd done both in order to keep her safe.

She should be grateful. Grateful, appreciative, and all the other words that described the way a woman felt toward a man who'd saved her life.

But she should not—should *not*—want to strip him naked and jump his bones every time she looked into his gray-blue eyes.

Except…I do.

A knock on the door made her jump.

"Jenna?" His deep, sexy as sin voice reverberated through the barrier. "You okay?"

"I'm fi—" Her voice cracked like a pubescent teenager's. Clearing her throat, she tried again. "I'm fine."

There was a slight pause and then, "I ordered some food. It should be here soon."

Her first thought was *how sweet*. Then she rolled her eyes at herself. Of course, he ordered food. The guy was probably starving.

"Okay." The word came out steady, thank goodness. "I'll be out in a minute."

A slight sound reached her ears, almost as if he'd placed his hand on the other side of the door. Her heart thumped hard inside her chest, and for a moment, she thought he might say something more.

For some reason, she felt disappointed when he didn't.

Gah! She'd never felt more confused—or turned on—by a man in her life!

Angered by the jumbled concoction of emotions rolling through her, Jenna grabbed the hotel's hairdryer and flipped the switch.

Normally, she let her hair air dry. But it was thick and long, which meant doing it this way would buy her more time.

Despite her efforts to think of anything *but* Adrian, her mind continually travelled back to him.

She thought of his handsome face and tortured eyes. His tall, powerful body and the way he'd hovered over her protectively since she'd woken up in the hospital.

And it hadn't ended there.

In the cab to the hotel he'd been staying at just down the street, through the lobby, and during the elevator ride up to his room, while he threw his stuff together, and during the cab ride back here, to *her* hotel…

That entire time, Adrian had stuck to her like glue.

She couldn't help but notice the way he was always on constant alert, too. Like he was ready to put himself between her and anything—or anyone—he perceived as a threat.

With all of that, Jenna could no longer deny the fact that Adrian Walker was the complete opposite of any other man she'd ever dated.

The men from her past—which was a very short list—had all been perfectly nice. They'd been smart, attractive, held steady jobs… Everything Jenna *thought* she wanted.

But Elle was right. They were also boring as hell.

Adrian, on the other hand, was well above average in both

the looks and intelligence departments. He was also rough and rugged. Mysterious and powerful.

Not to mention really, *really* good in bed.

And despite his deadly resume, he made her feel safe.

As if that weren't enough, there was the kiss... *God*, when he'd kissed her earlier today, it felt as if it were his sole purpose for living.

Jenna lifted a fingertip to her mouth and traced her bottom lip. She swore she could still feel the singeing heat of his mouth on hers. But what continued to rattle her was what he'd said right before the soul-reaching kiss.

I stayed because I was worried about you.

For the past two hours, those words had been playing over and over in her head. He'd seemed so serious when he'd said them.

Because he'd been telling the truth.

And there it was. The realization hit her like a grand epiphany.

Adrian hadn't used her for a few rounds of great sex. Or maybe, he had. The jury was still out on that one. But suddenly, that didn't matter. What *did* matter, what she'd finally come to realize—while sitting on a toilet in nothing but her robe—was that Adrian Walker, man of mystery, murder, and intrigue, cared about her.

Now she had to figure out what she was going to *do* about it.

You know what you want to do. So what's stopping you?

Jenna turned off the hairdryer and slid it back into its cradle. Using her brush, she tamed the thick locks until they were shiny and smooth.

Her body slightly trembled, but she drew in a deep breath and forced herself to meet her own gaze one final time.

The corners of her lips—just the corners—curved upward into the slightest of smiles.

The eyes reflecting back at her were no longer confused or angry. Instead, they shone bright with acceptance and conviction.

It's now or never.

With one final breath, she opened the door and stepped into a room crowded with carts filled overflowing with food.

Adrian stood near the bed, his eyes widening before skimming over her body as he took her all in. A short second later, their grays darkened as a look of smoldering heat swept across his face.

"You hungry?" He lifted his stare back up to meet hers.

There was a roughness to his voice. One that made her body ache with need.

Jenna nodded. "Yes."

Just not for food.

Adrian cleared his throat. "I, uh…I wasn't sure what you liked, so I ordered—"

"Everything on the menu?" she teased, hoping it might ease the tension coiling inside her.

"Not quite." He briefly smirked. "I know it's a lot but eat whatever looks good."

Was that a subtle innuendo? Jenna wasn't sure, but she hoped so. She had plans for the complicated man. Big, big plans.

But first…

"Why didn't you kill that man?"

His dark brows turned inward. "What?"

"The man who murdered the cab driver." She took a step toward him. "The one who almost kidnapped me. You said you shot him. I'm asking why you didn't *kill* him."

Adrian's cobalt eyes searched hers. "I didn't have a clear kill shot."

"You're a government trained hitman—"

"Former hitman." He cut her off. "What's your point?"

Jenna advanced on him until her bare toes were inches away from the tips of his boots.

"My point is you could've easily taken that man out and the driver. But you didn't. I want to know why."

Just say it.

But Adrian didn't *say* anything. He remained silent and stoic, his gaze appearing even more tormented than normal. It was as if there was a war brewing inside him, and he was trying to choose which side to fight for.

Choose me.

His throat worked and his jaw tightened. Slowly, he lifted his strong, callused palm to her cheek.

"I was afraid my bullet would hit you." Adrian's thumb gently caressed her skin as he spoke.

Jenna hid the hitch in her breath. "It wouldn't have."

"I couldn't risk it." He leaned in closer. "I couldn't risk *you.*"

A stretch of silence passed before Jenna whispered, "I shouldn't want you."

"No." He swallowed hard. "You shouldn't."

"I'm a nurse. I took a vow to save lives, and you're a—"

Adrian's entire body stiffened, the heat in his eyes cooling instantly. "A what?"

"A killer."

There. She'd said it out loud.

"Yes." His voice was flat, now. "I am."

He started to drop his hand and step away, but Jenna grabbed his thick wrist and held it there. "If I hadn't been in the way, you would've killed that man trying to take me."

"Yes." His chest began rising and falling at a more rapid pace.

She knew what he was thinking, but he was wrong. So, so wrong.

"Why would you do that?" Jenna searched his eyes for the truth. "Why do you even care about what happens to me?"

His lips parted. "Because."

"Because?" She snorted. "I deserve more of an answer than that."

A muscle in his jaw twitched. "What do you want from me, Jenna?"

"I want to know why." *Come on, big guy. Just. Say. It.* "Tell me why it matters to you, Adrian."

"Because, damn it!"

"Because why?"

His nostrils flared, and when he finally *did* say it, his words sounded like they were being torn free from somewhere deep inside.

"Because I care!" Adrian bellowed, his words echoing off the room's thin walls. He blinked, clearly surprised by his own admission, but then, "It matters because *you* matter. And I didn't want to lose you like I lost…" He cut himself short. Brought his other hand up to frame her face. He leaned in, his lips brushing against hers as he whispered, "It matters because…I fucking *care.*"

He lost someone. Someone very important to him.

Her heart ached for him. Jenna wanted to ask who it was he'd lost but decided to hold off. For now.

In the meantime…

She smiled. Feeling triumphant, she rose onto her tiptoes, her mouth nearly touching his. "Good. Because I care about you, too, Adrian."

She was going to kiss him. Had *planned* to kiss him. But it was too late.

He was already kissing her.

CHAPTER 6

I shouldn't want you.

Jenna was spot fucking on when she'd said those words. Of course, he'd known that shit from the start.

She *shouldn't* want a man like him. She should be with someone who was safe. Trustworthy. A banker or a doctor. An accountant, maybe.

Someone whose life didn't revolve around death and deceit.

But by some miracle, she'd chosen him. And God help her, he was too weak to walk away a second time.

Adrian did, however, find the strength to tear his lips from hers long enough to look her in the eye. He needed to be very clear when he told her this next part. Needed to make *sure* she understood what she was signing up for.

"You were right." He pulled in a ragged breath.

"About what?"

"You shouldn't want me."

Jenna started to shake her head. The argument was already there, brewing behind her determined gaze.

Make it clear, shithead. Tell her the truth and let her decide.

"I've done things." He clenched his jaw. "Terrifying things that would send you running in the opposite direction."

Her auburn brows fell inward. "Why are you telling me this now?"

"Because I'm not a good man, Jenna." He swallowed hard. "Not the kind of man you deserve."

The lines on her forehead smoothed as a look of understanding crossed over her. "Is that why you left after our first time together? Because you think I deserve someone better?"

I know you do.

"I thought if I could have you that one time I'd be able to forget you. I thought..." Adrian pulled her flush against his chest, holding her so tightly, his fingers dug into her back. "I thought these flames burning me up inside would go away, and I could move on but..."

"But what?"

He stared deep into her emerald eyes and shook his head. "The fire grew."

"Adrian..."

She needs to know.

"You shouldn't want me," he reiterated the point. "You should go back to California. Stay as far away from me as you can."

Her eyes softened and...was she smiling?

She's not listening.

"I'm giving you an out, Jenna."

"Funny." The corners of her lips definitely curved. "I don't recall asking for one."

"I'm serious." His voice came out rough. "You said it yourself...I'm a killer."

"I know."

Why isn't she listening?

"I'll kill anyone who even thinks about hurting you and not lose a wink of sleep."

His declaration didn't send her running. She didn't flinch or tear herself from his arms. Instead, she seemed to hold him closer.

Didn't she hear what I just said? Can't she see the darkness living inside me?

"I've walked away from you once before." He laid it all out there. "I don't think I can do it again."

"Good." She cupped one side of his face. "I don't want you to walk away. And, whether you want to believe it or not, I know exactly what kind of man you are."

"No, you—"

"You're the kind of man who gave up the life he knew for his country. You risked yourself to save my friend." She rose up, her lips a hair's breadth away from his. "You risked your life for me."

I'd risk everything for you.

"Jenna—"

"*That's* the kind of man I want to be with. That's the kind of man I can see myself falling for."

His heart punched his ribs like a prize fighter. "Be sure, baby. You need to be sure."

Because he was pretty sure he'd already fallen.

"I *am* sure, Adrian." Her lips whispered across his as she spoke. "I want you." A simple kiss. "I want all of you."

And just like that, his control snapped.

Adrian slammed his mouth against hers in a kiss that ignited his soul. He tasted and took, and when she opened for him, he wasted no time feasting on what was his.

Mine!

Jenna melted in his arms. A tiny moan escaped her throat, and like the greedy bastard he was, he swallowed it whole.

Releasing a guttural sound of his own, Adrian reached between them, releasing the tie on her silky robe. He reached up, gently pushing the material off her delicate shoulders and letting it fall.

A second later, the garment was lying in a pool of satin by her feet, and she was standing before him, completely naked.

Fuck. Me.

He sucked in a breath and stared. Yes, he'd already seen her without her clothes, but that night had been a whirlwind of hard, fast, primal sex.

Tonight, he wanted to take things slow. He needed to savor every second he had with this amazing woman and relish in the fact that—though he'll never understand why—she'd chosen him.

Adrian took a moment to let his gaze fall over every visible inch of her. "Jesus, you're beautiful." His eyes met hers once more.

A slight blush crept into her cheeks, but then she smiled and arched a single brow. "And you're overdressed."

Easy fix.

Moving with lightning speed, he stripped himself of his shoes and clothes. He thought of the new box of condoms he'd packed for the trip here—on the off-chance Jenna forgave him and invited him back into her bed.

What was it his high school shop teacher always said? *Prior proper planning prevents piss poor performance.*

But, looking at the woman before him, Adrian decided the condom could wait. He needed to make this an *unforgettable* performance. Not just a quick fuck.

She deserved nothing less.

Scooping her up, he carried her the two feet to the bed and laid her down in the center. He took one more precious second to soak up the way she looked right then, committing the image to memory.

Jenna was sprawled out on the mattress, her red, wavy

hair fanning around her head. Her firm breasts and rock-hard nipples rose with each breath.

It was as if they were reaching for him. As if they were as desperate to be touched as he was to touch them.

Then she *did* reach for him.

"Make love to me, Adrian," She rasped, her voice deepening with desire.

Make love.

His swollen cock twitched, and his heart raced. He didn't make love. He *fucked*. And he was damn good at fucking.

But this? This was unfamiliar territory. Despite the fact that he wasn't an expert—not fucking close—he did know making love took patience and finesse. Two things he'd never been good with.

I can do this. I can be gentle and in control.

Determined to make her feel as good as she deserved, Adrian laid on the mattress beside her. Using his fingertip, he began tracing her hairline, her jawline…her bottom lip.

Just before he leaned in for another taste, he whispered, "Don't worry, baby. I'll take care of you."

Just like that, it became his new mission in life. To take care of this woman in every way possible. From this moment on, whether it be pleasure or protection, Adrian would make sure she had whatever she needed.

Adrian pressed his lips to Jenna's chin, down the side of her neck, and lower. Leaving a trail of kisses, he made his way down to the breasts he'd been dreaming about for weeks. He took the crest of one into his mouth.

Jenna's breath hitched, the movement pushing her body even closer to him. Using one of his hands, Adrian held the perky globe in place while he teased and sucked her taut, rosy bud. While he continued feasting, he used his free hand to gently knead her other breast. Carefully massaging it with his palm and rolling the distended nipple between his thumb and forefinger.

Her low moan sent a vibration against his mouth, the sound sending a rush of blood to his already-filled erection.

"Please," she begged breathlessly. Her hips lifted toward him in search for the release.

Her plea reached into his chest and tugged at his heart. Adrian pushed himself back up, his lips on hers in an instant.

"You won't ever have to beg with me, baby." He kissed her again, praying she understood. "Not ever."

Her eyes softened and she looked up at him as if his words surprised her.

Christ, had the men in her past been such selfish bastards, they'd made her beg? Had they even bothered to make sure she was taken care of at all?

A surge of anger struck. He wanted to find each and every one and beat their asses, and—

"Adrian?" Her sweet voice broke through his thoughts. "Is everything...okay?"

Focus, asshole.

He smiled down at her. "More than okay."

And it was about to get a whole lot better.

With a playful nibble of her bottom lip, Adrian retraced his earlier steps. Only this time, he didn't stop at her breasts —although, he could spend hours on them. Instead, he continued a downward path along her flat, toned abs, not stopping until his head was between her thighs.

Jenna's sex was bare, her musky scent of arousal driving him wild with need. He'd dreamed of it ever since the day he'd showed up at her apartment. Would wake up and swear he could still smell her.

As if she'd been there, in his bed, all along.

She hadn't, and that had been his fault. But she was with

him now, and he wasn't about to waste a single, solitary second on regrets of the past.

His impatient dick throbbed painfully, ready to slide into her body and never, ever leave. Instinctively, his hips started to surge forward, but he regained control and held back.

Make love to me.

Right. He needed to take things *slow*. Needed to show her he could be the kind of man she wanted. The kind she deserved.

Adrian leaned in for a taste. He put his mouth on her and closed his eyes. Using his tongue and lips, he began savoring the taste he'd been craving.

Heaven.

Jenna cried out, her fingernails digging into his scalp as he licked and laved to his heart's content. She moaned again, her body writhing beneath his mouth with every swipe of his tongue.

God, he loved how responsive she was to his touch. Loved how she was hot and wet, and ready for more.

He slid a finger inside her molten core. First one, then another. Her inner muscles clamped down on his hand as he moved slow and easy. He was amazed when her body begin to tremble with her impending climax.

Memories from their first time together seeped into the present, and he drew upon them for guidance to what he knew she liked. What he knew she *needed*.

"Oh, god," she panted the words as he continued working her. "So…close."

I know you are, baby.

Adrian held off just a little longer. For her.

He continued thrusting his fingers in and out of her tight sheath. *In. Out. In. Out.* And when he sensed her impending orgasm, he put his mouth on her swollen clit and sent her to the stars.

"Adrian!"

Her climax hit with magnificent force. Jenna bowed off the mattress as she cried out his name—*his*—when she came.

Her muscles stiffened, and when a rush of hot liquid covered his fingers, he quickly replaced his hand with his mouth.

Adrian didn't even try holding back his growl of pure, male satisfaction. He got drunk off her essence, consuming every last drop of pleasure he could.

Leaving a trail of kisses up her inner thigh and higher, he made his way back to her. Locking his arms on both sides of her, he held himself up and stared, taking in the most beautiful sight he'd ever seen.

Jenna was looking up at him. Her eyes were heavy-lidded, their greens dark with the satisfaction *he'd* given her.

It was a look he wanted to see again. And again. Every single night for the rest of his life.

Whoa.

The thought took him by complete surprise. Adrian Walker didn't do relationships, let alone forever. Except, lying here, next to *this* woman, he realized...

I want to try.

A relationship. Commitment. Happily ever after...Adrian wanted all of that and more. And he wanted it with Jenna.

Holy shit.

"That was incredible." Jenna reached for him. "Thank you."

Her words pulled him away from the shocking revelation.

She was thanking him for an orgasm? *Oh, hell, no.*

"I should be thanking you." He kissed her softly. "Watching you fall apart in my arms the way you just did...*that* was incredible."

Her lips spread into a lazy smile, and she pushed against his chest. "Lay down on your back."

"Why?"

"Because it's my turn to taste you."

Fuck. Me.

"Baby, you put your mouth on me it's going to be over before you even get started."

"Okay." Jenna climbed onto her knees and positioned herself between his thighs.

He nearly choked. "Okay?"

"Sure." Smiling down at him, she began tracing a finger down the center of his chest, across his abs, and lower. "Just means we'll have to do it again." She leaned down and flicked her tongue across one of his nipples. "And again." She did the same to the other one, only this time she reached down and took his pulsating dick into her hand. "And again."

"Jenna—" he growled.

She began pumping her fist up and down his length. Adrian grabbed hold of her narrow waist, his fingertips digging into her skin there.

He tried to be careful. The last thing he wanted to do was hurt her. But Christ *Almighty*...

"You're playing with fire, sweetheart," he warned her.

She moaned, her tongue tracing the thin layer of hair leading from just below his navel to where his weeping cock waited eagerly.

"If I'm lucky, maybe I'll get burned," she purred.

"I'm serious, Jenna." He hissed when she blew on the tip of his swollen length. "You wanted me to make love to you, but I won't last if you—"

"You did make love to me." She ran her tongue over the crest. "Now, I'm making love to you."

Holy. Hell.

"I'm clean," he blurted.

"I know."

They'd already had the talk about being clean and birth

control the first time they were together. They'd still used a condom, because even then, he'd wanted to do everything he could to protect her.

"I haven't been with anyone since you." He needed to be very clear about that.

"Me, neither."

She licked him again.

Adrian sucked in another breath.

"I've never gone without a condom before." Not ever.

But the idea of going bareback with this woman had him becoming impossibly fuller.

"Me, neither."

His cock jerked. "Okay. But you don't have to—"

A wicked smile formed just before she leaned down and wrapped her lips around the tip.

Holy. God.

A low moan escaped the back of his throat, and somewhere in the back of his mind, Adrian wondered if it was possible to die from too much pleasure.

He had a feeling he was about to find out.

Jenna took more of him in, going as far as her throat would allow. And when she began sliding her hot, wet lips and tongue up and down his length, Adrian felt his eyes roll in the back of his head.

CHAPTER 7

Jenna loved the way Adrian tasted. All male and heat and passion. She loved the way he'd laid his head back onto the mattress and gave himself over to her, and she—

Was being lifted by her shoulders and tossed onto her back.

"Hey!" She licked her lips and frowned. "I wasn't finished."

Adrian loomed over her with a smirk. "No, baby, but I almost was. And I want to be inside you." Heat filtered through his eyes as the blunt tip of his cock pressed against her entrance.

Works for me.

Jenna laid her palms on his defined chest and spread her legs wider. She lifted her hips and grinned. "Well, then. What are you waiting for?"

He didn't wait.

Adrian surged forward, filling her in one, powerful thrust. His guttural moan mixed with hers, the satisfying sound reverberating throughout the room.

"God, baby." He stilled long enough to kiss her. "You feel fucking fantastic."

"So do you." She brought her mouth to his.

Their tongues swirled and danced in the most perfect of kisses. Demanding, yet gentle. Greedy, yet giving.

Lying beneath Adrian, his body stretching hers to its limit, Jenna had the fleeting thought that she could spend hours doing nothing *but* kissing this man and be perfectly happy.

Then Adrian began to move.

It was much different than their first time. Not better or worse. Just *different*.

The day he came to her apartment, they'd touched, and her world had ignited. The sex was hard and rough. All-consuming and absolutely amazing.

Exactly what they'd both needed at the time.

But what was happening between them now was neither hard nor rough. It was tender and warm. Gentle and unhurried. Adrian was kissing and touching her in a way that made her feel...*loved*.

Make love to me.

And he was.

With every thrust. Every kiss. Every brush of his strong, callused hands, Adrian continued making slow, sweet love to her. And though he believed himself undeserving—they'd have to work on that—Jenna fell a little harder with every moment that passed.

"Baby." Adrian panted. "Can't...wait. Need...you...there."

His words were like a command. One her body was more than willing to obey.

Picking up the pace, he shifted his lower body in a way that it rubbed against her swollen bundle of nerves with every thrust.

That's it, right there. Just...a...little...more...

Jenna cried, her eyes squeezing shut as her second orgasm hit with a vengeance. Adrian followed her almost immediately.

He gave one final, hard thrust. Growling her name as he came. *"Jenna!"*

I've never gone without a condom.

A primitive sense of satisfaction rolled over her as his hot seed spilled inside her. The weight of his body making her feel safe and protected, even now. Even like this.

Much too soon, Adrian withdrew from her sensitive core and fell to his back beside her. His breaths heaved in a rhythm matching her own.

He rose from the bed and disappeared in the bathroom. A few minutes later, he returned, warm washcloth in hand. Without a word, he carefully began cleaning *her* up.

She wanted to tell him he didn't have to, but it felt so good she couldn't seem to find the words.

When he was finished, she smiled up at him and mumbled, "Thank you."

A strange look crossed over his face, but he didn't speak. With an expert throw, he tossed the washcloth back into the bathroom and settled in beside her.

His strong arms pulled her close. His front to her back.

Satisfied beyond measure and wrapped in the comfort of his strong arms, Jenna had just started to doze off when she felt his lips press against the back of her head.

Then, in a low rumble, he told her, "You don't ever have to thank me for taking care of you."

His sweet words were the last thing she heard before falling asleep.

Hours later, Jenna woke feeling more rested than she had in...forever. She stretched, smiling at the way certain muscles felt deliciously sore.

"Sure hope that smile has something to do with me."

She turned and found Adrian sitting at the room's small, round table. Dressed in a pair of well-worn jeans and a dark gray t-shirt that did nothing to hide his broad shoulders and sculpted chest, he was drinking coffee and staring back at her in a way that made her wonder…

Has he been watching me sleep?

"Good morning." She cleared her husky throat and sat up.

The curtains were drawn, so the room was still fairly dark. But from the light seeping through the edges suggested it was well past sunrise.

Jenna frowned.

That couldn't be right. She'd gotten released from the hospital at like two yesterday afternoon. Then she and Adrian had come here, she'd showered, they'd made love, and then…

Her eyes shot to his. "What time is it?"

He sat his coffee cup down and looked at his watch. "Almost ten."

"Ten?" She shook her head. "That would mean, I slept for almost—"

"Fifteen hours." Adrian shrugged. "Give or take."

Holy shit.

"Why did you let me sleep so long?" She threw off the covers…then remembered she was naked. Pulling the sheet back up to her chest, she stood and yanked it from the bed.

"You obviously needed it." His heated eyes trailed down the length of her body. "Don't cover yourself on my account. I rather like seeing you naked." As casually as can be, he took another sip of coffee.

A ridiculous blush crept up her neck. "I…um…"

Trouble talking, much?

Jenna cleared her throat and started to try speaking again, but her stomach decided to let out an embarrassingly loud growl at the same time.

His lips curved into a sexy half-smile. "Hungry?"

"Starving, actually." Jenna looked around the room and back to him. "Oh my gosh, the food!" The room had been filled with it last night. "I completely forgot about it."

"In your defense, you were a little pre-occupied."

Her heart stuttered from the memories. "Yeah." She stared back at him. "I guess I was."

"I ordered breakfast. It'll be here in twenty. Our flight isn't until one, so we have time."

"Flight?"

"I booked us on a flight to San Diego. Figured you'd want to get outta here as soon as possible."

They'd revisit that, but first, "I feel guilty."

A guarded look flashed across his face. "Why?"

"Because we wasted all that food."

Was that relief she saw in his eyes? It took her a second to realize he thought her comment about feeling guilty was about *him*.

She nearly smiled. Jenna felt a lot of things about what they did last night, but guilt was definitely *not* one of them.

"It didn't go to waste."

"Huh?" She shook her thoughts away.

"The food." Adrian explained. "It didn't go to waste. There's a center for homeless Vets a couple blocks from here. While you were sleeping, I called the guy who runs it. He and a buddy of his came and got the food."

She'd slept through someone coming into the room and taking all the food? Adrian was right. Apparently, her body really did need the extra rest.

"That was nice of you."

"What can I say?" He winked. "I'm a nice guy."

Jenna's insides tingled because, damn. When he winked at her like that, it made her want to drop the sheet and demand a repeat performance.

Instead, she smiled and said, "I'd better go shower and get dressed. Wouldn't want the guy delivering our breakfast to see me in nothing but a sheet."

The playfulness that had been in his eyes a second before vanished. "No one gets to see you like this, but me."

Jenna started to chuckle but stopped when she caught sight of his hardened jaw. "You're serious."

"Damn straight, I'm serious." Adrian got up and stalked toward her. "I don't share, Jenna. We need to be clear on that. This..." He ran a finger over her collar bone, dipping down to the crevice between her breasts. "You're mine, now. No one else's."

Her breath hitched. "And you?" She studied him closely. "Are you mine?"

"For as long as you want me."

Oh, my.

"Okay."

It was a totally lame response, but what else could she say?

Adrian's eyes lit up with a smile that made him look years younger. "Okay."

Jenna turned for the bathroom to avoid doing something stupid, like blurting out *I love you.* She wasn't sure she was ready to go there yet, but her heart was definitely headed in that direction.

Which was probably crazy, considering they barely knew each other. Still, in some ways she felt like she'd known him forever.

Standing beneath the hot water, Jenna wondered what her psychologist friend would say.

More than likely, Elle would probably say it was just some sort of hero worship thing. That or she'd spout off some other clinical term to explain why Jenna was feeling what she was feeling about a man who was clearly dangerous.

Something other than the fact that she was falling for a man who used to kill people for the government. Who would've killed for her if he hadn't been so worried about hurting her.

That. That right there. That's *why you're falling for him.*

Not the killing part, of course. No, Jenna was falling hard for the man because he *wasn't* the uncaring bad boy he wanted everyone to believe him to be.

He could put on a damn good show. She'd witnessed it on more than one occasion. But there was more to Adrian Walker than most people knew.

Almost from the very beginning, she'd seen past the walls he'd built to the man she was now certain existed. If there was any doubt left, they were long gone, now.

Because there was a moment last night—several moments, in fact—when Jenna saw the *real* Adrian. The man who was attentive and kind. Who put her pleasure before his own. The man who, with a gentle touch and soft caress, had made her believe she truly meant something to him.

You're mine, now.

Jenna reached up and turned the water to cold. Gasping at the sudden change in temperature, she forced herself to stay under a little longer in order to douse the burning desire she felt for the sexy man.

Like that's going to work. The guy looks at you and you melt.

The tiny voice may be right, but she pushed those thoughts away and focused on what needed to be done.

First, she needed food. They both did. And then she needed to get to work.

Because Jenna had woken up with an idea—one Adrian

was almost certainly going to hate—and she'd wasted enough of the day, as it was.

A few minutes later, she was dressed in a pair of ripped jeans and a cream-colored sweater. She had just a touch of makeup on and her hair was gathered in a thick braid that fell over her left shoulder.

With a final glance at herself in the mirror, she exited the bathroom and stepped into a major case of déjà vu.

Adrian stood near the cart—just one, this time—waiting for her return.

"Smells delicious."

"Eggs, bacon, sausage, and French toast. Hope that's okay."

"Uh, more than okay." Jenna made a beeline for the cart. "French toast is my favorite."

"Good to know."

Over the next several minutes, the two of them enjoyed their breakfast while making casual conversation. Rather than dive right into her plan, Jenna used that time to try to learn a little more about the man sitting across from her.

"Tell me something about you."

Adrian swallowed a bite of scrambled eggs. "Like what?"

"You know, things like where you're from. What's your family like? Why you decided to go into the military."

How you became a super-secret government hitman.

He stared back at her with an unreadable expression. The silence that stretched between them seemed deafening, and Jenna was about to think he wasn't going to tell her *anything* when he finally began to speak.

"Not much to tell."

Okay, so he wasn't going to make this easy. Well, neither was she.

"Huh," was all she said.

"What?"

Jenna shrugged a shoulder and took a bite of her French toast. "Nothing."

Adrian sat his fork down and folded his hands on the table in front of him. "What?"

"Really, it's nothing." She continued acting as if it were no big deal. "I just thought the whole *you're mine* speech referred to more than just sex. Guess I was wrong. My bad."

"The whole…" He scowled. "I *was* referring to more than sex. I just—"

"Don't want to share your life with me." Jenna finished for him. "No, I get it."

"It's not that I don't want…" He sighed, the sound almost that of resignation. "My life before the military isn't remotely interesting. And after…well, you know what that's been like."

"Your life, before during, and after the military, interests me. Because *you* interest me." When he started to shake his head, she laid it all out. "If this"—she motioned between them—"has any chance of working, you're going to have to trust me."

Adrian stared deep into her eyes. "I do trust you."

Jenna picked up a piece of bacon and took a bite. "If that were true, you'd give me something. Even just a tiny piece of who you are. Who you used to be."

After a few seconds of silence, his voice softened. "Ellena didn't share any of this with you?"

Her friend knew the answers to those questions and didn't tell her? Jenna made a mental note to find out why the next time she talked to Elle.

"No." She shook her head. "Elle didn't tell me anything about your life before the military. She and Gabe just said you were working undercover for the government for the past several years. That Gabe and his team all thought you were a traitor… that the *world* thought that of you. But that it wasn't true."

He took a minute to process this and then he finally, *finally* started sharing.

"I grew up here."

"In *Gulfside Harbor?*" Jenna felt her eyes widen.

"Haven't been back in several years."

"How come?"

"My childhood was less than ideal." He paused. "My mom split when I was twelve and my sister was nine. Dad, and I use that term very loosely, was a worthless drunk and a junkie."

"You have a sister?" For some reason that bit of news was shocking.

"Had." A soul-deep sadness filled his eyes. "Bree died a few years ago."

Her chest ached for him. "You started to say you lost someone. You were talking about your sister."

Adrian nodded. "I basically raised her from the time our mom took off until I left for the military."

He seemed to become lost in his memories for a moment but blinked them away. Clearing his throat, Adrian continued with the heartbreaking story.

"So, my dad…he'd do pretty much anything for alcohol or drugs. Asshole couldn't hold a job to save his miserable life. Instead, he spent his time looking for ways to scam people out of money for alcohol. Drugs. Sex."

"God, Adrian." Jenna reached across the table and put a hand over his. "That must have been awful. How did you and your sister get by?"

Glancing down, he pulled his hand free. Jenna started to move hers back, but he surprised her by linking their fingers together.

He needs comfort. He needs you.

"I dropped out of high school after my sophomore year.

Schoolwork always came easy to me, so I got my GED and started working two jobs to pay the bills."

"You were what, sixteen?"

"Barely."

Just a baby.

"I waited until Bree graduated high school to enlist. She was smart." He gave her a ghost of a smile. "So fucking smart. Got a full ride to the University of Texas in Austin. She wanted to be a teacher."

"What happened?"

Adrian drew in a deep breath and let it out slowly. Jenna could tell this part was especially hard for him to talk about, but if he was willing to share, she wasn't going to stop him.

"It was her junior year. She'd just turned twenty-one and she'd come home for the weekend to celebrate with some of her old friends from here. My dad, uh…he heard she was coming back, and like always, he saw an opportunity to help himself, so he took it."

Though she was afraid to, Jenna asked, "What does that mean?"

"My dad knew somebody who knew this group of guys. They'd been taking prostitutes and runaways from the area and selling them to another group across the border."

Jesus. "You're talking about sex trafficking."

Adrian nodded. "Dad gave his buddy a picture of Bree. He showed the men her picture and they agreed to pay top dollar for her."

Horrified, Jenna squeezed his hand tighter. "Oh, Adrian."

What kind of father sells his own daughter?

"Bree grew up here, you know?" He looked over at her. "Knew the neighborhoods. The people. So she wouldn't have been scared to walk the few blocks from the bar back to the house."

"That's when they took her? While she was on her way home?"

Another sad nod.

"That was the last night anyone saw or heard from her."

"How did you..." Jenna swallowed the growing knot in her throat. "How did you find out what happened?"

"When Homeland and the CIA first approached me about taking the deep cover job, they knew my sister was missing. They also knew of a trafficking ring based out of Colombia. From some of the evidence they'd found, they suspected it was the same group responsible for Bree's disappearance. They gave me first dibs on the job."

"The job?"

A coldness seeped into his eyes. "The fall of an empire is like an avalanche. You start from the top, and the rest begins to crumble."

Jenna processed this before asking, "You went after the head of the ring, didn't you?"

"His name was Cesar Ortiz. I didn't just go after him, sweetheart." Adrian watched her closely. "I killed him. But not until after I *made* him tell me where Bree was."

"Where was she?"

"In a shallow grave in the woods behind the bastard's house. He fucking used her. Raped and beat her. Then, when he was tired of her, he had one of his men put a bullet in her brain and bury her."

Shocked, Jenna gasped. Her free hand covering her mouth before she said, "I'm glad you killed him."

The words were out before she'd even thought about it, but she had no desire to take them back.

She'd always been a black and white kind of person. Something was either right or it was wrong. And for her, killing—unless it was self-defense—was *always* wrong. Period.

But Jenna was finally beginning to realize the world didn't exist in only black or white. She *finally* understood that there were a whole lot of grays mixed in there, too, and sometimes...sometimes people deserved to die.

"I tortured Ortiz, Jenna." He said it as though he was warning her. "I cut him. Broke his bones. I did whatever I had to in order to get the information I needed. Then, when he finally told me about Bree, I tortured him some more before I slit his throat from ear to ear."

The picture he painted was one of nightmares, but she knew what he was doing. She'd asked him to share more about his life. She wanted to know who he was, and this was his answer.

He saw himself as a ruthless killer, and while that may be partially true, Jenna needed to make him see he was so much more.

She stood and went to him. Sat down on his lap and wrapped her arms around his neck.

"I'm sorry you grew up the way you did." A tear fell down her cheek. "I'm sorry your sister had to go through something so heinous, and I'm so, so sorry you lost her. But I'm *not* sorry you killed that monster. As far as I'm concerned, he got exactly what he deserved."

"What about my dad?" He challenged. "Do you think he deserved to die for what he did?"

"Yes."

He didn't say he killed him, and she wasn't going to ask.

Adrian shook his head, looking up at her as if he hadn't heard her correctly. "Jenna?"

"I get what you're doing," she told him. "You're trying to scare me. I get it, but it won't work. You want to know why?"

A slight nod.

"Because I *see* you, Adrian. I've seen the walls you put up to protect yourself, and I understand why, but I'm here." She cupped one side of his face. "I'm here, and I'm not going anywhere. So you can tell me all the horrifying stories you want, but it won't change the way I feel about you. Because I see you. All of you. And I still want you."

One minute she was staring into a pair of tortured eyes. The next, his mouth was on hers, and she was being lifted in his arms and carried to the bed.

They stripped each other in a frenzy. Clothes flew in every direction until they were both lying naked on the mattress.

"Can't go slow." His voice was tense and gravelly.

Lying beneath him, Jenna leaned up and nibbled his bottom lip. "I don't want slow. I just want you inside me. Now."

Urging him on, Jenna lifted her pelvis, brushing her wet sex against his hard shaft. With a growl, Adrian positioned himself to her entrance and slid inside. Exactly where he belonged.

CHAPTER 8

"We missed our flight." Adrian ran his fingers up and down Jenna's arm. He smiled at the trail of goosebumps following in his wake.

He couldn't believe he'd dumped all his baggage on her the way he had. Telling her about his sister…revealing *classified* information that could get him tossed into fucking Leavenworth…that shit wasn't who he was.

But maybe that was the point. He'd changed since meeting Jenna. In ways he never thought possible.

They'd had sex twice in the last two hours, and his cock was already half-hard, again. Or maybe still. He felt like a damn teenager, his body always primed and ready whenever she was near.

I can't get enough of her. I see her and I want.

He was beginning to realize he never would.

With a lazy grin, she turned on her side to face him. Her eye makeup was a bit smudged, her hair was a mass of wild, red waves, and her lips were swollen and red from his kisses.

Hands down, the most beautiful thing he'd ever seen.

"I'm not going home," she announced matter-of-factly. "Not yet, anyway."

Adrian's entire body stiffened. He half-expected to hear the loud scratching sound, like a needle sliding across an old vinyl record, because she'd just dropped a major wrench into his plans.

With a controlled tone, he asked her, "What do you mean, you're not going home?"

He wanted to—no, he *needed* to—get her the hell out of this town. The sooner the better.

"Don't worry." Her smile made his heart kick against his ribs. "I'll pay you back for the tickets."

"I don't care about the tickets, Jenna." He pushed himself up and rested on an elbow. "I care about getting you as far away from this place as I can."

"Why?" Jenna sat up fully, resting her back against the padded headboard. She brought the sheet with her as she moved, gathering it just above her breasts.

Such a shame.

Jesus, he needed to focus.

"Why?" He looked at her like she was nuts. "You were drugged and damn near kidnapped less than twenty-four hours ago."

"That could've happened to anyone, Adrian. It's not like I was specifically targeted."

"Baby, you *were* targeted."

"You know what I mean. Unless..." She studied him a moment. "Do you know something about what happened to me? Something you're not sharing?"

"No." He answered truthfully. "If I did, I'd tell you."

"Okay, then." She got up and walked unabashedly to where her clothes still lay strewn on the floor. "It's settled."

"No, it's not." Nothing was even *close* to being settled.

She talked while she dressed. "I'm not leaving, Adrian."

"Yes. You are."

Buttoning her jeans, she zipped them with a narrowed gaze. "No. I'm not."

He shot out of bed and started putting on his own clothes. "After everything that's happened, why the hell would you want to stay?"

"I want to stay *because* of what happened to me."

"Okay, now you're not making any sense."

"I'm making perfect sense. You're just not listening." She ran a hand through her hair and sighed. "Look, I get that you're worried, and I appreciate everything you've done for me. More than you'll ever know."

"But?" Because there was definitely a huge fucking but coming.

Three, two...

"*But* I'm the one who was drugged. *I'm* the one who almost disappeared." Her voice cracked and damn if those weren't tears forming in her eyes.

Adrian could handle just about anything. But seeing this woman cry damn near brought him to his knees.

Thankfully, Jenna swiped them away before they could fall. "Marie told me one of the two nurses who went missing had been found, which is great. But the other one...she just vanished, Adrian. According to what little Marie and the other nurses know, the police have no leads, and she had no husband or kids. They made it sound like no one's even looking for her, anymore."

"Okay, so I'll talk to Gabe. I'm sure Bravo Team can track down the people who took her. Either that, or they'll know someone else who can."

"You're missing the point." Jenna took a step toward him. "I'm just like her, Adrian. A single woman with no family. No one at home to miss me if I'm not there." Her eyes glistened again, and this time when she blinked, a single tear streaked down over her cheek. "That could've been me."

"Like hell." He covered the short distance separating them. With his hands on her shoulders, he forced her to look at him. "You're not like that other nurse, Jenna. You have people who care. Who'd miss you like crazy if you were gone."

She was shaking her head before he'd even finished. "Gabe and Ellena don't count—"

"What about me?" he bit out. "Do I count?"

She searched his eyes, for what he wasn't sure. Rather than answer his question, she asked him one of her own. One that knocked him on his ass.

"Do you want to count?"

Do I want to...

"Yeah, baby." He swallowed. "I want to count."

In every way possible.

Despite his words, Adrian could still see a sliver of doubt still swimming around in those gorgeous eyes of hers. He needed to set that shit straight right the hell now.

"I've never been in love," he admitted quietly. "So I don't know if that's what this is. But what I do know is you make me feel things. Things I've never felt before."

"Adrian?"

"You make me want to be a better man, Jenna." He framed her face with both hands. "You make me want to be a better *person*. So yeah, when it comes to you, I want to fucking count. And baby, I promise if you went missing, I'd move heaven and earth to find you."

He took her mouth in his. He could *taste* the salt of her tears. And as their lips and tongues moved together in perfect harmony, Adrian put all his energy into showing her how he felt with that one, powerful kiss.

When they finally pulled apart, Jenna was breathing hard

—and blinking away more tears. When another escaped, he caught it with his thumb and gently swept it away.

"I feel the same way about you, Adrian." She whispered softly. "Except…"

"Except what?"

Her eyes locked onto his in a way that made him feel as though she could see into his soul. "I'm pretty sure I love you." Jenna's long hair swooshed around her shoulders as she shook her head. "I know it's crazy fast, and I'm not asking for you to say it back or to even try to figure out your feelings for me right now."

Holy. Shit.

Adrian could barely breathe, let alone speak. This woman…this crazy, wonderful woman…loved *him*?

Say something, dickhead!

"Jenna, I—"

"You know what?" She cut him off. "Forget I even said anything. None of that matters right now, anyway."

None of it…

Frowning, he opened his mouth to ask what the hell she meant but she beat him to it.

"What *does* matter is that missing woman," Jenna continued on as if she hadn't just filled him with more joy than he'd ever known. "And all the other women in this city who are in danger of going through what I did. I can't go back home and pretend like it didn't happen. I can't go to sleep at night and forget that those men are still out there, preying on innocent women."

Yeah, he was still back on the whole declaration of love thing. But she'd obviously moved on, so he let her.

For now, because baby…we will *be revisiting that particular conversation very soon.*

Clearing the emotion from his throat, he set it aside and asked, "What exactly are you wanting to do?"

"I want to stay here, in Gulfside Harbor. I want to go back to that club, and I want to find the man who drugged me. The bartender said the guy was his friend. I figured I could start there. Maybe the guy who drugged me is connected to the missing woman. Or maybe what he and the other two men did to me was a random, one-time thing. Either way, somebody needs to be out there trying to figure it out."

Adrian ran a hand over his jaw. He thought about his sister, and how he'd wished a million times over someone had been looking out for Bree when he couldn't. Someone like Jenna.

He glanced back down at her. Saw the determination in her eyes and knew. If he didn't help her, she was going to try to do this shit all on her own.

The idea of her going anywhere near that night club again left his gut churning. The thought of her going there *alone*?

That fucking terrified him.

"Fine." He finally gave in. "We'll go back to the club. Together. But first, I want to meet with my GHPD contact. See if they know more about your case."

"Okay."

"And when we do go to the club, or anywhere else for that matter, if I tell you to do something, you do it. No arguments. No questions asked. Understood?"

Jenna wasn't as quick to agree to those terms. Adrian could tell she wasn't keen on the idea of taking orders from him, but she didn't argue.

"Okay." A wide smile lit up her entire face just before she threw herself into his arms. "Thank you."

He hugged her back. "Don't thank me yet, sweetheart."

"Why not?"

"You need to go into this thing with your eyes open. We may not learn anything new or helpful. I just want to make sure you don't—"

"Get my hopes up. I got it." She leaned up and planted a sweet kiss on his lips. "At least we'll know we tried."

Adrian pulled out his phone, making a quick call to Jason Ryker. The Homeland agent was an arrogant prick, but he knew how to get shit done.

"Walker," Ryker greeted him on the first ring. "Didn't expect to hear from you again, now that you're a civilian and all."

"I need a car." Because he was done putting Jenna's life in anyone else's hands but his.

"Where are you?"

The question seemed foreign coming from him. For the past several years, Adrian hadn't been able to make a move without Ryker knowing exactly where he was and what he was doing.

"Gulfside Harbor," he clipped before sharing the name of the hotel.

There was a slight pause and then, "What? No Enterprise nearby?"

Adrian gritted his teeth. "Funny."

"I thought so." Several clicks from the other man's keyboard came through the phone and then, "All set. It'll be delivered within the hour."

"Thanks."

"That's it? Aren't you going to tell me—"

Adrian ended the call before Ryker could finish.

A little over an hour later, he and Jenna were sitting on a bench inside the Gulfside Harbor Police Department, waiting to talk with Adrian's contact.

The guy's intel had always been solid, and with his recent promotion, Ben would have easier access to the information they needed.

"Tell me again who it is we're waiting to see?"

Leaning against the brick wall behind them, Adrian

turned his head toward Jenna, who was sitting to his right. "Guy named Ben Campillo."

She nodded, though he could tell the name meant absolutely nothing to her.

"Known him a while." Leaning over, his shoulder touched hers as he spoke low enough only she could hear. "He's helped me out before."

"Oh." Jenna nodded again. Then her eyes widened, and she drew out another, "*Oh.*" She waited a beat before shifting on the bench to face him more directly. "Is he...like you used to be?"

"Undercover?" Adrian shook his head. "No. But he provided me with some much-needed intel once."

"So, he was your snitch."

For some reason her description made him smile. "Something like that."

Jenna took a moment to process that bit of news before asking, "You think he knows something about the missing woman?"

Movement over her shoulder caught his eye. With his hands on his knees, Adrian pushed himself to his feet. "We're about to find out."

Campillo was walking toward them. He'd put on a few pounds since their last meeting a few years back, his shirt bulging at the buttons in a couple of places. His hair was also a little grayer on the sides.

A native of Gulfside Harbor, Ben had been a beat cop when Adrian was younger. When Bree first went missing, he'd put in hours of his own time helping with the search.

He'd also passed along vital information that had led Adrian to the trafficking ring that had taken her.

"Adrian." Ben held out his hand. "What's it been, four years?"

Adrian shook the guy's hand. "Just over." With an

assessing glance, he took in the guy's freshly pressed, white shirt. "Congrats on the promotion…Chief."

"Thanks." The dimples on Ben's left cheek deepened with a smile.

He turned to Jenna, who was clearly surprised by his contact's position within the department.

"Jen, this is Chief Campillo." To Ben, Adrian said, "This is Jenna Shaw. The woman I told you about when we spoke on the phone."

"Nice to meet you, Chief."

Using a bit more grace than he had with Adrian, Ben shook Jenna's hand. "Please, call me Ben."

"Okay, Ben." She smiled.

"Why don't we go to my office where we can speak more privately."

"Office, huh?" Adrian slapped the man's back as they walked. "You really are moving up in the world."

"Yeah, well that move came with a lot more headaches and paperwork, trust me."

Down the hall and to the right, they stopped at a door with a nameplate that read *Chief Campillo*. Ben opened the door, stepping aside to let Adrian and Jenna enter first.

Following them in, he shut the door behind him and motioned to the two leather chairs in front of his desk. "Have a seat."

Adrian waited for Jenna to sit first.

"I don't mean to act so formal." Ben rounded his desk. "But I'm sure you remember how things are here, Adrian."

He did. "Prying ears and deep pockets."

"Too many to count, I'm afraid."

Not surprising. Just like any other border town department, this one had a history of officers and the like being bought off. At least that's how it was when Adrian still lived here.

"What do you know about the missing nurse?" Jenna spoke up beside him.

Both men turned their attention to her.

"Straight to the point." Ben smiled. "I like it."

"That's good, because I'm not one to beat around the bush, Ben."

No, she sure as hell isn't.

Adrian's dick began to swell behind his zipper. The woman's confidence and grit were a major fucking turn-on, but he needed to get himself under control.

Getting caught in the Chief of Police's office with a boner wasn't high on his to-do list.

"I assume you're talking about the woman who worked for Saje Staffing?" Ben was still looking at Jenna.

"I am."

The other man nodded. "I'm behind the scenes now, for obvious reasons, but I talked to the investigators on the case after Adrian called me."

He opened a manila folder and pulled out a five-by-seven picture of a pretty brunette. Sliding the picture across his desk, he told them what he knew.

"Stella Gallagher. Twenty-six. Single. No kids. She has a studio apartment in Lovington, New Mexico, where she was born and raised. Took a job with Saje last year, and according to the point of contact within the company, this was Stella's third travel gig with them."

"Her third?" Jenna's forehead scrunched as she thought. "Sounds like she was a stable employee."

Ben nodded. "I agree."

"Stable employees don't just up and leave two weeks before their contracts are completed, Chief."

"You're absolutely right, Jenna. They don't. Unless…"

"Unless?"

Ben closed the file and rested his elbows on his desk.

Steepling his hands, his expression softened. "My investigators discovered Stella met someone shortly after she got into town."

"A man?"

"That's correct."

Adrian knew exactly where his former asset was headed. He also knew Jenna wasn't going to like it.

"So?" Jenna's eyes bounced between him and Ben. "What does that have to do with her disappearing?"

"The man she was seeing disappeared at the same time Stella did." Ben sat back in his chair with a sigh. "Unfortunately, this sort of thing happens more than people realize. Especially in a town like this. Single woman with no ties meets a single man with no ties. They hit it off and decide to run away together. Start a new life somewhere else."

"If that's what happened, there should still be a trail," Jenna pushed on. "Credit card transactions, a canceled rent agreement on Stella's apartment. I mean, what about the guy? Where did he live?"

"He owns a house here in town. Neighbors haven't seen or heard from him since he left. But again, that doesn't equal foul play. They could be using cash to stay under the grid. Hell, for all we know, they're both happy as clams and living it up on a beach somewhere."

"Doesn't sound to me like you know much of anything."

"Jenna." Adrian put a hand on her leg.

"No." She shook her head. "This isn't right, Adrian. Someone should be looking for her. And this guy…what if he's the one who took her? He could be some sort of serial killer or something."

"He was a tech at the hospital here in town," Ben shared more. "Name's Tim Watson, and trust me when I say, my detectives did a thorough background on the man."

"How thorough are we talking?" Adrian asked.

Ben's dark eyes slid to his. "The works. No criminal record, solid work history. Watson even paid his taxes early every year. Guy's clean as a whistle."

"So was Ted Bundy." Jenna arched a single brow.

Adrian noticed the smile teasing the corners of Ben's lips, but the man cleared his throat and got serious. "Look, Jenna. I appreciate your concern for Miss Gallagher's safety, and I wish there was more I could do. But unless there's actual evidence that a crime has taken place, our hands are tied."

Jenna turned her head, her eyes lifting to his. Even though she hadn't spoken, Adrian knew what she was asking.

She wanted him to say something that would contradict what Ben had just said. It broke his heart that he couldn't.

"He's right, baby." He took her hand in his and squeezed. "Without some sort of proof that foul play was involved..."

Her disheartened expression told him she understood.

Without a witness or evidence—signs of a struggle or blood, *something* to prove the Gallagher woman had been taken against her will—there was nothing more that could be done.

"What about the other nurse?" Jenna asked. "I was told there were two who went missing, but one was found."

"Fortunately, yes. She was." Ben nodded.

"What happened?" Adrian asked before Jenna could.

"Nothing too surprising, I'm afraid. She went out dancing with a group of friends. They met some guys, she had too much to drink and ended up leaving the bar without telling her friends. Woke up the next afternoon in some guy's apartment."

Jenna shook her head as if she wasn't buying it. "The other nurses said she'd been missing several days."

"Apparently, the young woman was embarrassed and

ashamed about what had happened. So she went back to her hotel, packed her bags, and went to stay with her parents in Nebraska."

"Let me guess." Adrian put the pieces together quickly. "She didn't tell anyone she was leaving."

"Not a word," Ben confirmed his theory. "Didn't check out of her room or tell anyone what she was doing, so it took a few days to figure out what had happened. When we finally tracked her down, she told the detectives assigned to her case what happened."

A soft exhale hit Adrian's ears. He glanced over and found Jenna looking slightly less tense. "That's good news, at least."

"Very good news, indeed." Ben smiled.

A stretch of silence passed before Adrian stood and offered the man his hand. "Thanks for sharing what you know about this."

"Of course." Ben stood and returned the gesture. "Sorry I couldn't be more help."

"It's okay." Jenna's mouth curved into a smile that didn't reach her eyes. "I appreciate you taking the time to meet with us."

"This guy and I go back a long way."

Using that to his advantage, Adrian picked up the photo of Stella Gallagher and asked Ben, "Mind if I take this?"

"Sure. We have it saved in the system, so I can just print another copy."

"Thanks." He slid it into his back pocket.

"Let me walk you out."

Ben started around the edge of his desk when his phone began to ring.

"Saved by the bell," Adrian joked.

Ben's rounded belly bounced as he scoffed. "Saved or slaughtered. Depends on who's calling."

With a tip of his chin, Adrian took Jenna's hand in his. "We'll find our way out."

Back at the rental car, he pulled the photo out of his pocket and set it on the hood. Using his phone, he snapped a picture.

Standing across from him by the passenger door, Jenna asked, "Why'd you do that?"

"I'm sending it to Gabe." He typed out a quick text that included the Gallagher woman's basic intel.

"For…" Jenna let the word linger.

Adrian hit send. "I asked him to have Nate find out what he could about her."

Nathan Carter was former Naval intelligence and Bravo Team's technical analyst. The guy was crazy smart, and his computer skills were more than a little impressive.

"You think there's more to the story than what Ben told us?"

"If there is, Nate's the guy to find it." Adrian started to reach for his door, but Jenna's next comment stopped him.

"Isn't Nate the name of the Bravo Team guy you shot?" Her expression was unreadable. "I thought that's what Elle said, anyway."

Shit.

He wondered what else Elle had shared about him. Not that it mattered, because he wasn't going to lie.

Not to Jenna.

So he nodded. "Shot him in the shoulder."

Shot him, kidnapped his wife…almost got her killed.

"She said it was so you wouldn't blow your cover. That it was all part of the job and that you actually did what you could to protect Nate's wife."

Gracelynn wasn't Nate's wife at the time, but yeah. That's exactly what he'd done. Still, his gut tucked in with regret.

So many regrets.

"It was."

A long, painful moment of silence passed before she said, "I'm glad you quit. 'Cause it sounds like your job really sucked."

The comment took Adrian by such surprise, he threw his head back and laughed. "God, I love you."

It took two full seconds for him to realize what he'd just said.

His smile fell flat. His jaw dropped, and he stared at her from over the car.

Adrian opened his mouth, but he wasn't even sure why.

To deny it?

To blow it off as an offhanded remark that meant nothing?

Or had he come close to telling her the truth?

The truth being he *did* love her. Probably had from the moment he first saw her. He just hadn't realized it fully until that very moment.

Another truth was that the idea of letting someone get that close scared him more than bullets flying from an AK-47 with a Russian terrorist pulling the trigger.

He couldn't tell her that, though. Right? Couldn't actually admit *out loud* that just the thought of letting her into his fucked-up world terrified him.

No, he couldn't tell her that part. But he *could* man up and tell her how he really felt.

Here goes nothing.

Drawing in a deep breath and said, "I lo—"

"Look out!" Jenna yelled, her eyes growing as big as saucers. A fraction of a second later, the driver's window shattered into a million tiny pieces.

She screamed as Adrian yelled, *"Get down!"*

He was already in the process of ducking when a bullet slammed into the back of his left thigh. The impact threw him off balance, and he fell onto the road's cool, rough pavement.

"Adrian!" Jenna's terrified voice called for him from behind the car's protection.

"Stay...down!"

Tires squealed in the background as Adrian reached for his gun...and came up empty. *Fuck!*

His pistol was locked in the rental's glove box. If he'd tried taking it into the station, the metal detectors would've gone off, and he probably would've been cuffed and hauled off to interrogation.

Adrian hadn't wanted to risk that happening, because if that had, Jenna would've been left alone. So he'd locked it in the glovebox before they went inside.

Have to get to her. Have to keep her safe.

Those words became Adrian's mantra as he gritted his teeth and rolled to his stomach. He started dragging himself around the car's back bumper. There was a truck parked behind him, which provided even more cover.

Pushing through the pain, he ignored the tiny rocks digging into his palms and uninjured leg and kept moving. He didn't wonder how bad he'd been hit, or think that, given the impact he'd felt, the bullet may have hit his femoral artery, and he'd be dead within minutes.

The only thing he thought of—the *only* thing that mattered—was getting to Jenna and keeping her safe.

With the curb as leverage, he'd just started to push himself onto the sidewalk when he saw her. Bent over at the waist, Jenna was standing on the sidewalk between the two vehicles with an outstretched arm.

"Here." She reached for him.

The fuck is she... "I said get down!"

"I *am* down, and you're hurt. Besides, the car already took off. Come on."

Rather than wait for him to get his ass in gear and move, she grabbed his hand with both arms and dragged him with surprising strength up on the sidewalk and behind the rental.

Letting him go, she immediately began to examine his wound. Adrian hissed a breath when her fingers came damn close to the place where he'd been hit.

"Sorry." Her brow furrowed. "Shit."

"Not exactly the kinda thing…you wanna hear…from a…nurse."

Her emerald eyes found his. "Sorry," she apologized again. "It just…the bullet's still in there."

Yeah, he'd figured that one out already.

Fuck. He'd almost forgotten how bad getting shot hurt.

Ben burst out of the station's entrance. He spotted Adrian and Jenna almost immediately, and Jesus. By the look on the other man's face, you'd have thought he was dying.

He wasn't dying. Not today.

Not when he'd finally found something worth living for.

With two uniformed officers flanking Ben's sides, the three men had their guns drawn, and they were running down the sidewalk toward them.

"You two okay?" The man in charge yelled.

"He's been hit!" Jenna hollered at him. "He needs an ambulance."

Christ, she's something else.

Bullets had been flying around them and her hands were covered with his blood, yet she was calm as a fucking cucumber.

He would've fallen in love with her that very second, if he wasn't already there.

"I'm…fine," Adrian told them through his clenched teeth.

Jesus, he felt dizzy.

Quickly, before he did something ridiculously embarrassing like pass the hell out, Adrian gave Ben a rundown of what he knew.

"Black four-door…tinted windows…no plates."

Using his department-issued radio, Ben passed the information along. The man then requested EMS on the scene.

Adrian was about to argue that it would be faster if Jenna just drove him to the hospital herself when the world around him started to spin.

Okay, so maybe *fine* was a bit of a stretch.

"Adrian?" Jenna's soft palms cupped both of his cheeks. "Hey, stay with me, okay?"

He was. Or at least he *thought* he was.

Working to keep his eyes open, he saw Jenna reach for his belt. In a rush, she had it unbuckled and was pulling it free in seconds.

"'smuch as I like where you're…going with this, sweetheart…there's a bit of an…audience. Don't ya…think?"

He wasn't lying. The area was now swarming with cops and other department staff.

"Jokes? Really?" She slid the end of the leather strap between his leg and the sidewalk. "You're bleeding all over the place, and you're making jokes?"

"Just a…scratch. *Ah!*" He winced when she cinched the belt as tight as it would go, just above his wound. "Not like I'm…dying."

Jenna gave the belt another tug—*motherfucker, that hurt*—before latching the buckle. Taking his face in her hands, her watery gaze staring back into his.

"You'd better not be."

Getting weaker by the second, Adrian wrapped a bloodied hand around her tiny wrist and squeezed. "Not going…anywhere."

Sirens blared in the distance. Minutes later, Adrian had

an IV in his veins, and he was being strapped to a gurney and rolled toward the back of an ambulance.

Jenna was by his side, spewing off a bunch of medical jargon about his condition to the medics as they moved. He tried focusing on what she was saying, but his head had become even foggier than before.

One thing he *could* make out were the tears in her eyes and the worried expression on her face. She was breaking his heart.

Didn't she know? He'd waited too damn long to find her to simply up and leave her behind, now.

Leave her...

His heartrate spiked, and he sucked in a breath. In a sudden moment of clarity, Adrian realized if they hauled him off for surgery to remove the bullet, Jenna would be left alone and unprotected.

"Stop!" He wrapped his hands around the gurney's metal railing and attempted to push himself up.

"What are you doing?" Jenna pushed against his shoulders. "Adrian, you need to lie down and let the pain meds do their job."

Pain meds?

That would explain the cool, floaty sensation spreading through his body.

"Can't leave…you," his words came out slurred.

"You're not, remember? You already told me you weren't dying, and I'm holding you to that, mister. So just lie back down and—"

"No." Adrian squeezed his eyes and then opened them again in an attempt to focus on her face and his words. His fingers fumbled to grab her hand because, he *had* to get this out. "Can't leave you…unpro…tected."

"She won't be," Ben assured him from the other side of the gurney. "She'll be with me."

The two men shared a look, and through the fog, Adrian dipped his chin in agreement.

He fucking hated the idea of anyone else watching over her, but his current situation didn't give him much choice.

"Anything happens to…her…"

Ben's expression was unreadable. "It won't."

Something tugged at Adrian's gut, but he didn't know what it was. He wasn't sure if it was the situation or the drugs, and unfortunately, he didn't have time to question it.

Ben stepped back as one of the medics hopped into the back of the ambulance. Jenna started to pull away from him, too, but at the last second, Adrian grabbed her hand and kept her where she stood.

The man behind his head put a hand on his shoulder and said, "Sir, we have to go."

And I have something I need to say.

Ignoring the anxious medic, Adrian used all the strength he had left to keep his grip on Jenna's hand. He locked his hazy gaze with hers. "Stay with…Ben," he ordered. "Don't…leave…side."

"I won't," she squeezed his hand back.

"Promise…me."

"I promise." With a soft smile, she leaned in and gave him a gentle kiss. "Be a good patient, okay? Do what they tell you, and I'll…" Her voice cracked. "I'll be there when you get out of surgery."

With the sweetest of kisses, she pressed her lips to his forehead and let go of his hand. She stepped back to make room as he was rolled inside the ambulance.

No!

A tugging in his gut told him he shouldn't wait. He needed to say the words *now*, before it was too late.

"Love…you." Adrian uttered the words out loud.

It was the first time he'd said them to a woman who wasn't his sister.

He looked to where Jenna had been standing. His heart dropped into his stomach when he realized she hadn't heard his precious words at all because the doors to the ambulance had already slammed shut.

CHAPTER 9

Jenna's hands were covered in Adrian's blood. Her pulse raced and her body trembled as adrenaline still spread through her system.

The situation was so surreal, she was still trying to process everything that had happened.

One minute, she and Adrian were talking and laughing. The next, Jenna was crouching down to avoid flying bullets and screaming for the man she loved.

"He's a fighter."

She tore her gaze away to look at the man behind the wheel. "I know," she told Ben quietly.

Adrian was more than a fighter. He was one of the strongest men she'd ever known.

Even the mighty fall sometimes.

Ignoring the negative thought, Jenna glanced back down at the stain on her hands. Her stomach clenched with terror. The mere *thought* of him not making it out of this alive had her heart stuttering and her lungs breathless.

Adrian was shot. I have his blood on my hands. He was shot, and then they took him away.

"I've known him a long time," Ben spoke up again. His knuckles became white as his grip tightened around the steering wheel. "Adrian's survived things most people wouldn't. He'll make it through this, too."

Jenna studied the man's odd expression. He seemed confident in his statement, but at the same time he looked worried. And the tone of his voice…

It was almost as if he were trying to convince himself that Adrian would be okay, rather than her.

He lost so much blood.

For the millionth time since it happened, Jenna ran through the steps she'd taken to stop the bleeding. The homemade tourniquet had seemed to help. Between that and the speedy arrival of the EMS crew, he *should* make a complete recovery.

Of course, that was assuming the surgery to remove the bullet went off without a hitch.

It's only a flesh wound. They'll go in, extract the bullet, and sew him back up. Easy peasy.

Looking out the passenger window, Jenna mentally replayed those words over and over, until her pulse slowed, and her breaths steadied.

She glanced down at her watch and wondered if he was already in surgery. She'd wanted to go with him so badly, but contrary to what they showed in the movies, most EMS departments didn't allow third parties to ride in the back with the patients.

Too much liability.

That meant she was relying on Ben to get her to the hospital, and he'd needed to stick around to tell his officers how he wanted the crime scene to be processed. By the time he was finished delegating and giving orders, the ambulance was already long gone.

Chomping at the bit to get there, Jenna turned back to Ben and asked, "How close are we to the hospital?"

"It's not far." He kept his eyes straight ahead. "But I need to make a quick stop first."

He's making a stop? Now?

"I don't mean to be rude, but do you think you could just drop me off at the hospital and then go do whatever it is you need to do?"

"I told Adrian I'd watch over you."

As they approached an upcoming street, Ben flipped his blinker and pressed his foot against the brake.

"I'll be surrounded by hospital staff the entire time," Jenna assured him. "You could even ask one of the security guys to watch over me while you're gone."

"This will only take a minute."

Jenna pulled her bottom lip in between her teeth to keep her frustrations inside. She understood the man was in charge of an entire police department and probably had other responsibilities that needed his attention, as well.

Knowing these things did nothing to ease her anxiety.

I need to be at the hospital. I need to find out Adrian's status, and I need to be there in case something happens.

Doing her best not to let her emotions take over, Jenna drew a deep breath in through her nose and let it out slowly.

One quick stop. That's what he'd said. Surely, she could handle that.

The car turned onto the side street. Her brows pulled together when she realized they were driving through a residential area.

An unsettling feeling began to seep in.

They went down two blocks and turned right. After driving another block, they took a left, and after passing several more homes, they turned right, again.

It was a dead-end street with only two houses—one across from the other.

The one on their left appeared empty and had a for sale sign posted in the front yard. The house to their right had its windows boarded up, and the overgrown grass and foliage around it made the home's abandonment obvious.

Ben turned into the driveway of the house listed for sale. The large, double door to the attached garage began to open, revealing a dark SUV parked inside.

As soon as there was enough clearance, Ben slowly pulled his car into the empty space on the right. The garage door closed behind them, essentially locking them inside.

Jenna's pulse skyrocketed. Alarm bells filled her head.

This isn't right. We shouldn't be here.

Just then, two large, intimidating men exited the SUV. They wore matching black suits, and both were carrying guns.

Jenna's eyes flew to Ben's. "What's going on?"

She'd been hoping he'd say something—*anything*—to explain what was happening. Instead, she found a gun pointed directly at her chest.

Oh, god.

"Ben?"

"I'm sorry, Jenna." He held his pistol steady. "I didn't have a choice."

He didn't have...

"Choice with *what?*" Confusion and fear assaulted her. "Ben, what the hell are you doing?"

Beads of sweat formed on the man's forehead. "He threatened my family. My wife and two daughters. I had to protect them."

Through the windshield, Jenna watched the other two men closely. One stood guard outside Ben's door while the other walked around the front of their car.

Shit. Shit. Shit.

Panic set in. "What are you talking about? Who threatened you?"

"A man with the power to destroy everything I hold dear."

"But why?" Jenna's voice rose an octave. "Why me?"

"I don't know." Pale and pasty, now, Ben looked like he was going to be sick. "But when a man like Matais Ortiz gives you orders, you don't ask questions."

Matais *who?*

Jenna's mind raced to place the name, but she couldn't. However, one thing was clear. Adrian was right.

What happened at the club wasn't random at all. She *had* been targeted. And because she hadn't listened when he wanted her to leave town, he'd been shot and was on his way to surgery.

All because these men wanted to get to her.

I should've listened to him. I should've gone back to California instead of sticking my nose where it didn't belong. Damn it, Jenna...why didn't you listen?

The passenger door opened. Jenna swung her gaze to the man standing behind her. Tall and broad, the Hispanic man's cold eyes met hers as he reached in and grabbed her arm.

"Hey!" Jenna tried pulling herself free. "Let go of me!" Facing Ben again, she began screaming at the cowardice traitor. "You son of a bitch! How could you?"

"I'm sorry."

He looked and sounded remorseful, but the gun in his hand said something entirely different.

"You're *sorry?*" She was yanked forcefully from the car. Terror fueled the anger erupting inside her. "Adrian trusted you!"

"I know." Ben nodded. A sorrowful resolve filled his eyes.

A sudden understanding stole Jenna's breath.

Though Ben didn't say it, the guilt and shame pouring

off of him was as good as a confession. This man—the same man who'd *helped* Adrian in the past—had set them up.

"They were waiting for us to leave the police station." She spoke even as she fought against the jerk pulling on her arm. "You told them where we were. *You* did this to us!"

The gun in Ben's hand shook. "I told you, I had no *choice!*"

"Let's go." The big brute pushed her forward.

For a second, Jenna thought he sounded familiar, but before she could figure out why, she lost her balance and nearly went down. On reflex, she spun on her heels and pushed against the guy's massive chest.

"I said, don't touch me!"

She may as well have hit a brick wall. A very large, very pissed off brick wall.

With a snarl, the man's hand snaked out again. He grabbed her upper arm like before, only this time he pulled her body flush with his.

Lifting his other hand to her face, the asshole shoved the barrel of his gun beneath her chin. The cold, hard metal bit into Jenna's skin, making her wince.

"Boss said to bring you in alive." His hot, smoker's breath nearly made her gag. "But he didn't say what condition you had to be in."

Jenna's heart fell into her stomach. Despite the odds being stacked against her, Jenna's first instinct was to fight. But these men were too big and too *armed* for her to take them on alone.

Getting beaten or shot would do nothing to help her cause. So unless she wanted to make the situation worse—and given the gun currently pressed against her face, that was quite possible—she had no choice but to do what they said.

For now.

The first chance she got to escape, Jenna was damn well taking it.

There were too many things she wanted to do with her life to just give up. Memories she needed to make. Moments she longed to experience.

And while Jenna may have questioned her goals before, that was no longer the case. She knew exactly what she wanted…and who she wanted it with.

I want a life with Adrian.

Sweet, complicated, pain-in-the-ass Adrian. He was all she wanted. And everything she needed.

She was struck with the image of him laughing—right before all hell had broken loose. She could still hear those precious words falling from his lips.

God, I love you.

Sure, he'd uttered them in jest, but the shocked expression that had crossed over his face was telling.

Adrian loved her. Even if the stubborn man wasn't ready to admit it to her—or himself—he loved her.

So, no. Jenna would *not* give up. She'd simply bide her time until she could find a way back to him. Because right or wrong, too soon or not, she loved him, too.

With renewed determination to survive whatever this was, she quit fighting against the big buffoon's hold and allowed herself to be led into the SUV. With a not-so-gentle boost, Jenna was helped into the back seat by the man still holding her at gunpoint.

Forcing her to scoot over, he slid onto the seat beside her and shut the door. Without a word, he shoved the end of his gun against her ribcage.

A silent but effective warning.

Though it was damn hard, Jenna held back her reaction. She would not—would *not*—let these men see how scared she was.

And she was fucking terrified.

For herself. For Adrian. And despite the fact that he was a betraying bastard, Jenna also feared for Ben.

She hadn't missed the look the police chief had given her right before she was shoved into the SUV. It was the same haunted look of acceptance she'd seen in patients who knew they were about to die.

Jenna kept her gaze forward, refusing to watch. Knowing there was nothing she could do to help, she closed her eyes and waited. Her heart broke when she heard Ben's muffled voice carry through the enclosed vehicle.

"Please. You don't have to do this. I did as Matais instructed! Please! I have a family. My children need me. *Please!*"

The echoing gunshot made her entire body jolt.

Oh, god!

Tears fell down Jenna's cheeks, but she silently wiped them away. She didn't have to look to know Ben Campillo was dead.

First the cab driver. Now Ben.

You'll be dead, too, if you don't find a way out of this mess.

The second man opened the driver's door and climbed behind the wheel. Ever-so-casually, as if he hadn't just taken someone's life, he started the engine and opened the garage door.

Backing the vehicle out of the enclosed space, the man pressed the remote a second time. Jenna watched the electronic door close, hiding Ben's body and car inside.

Jenna couldn't help but wonder when the slain man would be found. She prayed it wasn't long. For both her sake and that of Ben's family.

The sooner they realize what happened, the better chances I have of being found.

"Why are you doing this?" she couldn't help but ask.

The gun dug even harder into her side. "Keep your mouth shut, or I'll shut it for you."

The two men began speaking in Spanish as they drove away from the house. Not wanting the man to make good on his threat, Jenna stayed quiet and buried herself in her thoughts.

She wondered how Adrian was doing and prayed he made it out of surgery without any complications. Her heart became heavy as she thought about him waking up to discover his friend had been murdered and she'd been taken.

He's going to blame himself.

God, more than *anything* Jenna wished she could talk to him. Let him know she was sorry and make him see that this —whatever *this* was—wasn't his fault. It was hers.

And the worst part was, she didn't even know why.

At first, she'd assumed it had something to do with their inquiry into Stella Gallagher's disappearance. But they'd only just spoken with Ben about that minutes before the shooting, so how would anyone have known?

Ben could've told them. He could've called them after you and Adrian left his office.

But even that didn't make sense because the shooter was already outside when they left the police station.

No, she was almost certain this had something to do with before, when she was drugged at the club and almost abducted. Maybe these were the two guys who'd tried to take her?

Jenna's guarded gaze slid to the man sitting next to her and then the driver. Was it possible? Were these the men from that night?

The chilling theory sent a shiver down her spine. It also made perfect sense.

She'd witnessed the murder of the cab driver. Sure, she didn't *remember* anything about it, but these guys didn't know that. So maybe…maybe they were doing all of this to silence her so she couldn't testify against them?

If that were the case, then why didn't they just kill you and leave your body with Ben's?

Obviously, Jenna didn't have all of the answers—or any, really. But for now, she needed to focus on the fact that she was still alive and do her best to stay that way until she either found a way to escape or someone came for her.

As she was driven out of the city, she stared out at the road ahead of them in silence. With nothing else to do but sit back and await her fate, Jenna thought of the man who owned her heart and wondered if she'd ever get to see him again.

I'm sorry, Adrian. I love you. I'm so sorry.

CHAPTER 10

Adrian peeled his eyes open, then immediately squeezed them shut. Readying himself for the bright, blinding light, he tried again. And again.

After a few more attempts, he was finally able to *keep* them open. Feeling dizzy and disoriented, it took him a minute to realize where he was.

I'm in the hospital?

Like a slow-moving wheel, Adrian's memories began to surface.

He and Jenna had gone to the police station. They'd met with Ben. Afterward, they were standing outside, talking and laughing. But then…

Some asshole shot me in the leg.

The wheel spun faster, bringing it *all* back to him.

Glass shattering. Jenna's screams. The white-hot pain spreading through his leg as the bullet lodged itself into his muscle.

Adrian let his heavy lids fall. As he lay there, fighting the drugs still running through his system, more broken memories flashed before his mind's eye.

His blood was on Jenna's hands. He could almost *feel* her fingers on his leg as she worked to save his life.

Adrian could see the worry that had covered her beautiful face as he was loaded into the back of the ambulance, and he heard himself whispering…

I love you.

Shit, that's right. He *had* said that to her. But Jenna hadn't heard him because he'd been too late.

Fucking figures.

He shook his head against his pillow. May have even laughed a little, too. Either way, the irony of the situation wasn't lost on him.

For his entire adult life, he'd done everything he could to avoid getting close to any woman. And up until the day he met Jenna, that goal hadn't been difficult to accomplish.

But with her, it was different. With Jenna, *everything* was different, and suddenly Adrian couldn't wait to say those three not-so-little words to her again.

This time, I'll make damn sure she hears them.

Through his blurred vision, he squinted toward the chair on the right side of his bed. Disappointment left his shoulders sagging when he found it empty.

Jenna had said she'd be here when he woke up. Or at least he *thought* that's what she'd said. Damn place probably had strict visitor policies. Since she wasn't family…

We'll have to see what we can do to change that.

Another wave of dizziness struck, making him feel even more lightheaded than before. Staring up at the tiled ceiling, Adrian gave himself another minute to gain his bearings. While he laid there, he made a mental checklist of his plans for the immediate future.

See Jenna and make sure she was okay. Tell her he loved her. Get her the hell out of this city.

In. That. Order.

Huh. What do ya know...I have plans.

Feeling ridiculously giddy, Adrian started to smile, but a dull ache in his left leg started to gnaw at him. He lifted the heavy blanket to inspect the damage, but he couldn't actually *see* the damage thanks to the miles of gauze wrapped around his thigh.

Wiggling his toes to make sure they still worked, he clenched his teeth and drew in steadying breath. Pointing his left foot forward, he stretched the muscles in his leg. There was a slightly painful pull, but nothing he couldn't handle.

Deciding to push himself a little more, he flexed his foot upward, bringing his toes back toward his chest. A sharp, burning sensation ran up the back of his thigh, stealing his breath.

Fuck me.

"About damn time you woke up."

What the...

Adrian turned to his left, his drug-induced haze forcing his vision to play catch-up. Blinking quickly, he hoped the man he'd seen was nothing more than a disturbing hallucination.

He looked again, and...nope. No such luck.

Gabriel Dawson was actually here. In his room. And he looked fucking pissed.

Shit. How did he not see him before now?

Probably because you're high as a morphine-fueled kite. Just a guess, though.

Adrian smiled at his unexpected visitor. "I'm touched, Dawson." Damn, his voice sounded scratchy as hell. "You come all this way to kiss my boo-boo?"

The Bravo Team leader crossed his arms in front of his broad chest and stared. Between Gabe's narrowed gaze and a jaw made of stone, it didn't take a genius to see that he was in no mood for jokes.

"Where's Jenna?"

"Have you checked the waiting room? 'Cause last I knew, that's where people went to…you know…wait."

Curling his fists at his sides, Gabe took an angry step toward him. "You were supposed to protect her."

"What the fuck do you think I've been doing?" He grimaced as he shifted his injured leg. "In case you haven't noticed, big guy, I'm the one who took the bullet. Not her."

It could've been her.

No. Adrian refused to let his mind go there. Jenna belonged to him now, which meant he'd kill anyone stupid enough to even think about touching what was his.

"Where is she?" Gabe interrupted his thoughts.

"With one of the few people in this world I actually trust."

A muscle in the man's jaw twitched. "Let me guess, Ben Campillo?"

"Damn. You *are* good."

"Walker, Jenna's—"

"Relax, Dawson." Adrian cut the man off. "Ben's a former asset and an old friend. He said he'd keep Jenna safe until I can get sprung from this place."

"Walker—"

"Seriously, man. Everything's fine." He looked around the room. "Look, where's my phone? I'll call Ben right now and find out where they are, so you can see for yourself that Jenna's—"

"Missing."

Adrian heard the word. He knew what it meant. But apparently, he was struggling to keep up because what Gabe had just said made zero sense.

"What are you talking about?" He pushed himself up the noisy mattress. "Who's missing?"

"Who the fuck do you think?"

Feeling as though he were on some sort of time delay, it took Adrian three full seconds to process the man's words.

Jenna's...missing?

The pieces finally started clicking together.

Gabe hadn't come all this way simply because Adrian had been shot. They weren't even friends. Hell, most days they barely *tolerated* each other, and that was mainly for Elle's sake.

No, the only reason Gabe would've flown here from Dallas was if…

"You're wrong." Adrian shook his head vehemently. The machines connected to him beeped a little faster. "That's not possible."

"You think I came all this way to bring you fucking flowers and a get-well balloon?"

Denial had already dug its claws into Adrian's heart, and it refused to let go. "I'm telling you you're *wrong*. I left Jenna with Ben." Adrian fumbled with the controls on the side of the bed to get himself into a full seated position. "He's the—"

"I know who the guy is, Walker," Gabe barked. Placing his hands on his hips, he shot Adrian a glare. "Are you even listening to me, or are you too stoned to comprehend a complete fucking sentence? Jenna is *gone*. No one has seen or heard from her or Campillo since they left the police station after you were shot."

Nausea rolled through his gut as he tried to make sense of what Gabe was saying. Jenna couldn't be missing. She *couldn't*.

"Jesus Fucking Christ, Dawson. Think maybe you could lead with that shit next time?"

Ignoring the pain in his leg and the incessant beeping, Adrian threw the covers off and swung his body around so that his legs were hanging over the edge of the bed.

A new wave of dizziness hit. Working his way past it, he

tried desperately to think of an explanation for the bomb Gabe had just dropped on him.

Preferably one that *didn't* end with the woman he loved disappearing.

Calm your ass down. Take a damn breath and think.

He swallowed the knot in his throat. "Ben knew I needed him to protect Jenna. If you can't find them, it's probably because he decided to take her to a safe house or something."

"Even if that were true, the guy's the Chief of Police, Walker. He wouldn't just take off without letting someone within the department know where he was headed. Or, at the very least, his wife."

"You talked to Ben's *wife?*"

"Not me." Gabe shook his head. "King went by the house."

Zade King was another member of Bravo Team. From everything Adrian had learned about the man, King was the most emotional and sensitive of the group. Made sense that he'd be the one to talk to Sheila, Ben's wife.

"Nate ran the check on the Gallagher woman, like you requested," Gabe continued on. "As soon as he was finished, I tried calling you. When you didn't answer, I tried Jenna, and when *that* didn't work, I tried the hospital."

"She doesn't work there…here. Not anymore."

"No shit." The man's angry gaze narrowed. "After finding out that bit of information, I called Chief Campillo."

Calling the Chief directly seemed like an odd leap for Gabe to take. "Why Ben?"

"A woman who's like a sister to me and the dipshit I sent down here to watch over her went MIA. I didn't want to waste even more time than I already had, so I went straight to the top. Except Campillo didn't answer, and when I finally *did* manage to get ahold of someone within the department, I was told he was busy working a shooting that had taken place near the precinct. My gut told me you were involved, so I had Nate access the traffic cam footage from the street in front of the station, and ta da! Guess what I saw?"

"I was going to call you."

"Before or after you let some asshole take her?"

"Fuck you," Adrian spouted back. "You don't even know for sure that's what happened."

With his hands on his hips, Gabe's fury sprung to life. "I know your ass was loaded into the ambulance after being gunned down in front of a goddamn police station. I know Jenna and Campillo drove off in his car, and I know a few minutes later, they disappeared into thin fucking air! So unless you've got a better explanation…" He trailed off, his broad chest heaving as he pulled in several calming breaths. "I've used every contact I have, including Ryker and his team. But so far, we've keep come up empty."

"What about traffic cams? Surely one of those—"

"How the hell do you think we know she left with Campillo? Nate accessed every camera in the area. Campillo's car can be seen turning into a residential neighborhood about five blocks from the precinct. And before you ask, there aren't any cameras on those streets."

"Residential?" Adrian frowned. "Why would they have gone there?"

"No clue. All we *do* know is the car entered the neighborhood but didn't come out. At least not where there were any cameras."

Fear trickled down his spin. "A car with two people inside doesn't just disappear, Dawson."

"And this isn't my first rodeo," Gabe seethed. "The police are canvassing the area now. If Campillo and Jenna are there, they'll find them."

"Canvassing the…" Adrian's fingers dug into the edge of the mattress. "They should be going door to fucking door searching every goddamn house!"

ANNA BLAKELY

"They *have* been going door-to-door, but the neighbor-hood's huge. That shit takes time, Walker. Hell, my team's been questioning the neighbors right along with them. So far, no one in that area remembers seeing Chief Campillo or Jenna. As much as I'd love to, we can't just waltz in and start searching people's homes without a warrant."

He shot Gabe an incredulous look. "The fuck we can't. And since when does Bravo play by the rules?"

"This isn't just about my team, Adrian," Gabe reminded him. "You think I don't want to be out there, busting through every goddamn door until I find Jenna? The cops are involved because one of their *own* is involved." Gabe hesitated a beat before adding, "Maybe in ways you don't want to consider."

Adrian blinked. "You think Ben's dirty? No." He shook his head. "No fucking way."

"This is Jenna we're talking about. So, like it or not, we have to consider *every* angle. Including the possibility that your guy was in on it."

Though he'd never admit it, Adrian knew Gabe was right. Someone had taken the woman he loved. And that person—whoever he may be—was a dead man.

"You said your team's searching the area." He looked back up at Gabe. "Then what?"

"Nate's at the hotel running every report he can think of. He started with Campillo's financials. They came back clean, which is promising. But you and I both know there are ways around that."

"Yeah, I do. But that still doesn't mean Ben's involved."

"Nate also hacked the security footage from the club you and Jenna went to the night all that other shit went down. Ran facial rec on those he could, but it was dark and, according to Nate, the system's quality sucks ass. While that runs, he's been digging into the people Jenna worked with at the hospital."

Jesus. A lot sure happened while I was under the knife.

A thought struck, smacking Adrian upside the head like a prize fighter's fist.

Dread gnawed at his insides as he forced himself to ask, "How long?"

The look in Gabe's brown eyes made Adrian's stomach turn.

"Two days. My team and I got in town early this morning."

His heart stuttered. "Two *days?*"

Jenna's been missing for two fucking days?

Bile rushed into the base of his throat. He gagged but managed to swallow it down at the last minute.

With his eyes squeezed shut, Adrian hung his head between his shoulders and sucked in air. For the next several seconds, he forced himself to draw in slow, even breaths to avoid puking all over his paper-thin gown. When he could formulate a sentence again, he lifted his eyes to back to Gabe's.

"How the hell did this happen?"

"I don't know." The stoic man's jaw twitched. "But you can bet your ass I'm going to find out."

"Two days," Adrian whispered his disbelief again. "I was out that entire time?"

"I spoke to your doctor. Apparently, there was some sort of complication during your surgery." Gabe shoved his hands into his jeans' pockets. "Something about a nicked artery and extensive blood loss. Doc said they had to put you in a medical coma for a stretch to keep you from moving around and busting it open again."

Sweet Jesus.

Jenna had been missing for days, and he'd been fucking *sleeping?*

Shaking, Adrian ran a hand down his face. His breathing became rough. Uneven. And he felt like he was going to pass out from fear and worry.

Get your shit together, Walker. Jenna needs you.

The voice in his head was right. He needed to lock his shit down and focus.

"Get me some clothes." Adrian began peeling the sticky-as-fuck cardiac leads from his torso. Alarms blared all around him as he yanked his IV from his arm and stood.

"What the hell are you...no, I'm not getting you clothes. Sit your ass down before you start bleeding again."

Adrian jerked his head back in Gabe's direction. "The fuck you mean no? Why'd you even come here if you aren't going to help me—"

"Mr. Walker!" A male nurse rushed into the room, his eyes wide and his voice high-pitched with shock and confusion. "What...what are you doing? You need to get back into bed!"

The guy—or *kid*—appeared to be in his early twenties and probably weighed a buck twenty soaking wet. Small or not, Adrian would demolish the guy if he got in his way.

"What I need is for you to find me something to wear so my ass isn't hanging out when I walk out of here."

"Walk out of...no, Mr. Walker." The nurse shook his head, looking even more confused than before. "You can't *leave.* You've just had surgery. You lost a copious amount of blood, and the doctor wants you to stay another two days, minimum."

"I don't give a shit what the doctor wants," Adrian growled. "I'll sign whatever I need to sign, but I *am* leaving, and I'd prefer not to be wearing this"—he motioned to the gown—"when I do."

"But sir—"

Jesus H. Christ. I don't have time for this shit.

Getting right up in the guy's clean-shaven face, Adrian glanced at his plastic name badge. "Brad, is it? Listen, *Brad*... you don't know me, and while it may not seem like it now, I'm actually a pretty nice guy." Behind him, Gabe let out a loud cough. He ignored it. "That being said, I'm having a really shitty day. So I'm gonna need you to get me those discharge papers and a pair of scrubs so I can get the hell out of here."

"I don't understand...has there been some sort of emergency? Something I can maybe help with?"

"Emergency?" Adrian raised a brow as his gaze bounced between Gabe's and the young man's. "You could say that. I'm going to find the man who thought it was a good idea to put a bullet in my leg and then kidnap someone who means a great deal to me. And when I do, I'm going to end him. Now, you're welcome to tag along if you want, but my bet is you'd rather not be there for the whole torture and killing part. Just a guess, though."

Brad's wide eyes shot to Gabe's. "H-he's joking. Right?"

Gabe snorted. "About being a nice guy? Definitely a fucking joke."

"Papers and scrubs, Brad." Adrian snapped his fingers to refocus the kid's attention. "Right. The fuck. Now."

Looking like he was about to piss his pants, Brad stared slack jawed for another ten seconds before bobbing his head in a jerky nod. The kid damn near sprinted from the room.

Facing Gabe once more, Adrian opened his mouth to continue their argument about him staying put, but the asshole beat him to it.

"The *only* reason I'm here is because the hospital called and told me they were stopping the drugs that were keeping you under. I knew you'd be waking up, and I needed to find out what the hell was going on so my team and I could start putting together a plan of action."

Adrian didn't even bother asking Gabe how he managed to bypass the whole HIPPA bullshit. He did, however, need to make one thing clear.

"The *plan* is, I'm getting the fuck out of here, and then I'm going to find Jenna."

He took a step but stopped immediately when pain shot up his thigh. With determination and fear for his woman pushing him on, he took another step…and another.

Adrian continued like that—hobbling around the room with his bare ass showing—while he opened drawers and cabinets looking for something to change into.

"Jesus Christ, Walker. You heard what the nurse said. You're gonna end up busting open your stitches, which could mean you bleed out before anyone can do jack shit to help you. You won't do you or Jenna any good if you're fucking dead."

"I'm fine."

"You're not—"

"I said, I'm fine!" Adrian whirled on the other man. The pain in his leg begged to differ, but he used it and his fear as fuel and kept on with his search.

Gabe continued his efforts to talk him out of leaving. "There's nothing you can do that isn't already being done, so just sit back down and talk to me. Maybe something Jenna said or did will help give us a clue as to who'd want to hurt her." When Adrian didn't respond, Gabe asked, "What was going on with Jenna before all this shit happened?"

I'll tell you what was going on. I'm sleeping with her, asshole. I'm in love *with her. That's* what's going the fuck on.

With his frustration growing, the other man kept on. "I spoke to the woman from Saje Staffing. She told me Jenna parted ways with the agency the day before you were shot."

"Parted ways." Adrian snorted as he checked the small built-in closet. "That's one way of putting it."

"Goddamnit, Adrian!" Gabe's last string of patience snapped. "Will you please stop limping around the fucking room for five seconds and look at me?"

He did stop limping around, but only because there wasn't a stitch of clothing to be found.

Gabe blew out a breath. "Let's back up. Why didn't you tell me about what happened the night Jenna went to the club?"

"Because I was too busy getting her the hell out of there."

"You sure that's all there is to it?"

The fuck? "You think I had something to do with this? Christ, man. I thought we were past all that shit."

"What shit?"

"The you not trusting me bullshit. Have you forgotten your wife's alive because of me?"

"No, asshole," Gabe growled. "I *haven't* forgotten. But that situation has nothing to do with this one."

"Jenna didn't want you or Ellena knowing about what happened to her."

Something she'd shared with him when they'd laid in bed talking after one of their many rounds of incredible sex.

Adrian had mentioned filling Gabe in, but Jenna had immediately balked at the idea. To make sure he went along with her plan to keep the incident a secret from her two good friends, she'd then used her wild, wicked tongue to entice him to agree.

It had worked like a fucking charm.

"I don't give a rat's ass if she wanted us to know or not!" Gabe continued with his rant. "I sent you here to keep her safe, and instead, you—"

"What?" Adrian faced off with the other man. "What the hell do you want me to say, Gabe? That I fucked up? Fine. I.

Fucked. Up." The admission escaped through a set of clenched teeth. "You think I'm happy about the fact that Jenna was drugged and almost kidnapped right under my fucking nose? Or that it doesn't tear me up inside knowing she disappeared while my ass was lying in that damn bed, unconscious? *Fuck!*"

Adrian spun on his good leg and punched the closet door. The section of particle board below his knuckles caved in on contact.

His nostrils flared and…Jesus. He couldn't *breathe* for the fear running through him.

"I tried talking her into flying back to San Diego." He turned to face Gabe again. "After she was almost taken that first time. I tried, but you know how she is. I swear, that woman's so damn"—*amazing*—"stubborn."

He should've forced her to leave. He could've tried harder to convince her. Hauled her sweet ass over his shoulder and *made* her go back to California.

"That, she is," Gabe agreed. "But why was she so determined to stay in Gulfside Harbor?"

"She was hell bent on finding out what happened to Stella Gallagher. So, I set up a meeting with Campillo."

"Tell me about him," Gabe's voice held less of a bite than before. "About when he was your informant."

Adrian's brows turned inward. "What does that have to do with anything?"

"It may not, but we have to look at this thing from every angle. What did Campillo do for you?"

"Before he became Chief, Ben helped me on a case. Local gang was buying illegal weapons here. They'd make the purchase on the black market then move the cache over the border and sell it. The gang's main buyer at the time was Mexico's largest weapons dealer. Thanks to some vital intel

Ben shared, we were able to take down the entire organization."

"That's great and all, but that doesn't mean he's not—"

"Ben also helped me find my sister," Adrian blurted more loudly than intended.

"Bree, right?" Gabe studied him closely. "You mentioned her once before."

He had. Back when Elle was in danger and Adrian was still trying to convince Gabe and his team that he wasn't a fucking traitor.

"The guy risked his career...his *life*...by giving me the intel I needed to find her," he shared. "I didn't get to Bree in time to..." His voice cracked so he cleared his throat. "I wasn't able to save her. But, thanks to Ben, the men responsible for her death will never hurt another living soul again."

They shared a look only men like them would understand.

"That's why you and Jenna went to him for help." Gabe's anger seemed to falter. "Makes sense, but what exactly were you hoping he'd be able to do this time?"

"I thought..." Adrian raked a hand through his hair and sighed. "Hell, I don't know. I guess I was hoping he could set Jenna's mind at ease. Let her know the cops *were* still looking for the Gallagher woman. She was convinced no one was."

A line formed between the man's brows. "Why did she care so much about this particular case?"

Jenna's words from before rang through his ears.

I'm just like her, Adrian. That could've been me.

"Jenna saw herself in Stella," he explained. "Single woman. Nurse. No kids. No real family. After what happened at the club, she...I don't know. Related to her, I guess. We were talking about everything, and Jenna told me if she ever disappeared..." His damn voice broke again, so he cleared his throat. Again. "She was convinced no one would notice she was gone or even care enough to look for her."

"What the fuck?" Gabe's face twisted with disbelief. That Jenna would even *think* that had clearly hurt him.

"I told her she was wrong, but it didn't matter. For whatever reason, she was determined to stay in town and do everything she could to find out what happened to Stella."

"And you agreed to help her."

Adrian nodded woodenly. "It was either that, or she was going to do it on her own. I thought if I was with her, she'd be safe." *I was so wrong.* "Instead, I ended up taking a fucking bullet, and now you're here, telling me my woman's missing. That the man who was supposed to be *protecting* her is missing, and—"

"Hold up, *your* woman?" Gabe's brows arched high a split second before coming together in a nasty glare. "The hell, you say."

Shit. Had he really called her that out loud?

Yep. You sure did.

Great. The last thing he needed was Jenna's self-proclaimed big brother trying to kick his ass. Then again…

Fuck it.

Limping over to where Gabe was standing, Adrian didn't stop until he'd invaded the other man's space. Letting the last chunk of his protective wall fall, he made his intentions clear.

"That's right, Dawson. Jenna's mine, and I'm hers. So you bet your ass I'm going to do whatever it takes to find her."

"It's like that?"

Damn straight. "Yeah." Adrian nodded. "It's like that."

The two men stood nose-to-nose for the span of several seconds before Gabe cursed under his breath and looked away.

"Goddamnit." The former SEAL locked his fingers behind

his head as he paced the room. "You're telling me, of all the men out there, she actually picked your sorry ass?"

"That's what you're focused on right now?"

The pain and fear crossing the man's face mimicked what Adrian felt to his soul.

"Jenna's like a sister to me, Walker." Gabe set his jaw. "Which means, I'll do whatever it takes to find her, including beating your injured ass to get the intel I need. So if you know more than you're telling me, you'd better spill it right damn now, or I swear to Christ, I'll put a matching hole in your other leg."

The guy's brown eyes had hardened, and he looked like he wanted nothing more than to make good on his promise to shoot him. But that shit was going to have to wait, because Adrian had something *he* needed to say.

"You're not the only one who cares about Jenna." *Not even close.* "So you can toss around all the threats you want, but like it or not, she's mine. Way I see it, we can either work together on this, or I can do it on my own. Either way, I *will* find her, and I will bring her home."

"Or die trying?" Gabe's quip held a sarcastic tone.

The joke was on him when Adrian stared back and vowed, "Or die trying."

CHAPTER 11

Jenna woke with a start. She'd been dreaming of Adrian. They were together, and he was laughing. In her dream, he'd told her he loved her. He was about to kiss her when something ripped her from the blissful, unconscious state.

She waited in the dark, listening closely to try to figure out what it was. At first, the only sound filling her ears was that of her own, terrified heartbeat. But then she heard it again…a slight shuffle across the concrete floor.

Someone's coming!

On instinct, Jenna tried sitting up in case she needed to defend herself, but the nausea and dizziness made her regret the decision instantly.

You're handcuffed and weak as hell. What exactly did you think you were gonna do?

She squeezed her eyes shut, the metal cuffs biting into her tender wrists every time she tried shifting positions. They were wrapped around an old, metal pole. One that she'd tried —and failed—to pull and kick free.

But the damn thing wouldn't budge.

The only thing she *did* manage to accomplish at all during

her meager attempts to break free was to cut open the skin at her wrists.

At one point, Jenna had gotten so desperate to escape, she'd purposely continued with her futile efforts in hopes that the blood would allow her hands to slip free.

It didn't work.

She lost track of time a while ago, finally giving up on even trying to figure out how long she'd been here. She'd also stopped screaming for help.

No one had come for her. There'd been no interrogation or demands. Nothing but the cold, musty darkness she'd been tossed into and then forgotten.

After murdering Ben in cold blood, the man had who'd been sitting next to her in the SUV had waited a few blocks before shoving a needle into the side of her neck. At the time, Jenna had been so lost in her thoughts about Adrian, she hadn't seen the syringe until it was too late.

Sometime later, Jenna had woken up here, in what she assumed was a basement. Thanks to whatever drugs they'd put into her system, she'd had a massive headache and the worst case of cotton mouth she'd ever had.

There'd been no food or water. No explanation as to where she was or why she was here. The only light in the entire place was from a small, rectangle window on the wall to her right. One too high and much too small for her to even consider escaping through.

Jenna closed her eyes and breathed through the nausea. She was bone tired and severely dehydrated.

She was also terrified.

Over the course of her time here, the same two questions had replayed over and over again through her mind. She wondered if Ben's body had been found yet, and whether or not anyone was out there, looking for her.

I promise, if you went missing, I'd move heaven and earth to find you.

Adrian's promise had been a constant presence in her thoughts. She knew he'd meant every heartfelt word, but he'd also been shot. Was probably still in the hospital, recovering from his injury.

Even if he wanted to look for her—and she had to believe he did—chances were, he *couldn't.*

Jenna thought about Gabe and Ellena. They, too, would eventually figure out she was missing. When they did, Jenna had no doubt he and the rest of Bravo would begin their search.

Unfortunately for her, by the time that happened, Jenna had no idea where she'd be. Or if she'd even be alive.

"You're awake."

Her body jerked at the sound of the unexpected voice. Jenna looked up as the man who'd drugged her moved out of the shadows to come closer.

Reflexively, she shrank back as far as she could, her back hitting the cool, cinder block wall behind her. Fresh blood seeped from the cuts on her wrists as she pulled the cuffs to their limit.

"W-what do you want?" she croaked. Her throat was dry and scratchy from her earlier screams and the lack of water.

"Matais thought you might be hungry."

It's been two days since I had anything to eat, moron. Of course, I'm freaking hungry.

But information was more important to her than food, so Jenna ignored the tray in the man's hands and licked her dry lips. "I meant, what do you want with *me?*"

"Right now?" He tossed the tray down onto the floor near her feet. "I want you to eat."

The paper plate filled with rice and some sort of seasoned meat bounced, causing half of the food to fly off the tray and onto the concrete. The plastic water bottle that had been next to it tipped and rolled onto its side.

Her stomach *hurt* with hunger, and God she was so thirsty. But she had no way of knowing if any of it had been drugged.

Not willing to risk it, she looked away from the temptation.

"Eat," the man growled.

Jenna brought her gaze back up to his. "Tell me why I'm here."

Cursing, the man squatted down in front of her. Using his fingers, he scooped up some of the rice and meat and shoved it into his mouth. A few grains of rice stuck to his lips and chin as he chewed in a way that made her stomach churn.

"Satisfied?"

"You and your friend killed a man in front of me, kidnapped and drugged me, and then left me down here like a damn prisoner. Satisfied isn't quite the word I'd use."

He stood and nudged the tray with his foot. "Matais says eat, you eat."

Stubbornness, combined with a refusal to give this man even an inkling of pleasure, had Jenna jutting her chin. "Matais can go to hell."

With a snarl, he shook his head and hovered over her. "You have no idea what kind of man he is. What he's capable of."

"You're right." Jenna worked her parched throat. "I don't know, because this so-called boss of yours has yet to make an appearance." She swallowed again. "That tells me he either doesn't exist...or he doesn't have the balls to show his face."

Okay, so maybe poking the bear wasn't the *brightest* idea she'd ever had. But Jenna was just so tired.

Tired of sitting in the dark. Tired of breathing in dry, musty, dirty air. Tired of being terrified that, at any moment, they would come in here and put a bullet in her like they did Ben.

And that would be it.

No more life.

No chance to do all the things she still wanted to do.

And worst of all…no more Adrian.

Moving much faster than she would've expected for a man of his large size and build, the bastard grabbed the chain connected to the handcuffs and jerked her forward.

Reaching behind him, he picked up some of the food that had fallen onto the floor. Releasing the chain, he wrapped that hand around her chin and squeezed.

Jenna cried out, his painful grip making it feel as though her jaw was about to break. His strong hold forced her mouth to remain open while he shoved the rice and meat between her lips.

She attempted to spit it out, but the man used both hands to clamp her mouth shut. With no other choice, Jenna swallowed the food to avoid choking.

Giving her face a rough shove, the man let her go long enough to grab the water bottle and open the plastic lid. Though she tried to avoid it, the man held her jaw like before, forcing the water to fill her mouth and throat.

Unable to drink it all at once, Jenna coughed and sputtered, the excess liquid spilling out over her chin and dripping onto the concrete below.

"There. Was that so hard?" The man threw the bottle to the side and stood.

"Fuck…you," Jenna spoke between coughing fits.

"Maybe later." The asshole chuckled as he turned and walked away. "For now, you need to eat so you have energy for what is about to come."

That didn't sound good. Not good at all.

"Wait!" Jenna yelled, although in her weakened state it

sounded more like a whimper. "What do you want from me? Why am I here?"

He disappeared into the shadows.

A second later, she heard the door slam shut. Leaving her trapped in her own personal hell, alone and frightened.

Tears burned the corners of Jenna's eyes, but her body was too depleted for them to fall. Fear and frustration had her pulling wildly against her restraints again. She screamed to the point her voice broke, and her throat burned.

Was this their plan? Where they just going to leave her here to starve and go mad because she'd cared enough about a missing girl to ask questions?

Or could this be about something else? Something she wasn't seeing.

Jenna thought about the club. How she'd been drugged, and if not for Adrian, she would've been abducted that night, too.

Maybe *that's* what this was all about. Maybe…maybe she'd been targeted as part of some horrible sex trafficking ring.

Wouldn't there be other women here if that were the case?

Possibly. Or maybe this was what they did. Their attempt to 'break' the women they took before selling them.

That was the whole reason Jenna had talked Adrian into staying in town to begin with. She feared Stella Gallagher was being held somewhere against her will for that exact reason.

Someplace just like this.

Her stomach turned with the fleeting thought that Stella may have been brought here, to this *exact* place.

Oh, god.

A wave of helplessness and exhaustion struck simultaneously, and Jenna no longer had the strength to sit up. Ignoring the stinging in her wrists, she shifted her body in order to position herself onto her side.

Resting her head against the concrete floor, she laid in her cold, black prison. Jenna let her heavy lids fall shut.

As the darkness pulled her under, she thought of how upset Adrian would be, knowing she was gone. Her heart broke for him, knowing he'd be out of his mind with worry. And she worried *for* him. Because as soon as he was physically able, he *would* start looking for her.

Jenna just prayed he found her before it was too late. For both their sakes.

∼

"Bitch refuses to eat."

Matais looked up from his computer to address the man who'd just entered his office. Sebastian had been a part of the empire Cesar Ortiz—Matais' father—had built.

The same empire Adrian Walker singlehandedly destroyed.

"Ms. Shaw does not trust us." Matais stood and walked around what used to be his father's desk. "Can you blame her?"

The other man's square jaw clenched with anger. "She doesn't need to trust us. She needs to do what she is *told*."

"I understand your frustration, my friend." Matais rested his hand on his confidant's strong shoulder. "But we've come too far to let impatience get in the way of our plan."

"And what is the plan, Matais?" Sebastian asked boldly.

Not many men would have the balls to question him in such a manner. But Matais let it slide, because it was Sebastian. And because…

The woman will die, regardless.

"You're right." Matais let his lips curve upward. "The time has come. I trust you had no issues in delivering the package?"

"Left it in the middle of the bed, just as you instructed."

"Wonderful." He nodded. "I heard from my source within the hospital just before you walked in."

"And?"

"They informed me Walker is leaving early, against the doctor's recommendation. Just as I suspected he would."

Something else Matais learned from his father…you can never have too many eyes and ears working for you.

"I assume Walker's aware of Ms. Shaw's disappearance?" Sebastian inquired.

"He is. Authorities are searching for both her and Chief Campillo as we speak." Matais rubbed the stubble on his chin. "There is one possible complication we need to be prepared for."

"What is that?"

"There are other men in town. A group of former military operatives who now work for the private sector, though I've been told they take on government contracts, as well. Company called R.I.S.C."

Sebastian frowned. "What interest do they have in this?"

"According to my source, the leader of the team is a man named Gabe Dawson. He's in Walker's hospital room right now."

The other man blinked. "Walker is a known assassin. Why would this team be working with him? Are they mercenaries?"

"I haven't had time to research them yet. But my source informed me that Walker is getting ready to leave the hospital with Dawson. And he's out for blood."

"Which means, he'll have backup."

Matais tipped his chin. "If he doesn't follow our instructions, yes."

"I'll make sure the others are ready, just in case."

"Be sure that you do. When you've briefed them on the

situation, find Garcia and get everything set up like we discussed. Let me know when you are ready."

"Yes, sir." The man's cold eyes lit with anticipation as he turned to leave.

Matais stopped him just shy of the doorway. "Do you remember what it was like?"

Sebastian faced him with a questioning glance. "Boss?"

"When my father was still here." He slid his hands into the pockets of his designer dress pants. "Your time with him was quite limited, but he mentioned your name on more than one occasion. He was impressed with the work you had done for him up to that point. Your loyalty and sense of honor within the organization are the reason you are here now."

"Thank you, Matais." Sebastian looked genuinely humbled. "That means a great deal to me. And yes, I remember what it was like. Your father was a great man, as are you. He would be very proud of the way you've rebuilt what he worked so hard for."

Matais had no illusions to the kind of man his father was. Many called him evil. Monstrous. A ruthless drug and weapons dealer, as well as a seller of women and killer of men.

Cesar Ortiz was all those things, but he was also a brilliant businessman and charismatic leader. A loving father and husband who provided for both him and Matais' mother, may she rest in peace.

"Walker's death will be a defining moment for us both." Matais held out his hand.

The other man shook it with earnest. "I'm honored to be a part of it."

"And Garcia? How is he fairing?"

Garcia had taken one of Walker's bullets during his and Sebastian's first attempt at acquiring Jenna Shaw.

"His leg is still healing, but he will do what needs to be done."

Matais nodded. "I can imagine putting a bullet in Walker's leg was quite satisfying for him. Eye for an eye and all that."

Sebastian smirked. "It was."

"Good." Matais nodded. "He earned that moment and will be hailed for it."

"I'll let him know, Boss."

"Be sure that you do. Now, go. We have much to do in anticipation of our next guest."

With a wicked grin, Sebastian left the office to make preparations. Matais found himself smiling at the thought of Adrian Walker finding the gift that had been left for him.

It's all coming together, Papa. You will finally have justice soon. Very, very soon.

The day Walker murdered his father was the day Matais had begun to plan.

The first step in that plan was to rebuild all that his family had lost. Denying his primal need for revenge wasn't easy, but as he'd heard his father say many times over the years…

That which we need most is always worth the wait.

There had been days Matais had questioned his father's insight. Days when the doubt crept in and defeat threatened to take over. More than any other, *those* were the days he called upon his father's spirit for guidance.

Now, after years of pain, sweat, and tears, the time had come. The agonizing wait was finally over, and Matais was finally going to show those who still questioned his ability to lead in his father's shadow exactly what he was capable of.

He was every bit the leader his father was. And he would prove this—to those who doubted and to himself—by taking down the most feared hitman in existence.

Enjoy the breaths you are taking now, Walker. Because soon… very soon…you'll be taking your last.

CHAPTER 12

"I thought you guys were supposed to be the best of the best."

Standing just inside Gabe's hotel room—or suite, rather—Adrian put most of his weight on the set of metal crutches the doctor had insisted he take with him. His angry glare reached all five members of Bravo Team.

With an arched brow, Nate Carter stared up at him from over the top of his computer. "And I thought *you* were supposed to be in the hospital."

"I signed myself out so I could be out there, looking for Jenna and Ben. Not sitting on my ass in some swanky hotel room with you."

"Guess it's a good thing you're standing then, huh?" Matt Turner, Bravo Team's medic smirked.

Years ago, back before the CIA and Homeland recruited Adrian to work deep cover, he and Matt had served on the same Marine anti-terrorism unit. The guy was as solid as they came, and he now knew the truth about the whys and hows of Adrian's so-called desertion.

But there was a *slight* chance Matt was still pissed about the fact that, during one of his government-sanctioned ops,

Adrian had kidnapped the woman who was now Turner's wife.

Whatthefuckever.

They'd ironed all that shit out once, already. Adrian was not in the mood to do it a second time.

"You got a problem with my being here, Turner?" He faced off with the Bravo operative. "If so, say the word, and I'll go find them on my own."

"Oh, give it a rest, would ya?" Matt put his hands on his hips and scowled. "I thought we cleared the air like three months ago."

Adrian shrugged. "I thought so, too."

"Well, if anyone has the right to still hold a grudge, here, it's definitely not *your* sorry ass."

"I'm not holding a goddamn grudge, Turner!" He hauled himself over to the other man.

"Then what's your fucking problem, Walker?"

"My *problem* is we're standing around here with our heads up our asses while Jenna's going through only God knows what!" Adrian's voice boomed inside the open space. "She's out there somewhere, terrified and alone. She probably thinks no one is coming for her, and the truth is, we're not because we don't even know where to fucking start!"

"You mean 'they', right?" Zade King—one of Bravo's designated snipers—looked over at him from his seat across from Nate. Always the boy scout of the group, the former SEAL was calm, his voice low and steady.

"What?" Adrian snapped back.

"You said *she's* out there somewhere," Zade clarified. "That *she* probably thinks no one is coming for her. But I'm sure you meant to say 'they', since both Jenna *and* Chief Campillo are missing."

Who the fuck is this guy, the grammar police?

"Unless, of course, there's a reason he's more focused on

Jenna than Ben," Kole Jameson, Bravo's lead sniper joined in on the fun from across the room.

"You know"—Matt spoke up again—"now that you mention it, Walker did specifically ask about Jenna the second he got here. And is it just me, or did he used to be a lot less uptight?"

Adrian's knuckles became white as he gripped the crutches' small, padded bars tightly.

See? This is why I work alone. I fucking hate people.

"I'm just as worried about Ben, too, assholes," he spouted off the half-truth. "I only asked about Jenna first because she's—"

Mine.

"Yours?" The corner of Nate's smartass mouth lifted as if he could read Adrian's mind.

Adrian was about to tell the computer genius where he could shove his laptop when Gabe stepped forward, putting an end to the juvenile pissing match.

"Enough!" Gabe's voice echoed off the expensive walls. "We have two people missing with no leads as to what happened to them or where they could be. What we *don't* have is time to waste on this dick measuring bullshit. So put 'em away and get your asses focused on what's important. Understood?"

"Copy that, Boss." Nate went back to clicking on his keyboard.

The other Bravo men mumbled and nodded as they went back to whatever they were doing before he and Gabe arrived.

Adrian glanced around the room, the dread he'd felt before growing exponentially with every second that passed. Despite his sarcastic remarks, he knew deep down there was no other team he'd rather have working this case.

If these guys can't find her...

Gabe's phone rang. Every man in the room stopped and waited while he answered the call.

"Dawson." He listened a beat before sliding his unreadable gray eyes to Adrian's. "Where?" Letting out a low curse, he said, "We're on our way."

"What is it?" Adrian moved a step closer. "Did they find them?"

Gabe's expression was grim. "They found Ben."

Fifteen minutes later, Adrian was in some poor sucker's garage, staring at the body of a man he'd considered a friend. Someone had shot Ben in the temple at point blank range, and Jenna was nowhere to be seen.

Please let her be okay.

"He was executed," Adrian mumbled.

Beside him, Gabe nodded. "This was a professional hit. He was either in on it, or he was somehow lured here. Either way, Campillo pulls the car in, and then…"

The man's voice trailed off because really, there was no need to finish that sentence. Adrian understood perfectly.

They all did.

For whatever reason, Ben drove them here, was shot and killed, and Jenna had been taken elsewhere.

"Explains why no one saw his car leave the area," Matt commented.

He was right. The police and Bravo Team had all been around the neighborhood talking with residents about what they'd seen or hadn't seen. Because this was a dead-end street, and the only two houses on it were empty, no one had bothered looking here before now.

According to Gabe's contact within the department, the only reason they looked today was because some woman who'd been out walking her dog earlier had called it in.

Apparently, the dog was an overly large Goldendoodle, and the pet had all but pulled his owner toward the garage to investigate a scent he'd picked up. The woman then smelled it, too, and reported the strange smell coming from the house.

With fear turning his blood cold, Adrian studied the activity around them. Cops were everywhere. Some appeared to be frantic. Some sad.

Most were pissed that one of their own—their *chief*—had gone out in such a horrific way. Other officers and crime scene investigators bustled about as they tried piecing together the man's final moments.

Flashes of light burst sporadically as a crime tech took photos of everything in sight. The garage, the car…Ben.

Adrian stood there, his mind filling with questions no one had the answers to.

Who did this?

Why?

Where's Jenna?

Had she been sitting next to Ben when he'd been shot?

Did the bastard who did this hurt her, too?

The idea of her being touched by this level of violence —*again*— left Adrian feeling sick to his soul.

"At least we know she's still alive," Gabe commented, pulling him out of his thoughts.

He understood where the man's certainty came from. If they wanted Jenna dead, they would've left her here with Ben.

"I'm going to find her." Adrian brought his deadly gaze to Gabe's. "And then I'm going to kill the person who took her."

Gabe stared back at him. The cold calculated look in the man's eyes telling Adrian all he needed to know.

Despite all the shit from their past, the former SEAL had his back on this. And, though part of him hated to admit it, Adrian knew the entire Bravo Team did, as well.

"We have to start over," Gabe stated matter-of-factly. "Go back to the beginning, where everything first started."

"The club." Adrian swallowed the knot in his throat and got his head in the game. "Jenna and I..." He cleared the emotions from his throat. "We were headed there when I got shot."

"We'll go there, now. Together."

The two men shared a look before Adrian nodded. "Together."

And just like that, the two men put their differences aside for a common cause.

Following Gabe out of the garage and down the driveway to the twin SUV's Gabe had procured for his team, the formidable man motioned for the others to join them.

Once everyone was there, Gabe quickly explained the new plan.

"Chief Campillo's murder confirms our suspicions. Jenna Shaw is now officially considered to be the victim of a violent abduction. As you know, she's like family to me." He glanced at Adrian. "To us. Now, Campillo's body gives us a starting point, but we need to go back over every single detail, from the beginning."

Jenna wasn't like his family. She *was* his family.

Even if she doesn't know it yet.

Kole gave his leader a nod. "Whatever you need, Boss."

"Jameson's right." Matt spoke up next. Then, in a shocking turn of events, he looked right at Adrian and said, "Anything you need."

Well, I'll be damned. The devil must be sitting on a throne of fucking ice for this shit to be happening.

Adrian didn't know if Hell really had frozen over or if he'd somehow stumbled into an alternate reality. Either way, Ben was dead, and whoever killed him had taken Jenna.

Finding her was priority fucking one. If that meant playing nice with Bravo Team, so be it.

"There are only two ways in and out of this neighborhood. The street we came in on and another road east of that entrance." He looked at Nate. "Can you go back through the CCTV footage from where those two streets connect with the main road? Look at the vehicles that entered and left the day this all went down?"

Nate tipped his chin. "I'll start at the beginning of the day, too. When I was looking before, I focused on the time frame starting from when we knew Campillo and Jenna had entered the neighborhood. There were other vehicles that came in and out during that time, but our focus was on Campillo's car."

Adrian agreed. "If you go from earlier in the day, you may see someone else entering that looks suspicious."

"Plus"—Nate continued on—"since we now know for sure the chief didn't drive himself and Jenna out of there, I'll know to focus on the other drivers more closely."

"Thanks."

"Walker and I are going to go to the club where Jenna was drugged. Talk to the bartender and staff. See if we can pull anything from them. If the incident from that night is connected to this, and it's too damn big of a coincidence for it not to be, that means this whole thing started there."

"What do you want the rest of us to do?" Matt asked.

"Go to the hospital. Talk with anyone who worked with Jenna this past week. Maybe one of them heard or saw something that stands out."

"Roger that." Matt glanced at his watch. "Want to meet back at the hotel in say, two hours?"

"Make it three," Adrian answered for Gabe. "I want to go back to Jenna's hotel and see if the staff there noticed anyone suspicious hanging around."

"Three hours. Got it." Nate tipped his chin

Gabe dug his key fob from his pocket and unlocked one of the two SUVs. "See you boys then."

The afternoon traffic was heavier than normal, so it took several minutes to cover the few miles to the club. It was still early, and Adrian wasn't sure anyone would be there. But it didn't matter.

He was more than happy to wait.

"I get that you and Jenna are...whatever it is you are." Gabe slid him a sideways glance as he pulled up to the curb and shoved the vehicle into park. "But I care about her, too. A lot."

"Meaning?"

Shifting in his seat, the man's eyes locked on his. "This isn't just a job for me, either. But since it's now become an official Bravo Team op, I will be taking point."

"So...what does that make me? A silent partner?"

Gabe smiled. "Good. Glad we understand each other."

"I'm not allowed to *talk* to the guy?" Adrian brought his brows together. "Then what the fuck am I supposed to do?"

"What you do best." Gabe unbuckled his seatbelt and climbed out. "Stand there and look pretty."

Flipping his new partner the bird, Adrian moved more clumsily than usual as he got out of his side and slammed the passenger door shut. Grabbing the crutches from the back seat, he caught up to Gabe in a flash.

He'd play the part and let the big bad SEAL take the lead. For now. He just hoped Gabe understood he wasn't leaving here until he had the answers they needed.

Gabe pulled on the door to the club's entrance, pleased to find it already unlocked. The two men walked inside to find the place dimly lit with music playing in the background.

"Well, someone's here," Adrian mumbled as they made their way up to the bar.

"Let's just hope it's the same prick from the night you and Jenna were here."

Three seconds later, the prick in question came strolling in from the back. Singing along to the music, he carried a plastic crate filled with what appeared to be freshly washed glasses.

The guy nearly tripped over his own two feet when he spotted them.

"That's him," Adrian whispered under his breath.

"Uh…hey, guys," the bartender from the other night greeted them. "We don't open for another two hours, but feel free to come back later—"

"That's okay." Adrian grinned. "We don't plan on staying."

With a *what-the-fuck* scowl, Gabe wordlessly reminded him of the whole silent partner thing.

Silent. Right. Gotcha.

"Actually, Mr…."

"Slay." The guy set the glasses down onto the counter behind the bar. "You know, because I *slay* the ladies."

Oh, good lord.

"Okay, Slay." Gabe gave the man a friendly smile. "We have some questions about something that happened here a couple of nights ago. A young woman you served was drugged and then nearly abducted after she left your club. You wouldn't know anything about that, would you?"

Slay's left eye twitched ever so slightly. A tell most people would've missed.

Adrian wasn't most people.

"Really?" The guy started taking the glasses from the crate and stacking them on one of the lower shelves on the back wall. "Man, that sucks. But to be honest, this place is jam packed most nights, so it's not like I can keep an eye on everyone all the time."

"This woman look familiar to you?" Gabe held up his

phone for Slay to see. "She came in here with three other women. They're nurses at the hospital here in town."

Adrian's heart stammered against his ribs as he took in Gabe's picture of Jenna. She was with Ellena, and the two women were smiling wide.

I'll find you, baby. Swear to God, I will.

While his eyes were glued to her gorgeous face, Slay barely gave the phone a passing glance. "Nah, man. Like I said, we're crazy busy."

Adrian's back teeth ground together as his fists flexed against the padded hand grips. Gabe had about five seconds to get the guy talking before this 'silent partner' stepped in.

"Do yourself a favor and take another look." Gabe's voice had dropped to a level that caught the asshole's attention.

With an exhale that made Adrian want to throat punch the little fucker, Slay stopped what he was doing and looked at the phone again.

"Nope. Sorry." He looked up at Gabe. "I don't recognize her."

"You sure about that?" Adrian dropped the silent act.

Slay looked up at him and blinked, almost as if he'd forgotten he was even there.

That's right, asshole. Take a good, hard look.

"I just told you I don't know that chick."

Remember, Walker. Dead men can't answer questions.

"That *chick* has a name, asshole" he bit out harshly. "It's Jenna. And I was here the other night when you served her not one, but two drinks." Adrian set the crutches aside and leaned his elbows on the bar all casual-like. "I stood right over there and watched you with her. You talked and smiled. Looked like you were really laying on the charm."

Gabe cleared his throat, a clear signal for him to shut the hell up. Since the guy wasn't his boss, Adrian continued on.

"A man bought Jenna a drink. He sat at the end of the

bar, right over there." He pointed to where the man had been sitting. "Tall. Olive skin. Real good lookin' Hispanic guy."

"And?" Slay snorted as he broke eye contact. "Last I checked, it's not a crime to buy a woman a drink. I mean, I've kinda built a business on that shit."

Oh, it's going to be so *much fun beating your ass.*

"You took the guy's money, and *you* served her a drink that he paid for. A drink laced with Ketamine. I want his name."

The idiot eyed the crutches, and apparently decided it was a good idea to grow a set of balls. "What are you, her boyfriend or something?"

Adrian's voice lowered to an even deadlier calm. "Something."

Gabe crossed his arms, stretching the arms of his t-shirt to their limit. He was clearly ticked off because, yeah. Adrian hadn't followed the surly SEAL's orders.

Thankfully, the guy kept quiet and let Adrian take the bartender for a spin.

He started a countdown in his head. *Three...two...*

"Listen, man." Slay raised his hands palms up. "I'm sorry some guy dosed your girl, but I had nothing to do with it."

One.

Moving hell fast, Adrian reached out and grabbed the front of Slay's t-shirt. Pulling the scrawny asshat toward him, he didn't stop until the guy's body was halfway across the bar.

"Hey!" The shithead's eyes grew wide as he tried breaking the hold Adrian had on him. "What the hell, man?"

From beside him, he heard Gabe mutter a low curse followed by a resigned, "Here we go."

Getting right in the shithead's face, Adrian released only a fraction of the anger he felt.

"Give me a fucking name!" The order came out as an echoing growl.

"I told you, I don't know anythin—"

Using his free hand, Adrian grabbed the hair on the back of Slay's head and slammed the man's face against the top of the bar. The telltale sound of bones crunching was music to Adrian's ears.

"Motherfucker! You broke my damn nose!"

"Really?" Gabe's expression was deadpan.

Adrian's brow arched high. "You want to play nice, or do you want to find Jenna?"

The Bravo leader took all of one second to consider the question before motioning for him to continue his interrogation.

That's what I thought.

With his fist still full of Slay's hair, Adrian held the asshole steady. Leaning in real close, he made sure the fuckwad heard him loud and clear.

"Listen up, *Slay*. I'm going to ask you a few simple questions, and you're going to answer them truthfully. For every lie you tell, I'll break another bone. And I'll *keep* breaking bones until you're lying on that sticky ass floor of yours with your skeleton shattered into so many pieces, they'll have to scoop you up with a fucking spatula. Clear enough?"

"Y-yeah." Slay gave a jerky nod. "Whatever you say, man."

Watching the guy's left eye very closely, he asked, "Did you put the Ketamine in the lady's drink. Yes or no?"

"N-no."

And there it was. The twitch.

Tsk, tsk.

Releasing Slay's shirt, Adrian grabbed the lying bastard's left pinky and yanked it to the side until he felt a pop.

"Ah!" The dumbass yelled as he tried to pull himself free. "You crazy mother*fucker!*"

Blood and spit spewed from his mouth and nose, landing on the smooth and shiny countertop.

"Let's try this again, shall we?" Adrian curled his lips into a sinister smile. "Did you put the drugs in the pretty redhead's drink? Yes. Or. No?"

When Slay hesitated to answer, Adrian went for the ring finger. He had his hand wrapped around the digit and was just about to yank on it when Slay *finally* came to his senses and confessed.

"Yes, okay?" The pathetic jerk damn near cried. "I was the one who put the drugs in your girlfriend's drink. Jesus!"

The hold Adrian had on the finger loosened, but he didn't let go entirely. "Why?"

"The guy paid me a grand. A *grand!* I mean, what the hell did you expect me to do? That's more than I clear in a fucking week."

Don't kill him. Do. Not. Kill. Him.

"The man who paid you." Adrian kept his voice steady. "What's his name?"

"I can't. Please!" Slay begged. "The guy will kill me. Literally. Dude's got mad connections."

That finger snapped.

"*Fuck!*" Slay screamed again. "Ah, Jesus!"

He turned fifty shades of green, and unless Adrian's nose was mistaken, the mouthy prick had just pissed his pants.

Any other time, he would've loved to have wasted a few minutes giving the guy shit about it. Not today. Today, every single minute counted.

Because every minute he spent not knowing where Jenna was or if she was okay was a minute of pure hell.

"Name," Adrian growled. "Now."

"Slay, buddy." Gabe hopped on board the not-fucking-around train. "I've seen what this asshole's capable of. You keep holding out on us, you'd better believe he'll break you. Every. Fucking. Bone."

Done waiting, Adrian made a play for Slay's middle finger, but the guy finally caved.

"Wait!" Slay's face grew even more pale as he spoke through his pain. "Name's...Amanté...Perez."

The guy's name is the Spanish word for lover?

Rolling his eyes, Adrian asked, "Where can we find this Amanté?"

"I don't know."

He squeezed Slay's middle finger.

"I swear! I don't know!" The man's entire body shook with pain and fear.

"What do you think?" Adrian looked to Gabe. "You believe him?"

"Please." Slay was crying now. Actual fucking tears. "I'm telling you the *truth!* All I know is Amanté comes in here sometimes. He picks a chick...uh...lady he likes. Buys her a... drink. They dance...end up leaving...together. Except your... girlfriend. She left with...another woman."

Marie.

Gabe studied the man for a beat longer before nodding. "Yeah. I think his sorry ass is telling the truth."

Adrian released Slay's hair but kept his hold on the guy's middle finger.

"I am!" More blood ran from Slay's nose as he straightened himself up. It covered his lips and dripped off his chin, down onto the front of his shirt. "I swear."

"Okay." Adrian nodded. "I believe you, too."

Slay's tense shoulders sagged with relief. A second later, his middle finger snapped in two.

The guy screamed and cried some more as he used his right hand to hold the mangled one to his chest. "You said you believed me!"

"I do." Adrian took a step back.

"Then what the hell was that for?"

"Being a lowlife piece of dog shit who thought it was okay to put fucking date rape drugs into my woman's—into *any* woman's—drink."

Then, Adrian looked at Gabe and held out his hand. "Give me your gun."

"Ah, God. Please. Don't kill me. *Please!*"

"Would you relax?" Adrian shot Slay a look. "I'm not going to kill you." He turned back to Gabe and wiggled his fingers. "I'm *not*. I promise."

With obvious reservation, Gabe reached behind his back and pulled his pistol from his waistband. He smacked the gun into Adrian's outstretched palm.

"Thanks." Adrian smiled. He then aimed the weapon at the mirror behind Slay and pulled the trigger.

Once. Twice. Three times.

Slay screamed and ducked his head, covering it as best he could with his hands. Shards of the reflective glass shattered and fell all around him.

"*That* was a warning." Adrian handed the weapon back to Gabe and waited for the idiot bartender to look at him again.

When he did, Adrian very calmly said, "Something you should know about me, Slay. I, too, have 'mad connections'. If I *ever* hear of you putting anything stronger than alcohol into another woman's drink again, I'll come back. And next time, I won't bother with questions or broken bones. I'll just put a fucking hole through that dense skull of yours and be done. Understood?"

"Y-yes." Slay nodded.

"Good." He smiled. Nodding toward the bloody mess on the bar and the piss and glass on the floor, he added, "Might want to clean that up. You'll be opening, soon."

Not waiting for Gabe, Adrian grabbed his crutches and

started for the door. Before leaving, he stopped long enough to say, "Oh, and Slay? Find another nickname for yourself. One that's not so fucking ridiculous."

Once they were both back in the SUV, Gabe turned to him and shook his head.

"What?"

"You feel better?"

"No, actually." Adrian answered honestly. "I won't feel better until we find Jenna and I know she's okay."

Staring at him with an assessing glance, the man's lips almost curved into a ghost of a smile. Almost.

"You really care about her, don't you?"

Adrian nodded and told the man, "More than you know."

CHAPTER 13

"What the fuck?" Adrian took off his ski mask and stared at Amanté Perez.

After leaving their new buddy Slay, Gabe called Nate and asked him to find Perez's LKA, or last known address. Adrian hadn't put a lot of stock in finding him, mainly because he assumed the man was smart enough to use an alias.

He wasn't.

With Nate's impressive remote hacking abilities, they were able to breach Perez's residence without incident. Since Adrian's gun was currently in police custody, along with his rental car, as part of the evidence from the drive-by, Gabe had generously loaned him one, along with the mask.

Did he look ridiculous hobbling in on crutches while wearing scrubs and a ski mask? Sure did. Did Adrian give a flying fuck?

Not a single one.

Within three minutes of their arrival, both men had stormed into the above-average home, armed and ready for answers. Unfortunately for them, it didn't look as though they'd be getting any.

Not from Amanté, anyway.

"Anything about this seem familiar to you?" Gabe turned to him.

"You mean besides the smell?" Adrian's stomach turned. He'd never gotten used to the smell of death. Ironic given his past profession.

"One shot to the temple," he answered Gabe. "Point blank Range." *Just like Ben.*

They'd found Perez lying face-first on his bathroom floor wearing nothing but a towel. A large pool of coagulated blood had seeped into the Spanish tiles beneath the man's head.

He'd clearly been dead a while.

"They took him out before executing Ben." Gabe turned, his expression hard as he headed for the door. "Someone's cleaning house."

The other man was right. Adrian just wished like hell they knew *who* was doing the cleaning. And why.

"This doesn't make any goddamn sense," Adrian grumbled as he and Gabe began searching the house for evidence tying Perez to whatever the hell was going on.

Thankfully Gabe had also thought to grab a pair of disposable gloves to avoid leaving any fingerprints.

"No," Gabe agreed as he took out his phone and tapped the screen. "It sure as hell doesn't."

"Who you calling?"

"Nate." Putting it on speaker, he held the phone between them as they walked through the hallway to the main section of the house.

"Hey, Dawson." Nate picked up on the second ring. "I was just about to call you."

"Perez is dead," Gabe informed his teammate bluntly.

"You sure?"

"They guy's face down in a puddle of his own brains and

blood." Adrian's response was clipped. "So yeah, Carter. We're pretty sure."

He and Gabe entered a room that appeared to be Perez's home office. Leaning his crutches against the dead man's desk, Adrian began opening drawers while they continued their conversation.

"What the fuck?" Nate's question mimicked Adrian's recent thoughts. "Is it just me, or does something seem off with this whole thing?"

"We were just talking about that," Adrian spoke loudly as he rummaged through bills and other irrelevant papers. "Nothing with this case makes sense. Like the shooting. The more I replay that shit, the more confident I am that the shooter wasn't aiming for Jenna."

"Makes sense." Gabe opened a cabinet positioned against the far wall. "Like you said before, they obviously wanted her alive."

"That was actually why I was going to call," Nate chimed back in. "I went over the footage from the street cams outside the police station again. There were two shots taken. One right before you were hit in the leg, which took out your driver's side window. Jenna was standing directly across from you at the time, and given the bullet's trajectory, the shooter had to have had a clear shot at her head."

"Jesus, Carter." Adrian blew out a breath. Just *hearing* the possibility play out like that through the speaker made his gut tighten and his chest ache.

"Sorry." Picking up on Adrian's dislike for the conversation's direction, Nate quickly got to his point. "All I'm saying is, Jenna wasn't the shooter's target, and either the gunman was a horrible shot, or he wasn't actually trying to kill you, either."

Adrian halted his search, his mind replaying the scene one last time. "He could've easily shot me in the head or the back. Instead, he went lower." He slid his gaze to the set of metal crutches and then across the room to Gabe. "He purposely aimed for my leg."

"Maybe they didn't want a possible murder charge hanging over their heads," Nate suggested.

"Except they had no problem taking out Campillo and Perez," Gabe reminded him.

"Good point," Nate muttered. "Maybe they just wanted Walker out of the way so they could get to Jenna?"

Adrian nodded. "That makes sense. They had to have been watching us to know where we'd be."

The idea that he'd missed a tail burned his ass.

"Or they were tipped off by someone else." Gabe gave him a pointed look. "Someone who knew you were going to meet Ben."

He shook his head. "*Ben* was the only person who knew we were coming."

The raised brow on Gabe's chiseled face irked him.

"For the millionth time, he wouldn't fucking sell me out."

"He would if he didn't have a choice," Nate added quietly.

Gabe looked down at his phone. "You think he was being blackmailed?"

"I mean, it's a stretch, but it's always a possibility."

"It's a hell of a stretch," Adrian seethed. "That would mean the person responsible would've had to have gotten to Ben sometime between when I called to set up the meeting and the shooting. That's a small fucking window."

"It is," Gabe agreed. "But I think it's one we need to crawl through. Think about it, Adrian." He stepped toward him. "The guy drove himself and Jenna straight from the crime scene to that house. Why?"

"The big guy's right, Walker," Nate chimed back in. "That house has been empty for months. The owners moved to Wisconsin to be closer to family, and none of them...not even a distant relative of theirs, has a known connection to Ben."

Guess Carter's been keeping himself busy.

A stretch of silence spanned a few seconds before Nate spoke up again.

"I'll go back through Campillo's cell records and emails. Maybe I missed something."

"Check his work line and email, too," Gabe instructed. "If someone was forcing his hand on this, it's possible they contacted him that way."

Adrian felt sick even considering the possibility that Ben was involved with people who would do this sort of thing. It went against every single instinct he had about the man.

Everyone has a price when their hand is being forced. You know this better than anyone.

The voice in his head was right. The CIA and Homeland had used his sister's disappearance to force his hand. Maybe someone found something of Ben's to use against him

His wife and kid. Money. Something the man would've considered worth the cost of selling him out and handing over Jenna. Something that had cost the man his life.

While he hated even thinking it, Adrian had to accept it as a possibility. Because this was Jenna they were talking about.

Despite his efforts to the contrary, the sexy redhead had wormed her way past his concrete walls and settled herself deep inside his heart. She was a part of him, now. And without her, he realized he'd have nothing.

"Thanks, Carter," Gabe told Nate. "When you're done with Campillo, see what you can dig up on Perez. The guy was obviously connected. It would be nice to know how far that connection went."

"Roger that."

"Thanks. We'll finish up here and meet you and the others back at the hotel."

Ending the call, Gabe shoved his phone into his pocket and went about with his search. The two men completed their search in relative silence, allowing Adrian a chance to gather his thoughts.

Finding no evidence against Perez, they left the house—and the body—behind. Someone would discover the scene eventually, but as far as he was concerned, the bastard could lay there and rot.

Concerned about leaving him without any sort of backup, Gabe had insisted Adrian stay the night in his hotel suite. Though he was pissed that Dawson thought he could order him around, Adrian begrudgingly caved.

Logically, it made sense for them to all be in one place in case they caught a break and needed to head out as a team. Not that he was a part of their team.

He was almost part of something special, though. Almost. Something good and pure. Something *wonderful.*

Then she was ripped from his soul.

Hang in there, baby. I promise I'll find you. Just please, don't give up.

Since Adrian's clothes and things were still at Jenna's hotel room, they headed there first so he could change out of the ugly ass blue scrubs the hospital had given him. The plan was, he'd shower as best he could with the dressing on his leg, and then they'd meet up with the rest of Bravo in Gabe's suite at the other hotel.

Standing outside Jenna's door, Gabe reached into the plastic bag the hospital had used to hold Adrian's personal effects and pulled out his wallet. "Here."

"Thanks." Adrian took it and pulled out the plastic room key.

Ignoring the throbbing in his leg, he held the key up to the electronic sensor and waited for the light to turn green before opening the door. In an awkward move, Gabe brought his arm above Adrian's head and pushed the door wider so Adrian could go in first.

He'd barely made it into the room when Jenna's scent assaulted his system. Nearly stumbling, he recovered quickly, schooling his expression as his nostrils filled with a mixture of lavender and vanilla.

Right then, Adrian made a vow to buy a fucking case of the lotion she used…as soon as she was back in his arms, where she belonged.

"You good?"

Not even a little bit. "Yeah." Adrian moved further into the room. "Just not used to these damn crutches." That sounded believable, right?

Behind him, Gabe muttered a very *disbelieving*, "Uh, huh."

Fucker.

"Flip the lights, would ya?" he grumbled. "I can't see a damn thing."

"I'm sure you meant to say please, right?" Gabe turned on the lights. "I mean, I'm sure that word is in your vocabulary, somewhere. You might have to dig deep to find it, but—"

"What the fuck is that?" Adrian cut him off, his entire focus on the small gold box in the center of the bed.

Both men moved closer to get a better look.

There was a red bow tied perfectly around it, but he didn't see a card or a note with it.

"Maybe it's from the hotel." Gabe glanced around the tidy room. "Housekeeping's obviously been in here."

Adrian's gut said otherwise. "This hotel isn't the leave-a-mint-on-your-pillow type of place, Dawson." Still, wanting to be sure, he went to the bedside table and picked up the phone's receiver.

The woman at the front desk confirmed his suspicions.

"It's not from the hotel." He hung up the phone.

Gabe studied the box again. "Seems too small to be an explosive."

Adrian thought the same thing.

"Someone's playing with us."

"No." Gabe looked over at him. "They're playing with *you*."

Leaning on the crutches, the tops dug into his armpits as he ran a hand down his face. "Looks like it's my move."

Adrian's insides twisted. Looking at the box again, he did his best not to think of the different body parts that could fit inside the small package.

The idea that someone would torture his Jenna in such a way...

Not her. Jesus, not her.

With no choice but to look, he lifted his right crutch. Using the rubber tip, he lifted the lid before tapping the side of the box hard enough to make it fall over.

A loud breath escaped—one he hadn't even realized he'd been holding—when a small cell phone slid out onto the bed.

"Jesus Christ." He reached for the device.

There was no need to worry about destroying prints. The players in this twisted game wouldn't have left any behind.

Gabe picked up the box and looked inside. "There's a ring. Has some sort of crest on it."

Adrian glanced at the piece of jewelry and frowned. "That's a man's."

Confused, he grabbed it from Gabe's fingers. Fear clawed up his throat, its sharp talons ripping him to shreds as he caught sight of the familiar design.

His heart stopped beating. The air inside his lungs turned to ice, and his brain refused to accept what his eyes were seeing.

Fucking no!

A horrifying clarity struck with such force he could actually *feel* the color draining from his face. His knees buckled, and if it hadn't been for the damn crutches, Adrian would've fallen straight to the floor.

"Jesus, Walker." Gabe's hands helped steady him. "You okay? You look liked you've seen a damned ghost."

No, not a ghost. Just a ring that belonged to one.

"It's my fault," he rasped. He could barely get the words out.

"What the hell are you talking about? What's your fault?"

Adrian's stuttering gaze rose to meet Gabe's. "All of it."

Something inside him broke, then. *He* fucking broke.

Little by little, he began to shut down. Starting with the parts he'd only recently discovered. The ones Jenna had brought out in him.

Soon, the only thing left of the man Adrian *thought* he'd become—the man he'd always longed to be—was a broken, hollow shell.

"Sit your ass down before you fall and bust your leg open." Gabe grabbed the crutches and tossed them aside before guiding him down onto the mattress. He huffed a breath before asking, "You recognize that?"

He did. But the last time Adrian saw this particular ring, it had been covered in blood.

Blood I spilled in my blinding need for revenge.

"Hey!" Gabe gave his shoulder a hard smack. "Snap the fuck out of it and talk to me. Who does the fucking thing belong to?"

"Cesar Ortiz," Adrian muttered woodenly.

Silence filled the space as Gabe processed the information.

"Ortiz…you mean the *cartel* leader?"

He nodded.

"How the hell do you know that?"

Lifting his eyes, Adrian met Gabe's inquisitive stare and said, "Ortiz was wearing this ring the day I killed him."

The man's brown eyes grew wide. The move indicating that the bit of information Adrian had just shared had gotten his attention.

"*You* took out Cesar Ortiz?"

He nodded again. "It was my first assignment with the Agency."

"The CIA?" Gabe's spinning wheels were damn near visible. "Wait, you're talking about your sister's case, aren't you?"

Adrian was impressed the guy remembered.

Back when Gabe and his team first discovered Adrian had been working deep cover for the CIA and Homeland, he'd shared with them the story of how they'd enticed him with the promise to take down the organization they believed was responsible for his sister's disappearance.

"With intel the Agency and Homeland provided, along with Ben Campillo's help, I was able to track down the organization responsible for her abduction and death."

"And you went straight for the top."

Old memories—*painful* memories—had his teeth grinding together. "I found out Cesar Ortiz bought my sister Bree for himself. I found him and tortured him until he confessed to everything. Including killing her and where he'd dumped her body. Then I killed him. Slowly."

"Jesus." Gabe ran a hand over his salt and pepper scruff. "When you first told us how you got roped into becoming a government assassin, you didn't mention Ortiz had been your target."

The bastard's reputation preceded him. Even in death.

"I didn't mention his name, because I couldn't." Adrian huffed out a breath. "Hell I just broke about a billion laws by telling you now, but…" He swallowed hard. "If this ring means what I think it does…"

The two men shared a look, both understanding what had been left unspoken. That ring meant Jenna was in serious trouble.

"Who was left?" Gabe asked after waiting a beat.

"What do you mean?"

"Once you took down Ortiz. Who managed to walk away?"

"No one." Adrian shook his head. "Ortiz was the heart and soul of the organization. Once he was gone, the whole thing fell apart. People started turning on each other like crazy."

"There has to be someone." Gabe stood and began pacing the room.

"I'm telling you, there's not!" Adrian's voice boomed. "Everyone involved in the cartel is either dead or behind bars."

"How can you be so sure?"

His gaze narrowed. "I don't know. Maybe because I'm good at my fucking job."

Pushing himself off the mattress, Adrian rose awkwardly to his feet. He could feel the pull of his stitches but ignored the pain and limped his way over to where his crutches still lay.

Balancing on one leg, he bent over and grabbed one to help ease some of the pressure as he turned and faced Gabe again.

A muscle in the man's strong jaw twitched as he stared Adrian down. "Obviously *someone* connected to Ortiz is holding a goddamn grudge against you, Adrian. And Jenna's the one paying the fucking price. So if you could get your arrogant head out of your ass and work with me on this, we *might* be able to figure out who that someone is before they fucking kill her!"

The truthful words stole his breath as terror for the woman he loved stabbed at his heart.

Gabe was right. Not about his being arrogant. This had nothing to do with that.

Adrian had been pushing back because he couldn't face the fucking truth. He'd said the words out loud, but he still hadn't wanted to accept the fact that Jenna's life was in danger because of *him*.

It didn't matter who took her. Not really. Because when it was all said and done, *he* was the one to set this whole thing in motion. The minute he tortured and killed Cesar Ortiz for payback for what the man had done to his sister.

And now Jenna was being forced to pay for his sins.

Oh, god, baby. I'm so sorry. So. Fucking. Sorry!

"We need to call Ryker." Gabe pulled his cell from his pocket to call R.I.S.C.'s Homeland handler. "If this does have something to do with the job you did for him and the CIA, and it seems pretty fucking clear that it does, then he needs to know. Plus, if there's new cartel activity stirring, his people might know where to start looking."

While they waited for the call to be answered, Gabe looked back at him and asked, "You gonna be able to handle this? If not, I need to know, now."

Could he handle knowing that he was responsible for all this? That Jenna, *his* Jenna, could possibly die because of him?

No.

Was he going to admit that to Gabriel Dawson or anyone else?

Fuck. No.

"I got this," Adrian lied with brilliant form.

The CIA *had* turned him into a world-class liar, after all. They'd also been the ones who taught him how to let everything else go.

Fear. Emotions. All of it.

The Agency had shown him how to become more machine than man in order to focus solely on the mission.

And this mission?

Finding the assholes who took Jenna, taking them down, and bringing her home.

So he'd do as Gabe instructed. Adrian would get his head out of his ass and be a team player.

He'd work with Gabe, Ryker, the rest of Bravo…he'd work with the fucking *Coast Guard* if it meant finding Jenna and bringing her home.

And once he did that, once she was safe and those responsible had been dealt with, he'd walk away and never look back.

Because there was something he'd learned from all of this. One very important thing he'd been stupid enough to forget…

Happiness and ever-afters were never meant for guys like him.

CHAPTER 14

Jenna's head pounded. Her entire face throbbed from the sudden and unexplainable abuse she'd endured.

Her bruised cheek. Swollen eye. Split lip. It *all* hurt, and she had no idea what she'd done to deserve it.

When the one guy had stormed off earlier after her refusal to eat, she'd wondered if she'd ever see him—or anyone else—ever again. He'd left her alone for so long after that, Jenna had all but convinced herself she wouldn't.

She was wrong.

A little while ago—keeping track of time had become damn near impossible—the big jerk had come back. And this time, he'd brought a friend.

Jenna wasn't sure exactly what she'd expected when she saw them. It sure as hell wasn't being uncuffed, dragged to a chair, tied up, and beaten.

But that's exactly what had happened.

They'd taken turns hitting her. Laughing and taunting her when she'd finally broke down and begged them to stop. Then, as quickly as they'd appeared, the assholes turned and walked away.

There'd been no questions they needed answers to. No explanation as to why. They'd just beaten the crap out of her and then...they left.

Please, God. Let somebody find me soon.

Shivering, Jenna's body went cold with dread when she heard the door opening once more. She'd always considered herself to be fairly tough, but everyone had their limits.

And after being drugged, starved, and beaten for absolutely no reason, she was definitely close to reaching hers.

"Is she ready?"

Jenna barely had the energy to hold her head up, but the unfamiliar voice somehow gave her the strength to do it.

There's another one?

Fear threatened to choke her as multiple footfalls reached her ears. When they came into the dim light, she did her best to focus on their faces.

That's right, assholes. I want to memorize every last detail so I can identify your sorry asses. Assuming I'm still alive to do it.

"Excellent." The newest member of the Sick Fuck Club approached her with a smile.

Like the other two, the Hispanic man was dressed for success with his designer clothes, spit-shined shoes, and slicked-back hair. *Unlike* the pricks from before, this man was a bit older.

His black hair was accented with just enough silver at the temples to make him appear distinguished. The slight wrinkles on his forehead and around his eyes created an air of wisdom.

But it was his eyes that drew Jenna into the man's dark, disturbing web.

Their color was almost pure black, and when he stared down at her, it was as if he was looking straight through her.

There was no sign of emotion. No semblance of pity or remorse. Only cold, calculated evil.

"Who are you?" Jenna rasped.

Did her voice sound as weak to them as it did to her?

"My name is Matais Ortiz," he introduced himself. His accent was thick as he added, "It is a pleasure to finally meet you, Miss Shaw."

Gee, for a murdering psychopath, the guy sure has manners.

"What do you want from me?" she whispered softly. But only because she didn't have the energy to scream and yell.

"Exactly what you have been providing." The man took a step closer. "Fear. Agony. Psychological torture."

Okay, so this guy had clearly lost a few brain cells along the way because he was making absolutely no sense, whatsoever.

"I can see that you are confused." Matais linked his fingers together, letting his joined hands hang loosely in front of him. "No worries, my dear. You will understand perfectly soon."

He snapped his fingers—the smug asshole actually *snapped* them—and the first guy she'd dealt with came forward. He handed Matais something, and at first Jenna's heartrate spiked because she thought it was a gun, but she quickly realized it was only a phone.

"Gracias, Sebastian." The man in charge dipped his chin in appreciation.

"De nada."

Okay, so goon number one's name is Sebastian. Good to know.

After swiping his finger across the screen, Matais pointed the phone's camera directly at her. "Say cheese."

Jenna squinted and turned her head away as the camera's bright flash blinded her.

"Not your best side, but it will do."

His tone reminded Jenna of the sadistic killers she'd watched get taken down by Derek Morgan and the BAU.

Except this wasn't some random Criminal Minds episode, and she wasn't Derek's baby girl.

No, I belong to Adrian. And he belongs to me.

God, she wished he was here right now, because unlike some fictional character, Adrian Walker was very real. And very deadly.

He would snap these three men like the pathetic twigs they were.

Sebastian and the other man chuckled as Matais typed something out on the phone. With a smirk, he looked back up at her and grinned.

"It is done."

"What's done?" she demanded to know. "What the hell do you want from me?"

"Oh, it's not what I want from *you*." He came closer. "It's what I want from your boyfriend."

Shock reverberated through her entire system. Had she heard him wrong? She *had* to have heard the bastard wrong.

"Adrian?" His name escaped on a whisper. As if she were afraid to say it aloud. "W-what do you want with him?"

"Revenge, Miss Shaw." He reached for her, then. His evil eyes searing into hers as he brushed some hair from her face. "And when Mr. Walker comes to your rescue, I will finally get it."

Jenna jerked back as far as the chair would allow, a fresh wave of terror rolling over her as she tried to comprehend what the man had just said.

This man wanted to hurt Adrian? *Her* Adrian?

Shock and fear stole her ability to speak. Her mind whirled with the unfathomable reality that what was happening had nothing to do with her.

Matais Ortiz hadn't ordered Ben Campillo's death and her abduction for the purpose of selling her. And this clearly wasn't about her probing into the case of the two missing nurses.

This whole thing—the club, her being brought here, the picture Matais has just taken of her bruised and battered face…it was all being done for one purpose.

To lure Adrian into a trap.

God, no. Please don't let him come here!

For the duration of her captivity, Jenna had been praying for Adrian *to* come. Each time the darkness pulled her under, she'd dream of seeing his ruggedly handsome face.

She'd imagined him bursting through the door, taking out the bad guys, and carrying her away in his strong, comforting arms. More than once, Jenna had found herself begging God and the universe to show him the way.

But now…*now* that fantasy had turned into something horrible. A reality she would never wish on anyone.

Especially not the man she loved.

Because while she may not understand why, Jenna knew with utter certainty that Matais Ortiz planned to kill Adrian. And he was going to use her to do it.

"About damn time."

It was the only greeting Adrian gave the man who'd just entered Gabe's large hotel suite.

"Walker." Jason Ryker's lips pressed into a thin, arrogant. line. With a hint of amusement, his dark gaze lowered to Adrian's obvious limp. "Correct me if I'm wrong, but didn't you get shot the *last* time I saw you?"

Flipping the Homeland Security Agent the bird, Adrian passed by him to rejoin the others.

Looking past him, Gabe asked Ryker, "What do we know?"

ANNA BLAKELY

Adrian appreciated the man's desire to get right to it.

Dressed in his usual dark suit and white button-up, Ryker held out a thick manilla folder for the Bravo leader. "It's all in here."

"You expect us to read through that shit?" Adrian scowled. "We don't have that kind of time, Jason. *Jenna* doesn't have that kind of time."

Between the two days he'd lost while being in a fucking coma and spending all day today trying to figure shit out, it had now been damn near *three* days since anyone seen her.

Earlier, when he and Gabe were still back at Jenna's hotel room, Adrian had taken the fastest shower of his life—not an easy task while trying to keep his left leg dry.

Gabe had used that time to call the others and have them head to Bravo's hotel right then. He'd also informed Ryker of the fucked-up situation.

Once everyone was gathered in Gabe's suite, Adrian had filled Bravo Team in on everything he knew about Cesar Ortiz. They'd received no incoming calls or texts on the phone he'd been given, but it was charged and ready for when they did.

Since then, Nate had been working like crazy to find something—*anything*—that would give them a clue as to who from the old cartel would've had a reason to come after Adrian.

He'd first spent time hacking into the security feed at Jenna's hotel. As expected, the person who'd entered her room with the box had done a damn good job at keeping their face hidden from the hotel's cameras. In addition to that, Nate also had a separate program searching further into Amanté Perez's background.

Rather than dick with a bunch of back-and-forth phone calls, Ryker had chosen to hop on one of Homeland's private jets to come deal with whatever this mess was in person.

Something Adrian appreciated more than he'd ever admit.

"Well, I'll be damned." The Homeland agent gave him a long, assessing glance, and immediately Adrian realized Ryker could see too damn much. "I didn't believe you when you called, Dawson. I mean, this is *the* Adrian Walker we're talking about, after all. But you were right." Ryker slid an amused glance in Gabe's direction. "He's got it bad, doesn't he?"

Ryker and Gabe had been talking about him and Jenna? What was this, junior fucking high?

Forget it. I take my appreciation back, dickhead.

"What I've got"—Adrian limped closer to the other man— "is an innocent woman who's being held captive by someone connected to Cesar Ortiz."

"Don't forget a dead police chief and an asshole who likes putting date rape drugs into women's drinks," Zade chimed in.

"Amanté Perez." Ryker nodded. "Everything we know about him is in the folder, as well."

"How 'bout you give us the cliff notes version, yeah?" Adrian crossed his arms and waited. "Do you know who's behind all this or not?"

"The short of it? Yes." The man's dark eyes zeroed in on his. "Matais Ortiz."

The name was like a kick to Adrian's churning gut. "I take it the guy's is related to—"

"The late Cesar Ortiz," Ryker confirmed. "Matais is Cesar's son."

What. The. Fuck.

Adrian blinked before shaking his head. "Ortiz didn't have any children."

The man didn't have *any* family. Or so Adrian had been told.

"That's what we originally thought, but…" Ryker sighed. "We were wrong. Ortiz had both a wife and a son."

"You were *wrong?*" Shock and anger threatened to undo the careful control he'd forced into place. "You're fucking Homeland Security, Jason. For Christ's sake, the *CIA* was in on that op. How the hell does something that big get overlooked?"

After Adrian tortured and killed Cesar Ortiz, the United States government made sure pictures of the man's body were leaked to all the major news channels. The hope was that the horrifying images would reach the remaining members of the Ortiz cartel. Convince them it was a good idea to cooperate with authorities.

They'd also hoped the photos would act as a deterrent to anyone else who may have thought joining a cartel was a good life choice.

Adrian had been all for the plan, but now? Shit, now he realized Ortiz's own son had seen those images as well.

Matais knew exactly what had been done to his father. And somehow, he'd discovered Adrian was the person responsible.

"Trust me," Ryker attempted to empathize. "I was just as pissed as you when I found out Cesar had a son. But up until two months ago, Matais Ortiz didn't exist. Matais *Sanchez*, however, did."

"He used a different last name?" Matt asked from his seat at the corner of the room.

Ryker nodded. "His mother's maiden name. Rumor has it Matais was born in some shack in the middle of Cesar's in-law's family land. Cesar insisted they not list Ortiz as the baby's last name to protect the child from his enemies."

"That's surprising," Nate commented. "Usually guys like that are all about carrying on the family name."

"As was Cesar." Ryker turned to the other man. "However, he had the aforethought to focus on the long game. He knew our government had him in their sights, even back then. Since the man is dead, we can only go by assumptions. But our guess is he knew the risks that came with running a successful cartel, and he needed someone to take over the business should anything happen to him. Someone he trusted."

Gabe cursed beneath his breath. "Like a son."

Son of a bitch.

"So...what." Adrian looked to Ryker for more answers. "This secret son just suddenly appeared out of nowhere to claim his rightful place at the fucking throne?"

"Something like that. He's been working hard the past few years to rebuild what his father lost. Bastard's well on his way, too."

"Which is probably why he decided to take his father's name," Kole surmised.

The trained sniper was sitting at the table with Matt, and both men—every man in the room, actually—looked nearly as pissed as Adrian felt.

Actually, pissed didn't even begin to describe how he was feeling.

This was a major fuckup on the American government's dime. One that had already cost Ben his life. One that may very well cost Jenna hers.

No. Do not *go there!*

Adrian's subconscious was right. He needed to keep that shit locked down. If he didn't—if he allowed himself even a second to think about what could be happening to her—he'd lose his fucking mind.

"How long has the government known about this?" he demanded.

"Matais *Sanchez* has been under our radar for about eighteen months," Ryker explained. "At first it was just chatter. A new Colombian organization claiming its leader had the knowledge and power to rival that of El Chapo and Escobar."

"Jesus." Adrian shifted the weight off of his injured leg.

"The discovery that Sanchez was really Ortiz happened about six weeks ago." Ryker's intense gaze fell on his. "A CIA operative was already in place. It took a bit, but she managed to get close to Matais. According to her report, Matais likes to talk when he drinks. And when he has sex. He spouted off a few things that made her suspicious, and she was able to obtain DNA and pass it along to her handler. The report confirms Matais is a familial match to Cesar."

Jesus.

"Wait." Excitement shot through him. "If you have an agent on the inside, then that means you know where Ortiz is located."

Ryker shook his head. "We *had* a location. Up until a few days ago."

His excitement dissipated in a flash. "What happened?"

"The agent inside vanished. We were actually talking about bringing you in on the investigation," Ryker told him. "But then that shit went down with Dawson's wife and—"

Anger flooded Adrian's veins. "Are you shitting me? You could've at least *told* me about it."

"You quit, remember?" The other man took a step toward him. "There was no justification to read you in on an active case."

"Yet here you are." Adrian threw his hands out to the side. "I mean, you're telling us all now, right? So why the fuck couldn't you have given me a heads up when you *first* found out about all this shit?"

"Seems he's pretty good at keeping important shit a secret." Gabe's gaze narrowed as he stared Ryker down. "Especially from those of us who put our asses on the line for him."

"Oh, spare me the high-horse routine," Ryker defended himself. "What we do relies on discretion and secrets. You all know this. Hell, the only reason I'm telling you about Matais now is because *he* brought you into all this shit when he sent you his father's ring."

"Really?" Adrian got so close to the other man, their noses damn near touched. "So the fact that an innocent woman's *life* is at stake has nothing to do with it?"

"Of course, it does. And we're going to get Jenna back, but we have to go through the right channels. We can't just barge into his last known location without any sort of plan or backup. That's why I—"

"Fuck *you*, Jason." Adrian refused to listen to any more excuses. "And fuck your government agency bullshit."

Ryker opened his mouth to continue the argument, but Nate chose that moment to interject.

"I hate to break up this little love fest"—Nate interjected —"but...is it just me, or have we seen this episode once before?"

With his hand raised as if he were a kid in a classroom, he looked around the room for a response.

No one answered, but Kole did a piss poor job of covering up his smirk. One of the other guys—Adrian wasn't sure who—chuckled under his breath.

Nate wasn't wrong. The scene *was* a hell of a lot like the one that played out between Gabe and Ryker a few months back.

Still, this wasn't the time or place for jokes, and Adrian felt the need to convey that message loud and clear.

Spinning his rage-filled gaze toward the other man he said, "You think this is funny, Carter?"

"No, actually." Nate stared back at him with no sign of amusement. "I don't think it's funny at all. But I *do* think standing here arguing about who should've told who what, is a pointless waste of time. Time you, yourself, said we don't have."

Damn. The tech nerd was right.

Swallowing his anger, Adrian turned back to Ryker. He started to ask him for Ortiz's LKA when the burner phone that had been left for him dinged.

"Holy shit." Nate grabbed the phone from the table where he was sitting. His eyes rose from the screen to meet Adrian's. "You just got a text."

About fucking time.

He plodded over to the table and snatched the phone from the other guy's hand. Tapping the screen, Adrian held his breath and opened the text. Only it wasn't actually a text.

It was a picture.

"No." The image before him blurred from the red haze filling his vision.

Baby, no!

The other men gathered around the phone to see what had him so upset, but Adrian didn't notice them.

All he could see was Jenna.

She was in a chair, her wrist and ankles bound to it by thick rope. Her long, gorgeous hair was disheveled and there were bruises and dried blood on her beautiful face.

Someone had hit her. More than once, by the looks of it.

"Motherfucker," Gabe lashed out from behind him.

The phone shook in Adrian's fist. His murderous gaze rose to meet Ryker's. "I'm going to kill him. I'm going to find him and make what I did to his father look like a goddamn cake walk. Then I'm going to fucking *kill* him!"

Ryker yanked the phone from his hand and handed it to Nate. "See if you can run a trace on that picture."

Adrian's insides were an inferno of rage. He felt sick to his soul for what had been done to his sweet Jenna. And the fact that she'd been *hurt* because of him...

Ah, God.

A jagged blade ripped into the center of his shattered heart. The pain sharp and vicious, unlike anything he'd ever felt before.

Rubbing a hand against his chest, Adrian tried to ease the tormenting sensation. To fill his starving lungs with air. It didn't work.

Nothing was working, and Christ Almighty...was he having a heart attack?

He felt himself sway, but a set of strong hands grabbed hold of his upper arms and kept him steady.

"Whoa, brother." Zade kept his grip tight. "You're looking a little pale. Maybe you should sit down."

Matt added, "And take a damn breath before you pass out."

Despite the well-meant offer, Adrian shook Zade off and regained his composure. "I don't want to fucking sit. I want to find the son of a bitch who sent that picture!"

"You need to lock it down, Walker!" Ryker pointed a finger at him. The hardened agent's eyes zeroing in on his. "We're going to get your girl back, but in order to do that, you need to calm your shit and keep your head clear."

He heard the other man's words. Knew what he'd said was true. But *fuck.*

"Hey, I've got something," Nate spoke up, right on cue.

All eyes went to the man behind the computer.

"It's not much"—he bit his lip as he typed— "but it could be a start, at least. The number from which the text originated is a burner phone. No surprise there. But it looked familiar, so I cross referenced it with the reports I've been running and..." He turned the computer around for Adrian and the others to see. "The same number called Chief Campillo's private office line at the precinct around the same time you and Jenna got there for your meeting with him. According to the time stamp on the security footage from inside the building, the number called Campillo again, right as you and Jenna were walking out."

Adrian remembered he and Ben joking about the call. He'd told Ben he'd been saved by the bell. Ben's response held a whole new meaning, now.

Saved or slaughtered. Depends on who's calling.

He blinked, fighting the urge to deny the undeniable. "That's how they knew. Ben told them we were there."

"And he told them when you were leaving," Ryker stated what was now clear to everyone.

Sonofabitch. Ben *had* sold him out. Him and Jenna both.

Adrian closed his eyes and forced some much-needed air through his nostrils. Nausea from both his friend's betrayal and what he'd seen in that picture hit hard and fast. It was all he could do not to throw up.

Or punch something.

Or shoot someone.

He'd survived a lot of shit in his day, with both the Marines and his deep cover days. Adrian had seen and done things most people couldn't even begin to wrap their minds around.

Hell he'd shot two of the men standing in this very room in order to keep his cover and get the job done. But this?

If something happened to Jenna...if they hurt her worse than they already had or, God forbid she *died* because some asshole was pissed at him for killing the guy's sick fuck of a father...

Without a sliver of a doubt, Adrian knew he'd never come back from that.

Damn it, Adrian. Get your head on straight and fucking focus. You can fall apart later, but right now. Jenna needs the ruthless killer she knows you to be.

Though it proved difficult, Adrian listened to the tiny voice in his head and blocked out everything but the most important mission of his life.

"Is there any way to trace the phone's origin?" He shot Nate a hopeful glance.

"Sorry." The other man shook his head with obvious regret. "I've been trying, but there's a reason burner phones are used for shit like this. Whoever sent that pic knows what they're doing. The number's pinging off of multiple cell towers in different locations spread out all over the world."

"They're using a scrambler," Kole inferred.

Nate nodded. "A high quality one, too."

"Then what's the fucking point?" Grabbing the hair on the top of his head with both hands, Adrian was tempted to pull every single strand out.

"Of what?" Ryker frowned.

"Of any of this. Them trying to kidnap Jenna the *first* time"—because yeah, there was no way that wasn't connected to all this shit—"and then the drive-by. Amanté's and Ben's murders, and now this? They sent the picture, but there's no ransom note with it or any other type of demand. I don't understand the fucking point."

"This." Gabe met his frustrated gaze. His voice was calm and steady in the midst of Adrian's emotional storm as he pointed toward him. "This right here is the fucking point. The person behind all of this wants you to suffer, Adrian. And not just physically."

"He's right." Ryker agreed with the team's leader. "I think it's safe to say Matais Ortiz is the one we're dealing with.

And he's playing with you. He knows your weakness and he's using it…using *her*…to torture you."

"Because I tortured his father," he stated the obvious. "But how would he have known what Jenna means to me? Jenna and I…we were just starting to—"

"They've been watching you," Matt interrupted. "When did you and Jenna first become close?"

Adrian scowled at the other man. "Are you asking when we first had sex, 'cause that shit's none of your goddamn business."

"Easy, man." Matt quickly threw his hands up. "I'm not asking about the first time you slept together. I'm asking about the first opportunity someone had to *see* you two together. To realize what she meant to you."

Adrian thought back, the answer slapping him square in the face. "The first time we slept together."

"For fuck's sake," Matt muttered beneath his breath. "I *just* said, I'm not asking about—"

"No." This time he cut Matt off. "I'm saying the first night we slept together would've been the first chance anyone would've seen us together."

It had only been a few weeks ago, but so much had transpired between them since then, it felt as if a lifetime had passed.

"When was that?" Ryker put his hands on his hips.

"Three weeks before she came down here." Adrian stared back at him. "So about a month ago."

One of Gabe's brows rose, but thankfully the guy didn't choose that moment to give him shit.

"I only spent a few hours at her apartment that day, but…" Another thought struck. One that had his eyes closing. "Shit."

"What?" Several of the men asked in unison.

The admission tore loose from his protective layers. "I went by her place a few times before that."

Gabe looked confused. "And what...she wasn't home those times or something?"

"She was home." He sighed. "I just stayed outside."

There was another beat of silence before Nate ever-so-kindly offered up a quipped, "So what you're saying is you stalked her."

"I didn't stalk her, asshole," Adrian bit back harshly. "I went by her place a few times, that's all. Just to make sure she was okay after everything that went down before."

Okay, fine. Technically he'd stalked her. But not in a creepy ass, *I want to sneak inside your home and rearrange your panty drawer* kind of way.

Truth was, he'd been too damned chickenshit to approach her all those times before.

"When everything went down...you mean when you kidnapped her and then used her as bait?" Matt asked matter-of-factly.

Adrian took a step toward the other guy, but Ryker stopped him with a hand to his chest.

"All right, so we're looking at a timeframe of about, what. Two or three months, tops?"

Adrian nodded. "Give or take."

"So if Ortiz *did* have someone watching you back then, would they have been able to conclude that you cared for Jenna?"

He hesitated only a second before nodding a second time.

Ryker tipped his chin. "I'd say that's a solid theory, then."

A theory that provided even more confirmation of his colossal fuck-up.

He'd let his guard down. Focused on something *he* wanted for a change. As a result, he'd lead the bastards to Jenna.

Right. Fucking. To. Her.

"The hows don't really matter at this point, do they?" Zade pointed out. "Our focus should be on confirming the person who took Jenna and finding out where the hell they are so we can go in and get her."

Seemingly apprehensive, Ryker said, "I already have a team looking."

"What?" Adrian was seriously considering asking Gabe for his gun again. "What do you mean? What team?"

"The same Delta Force team that worked with Bravo to get you and Ellena back."

"Ghost?" Nate spoke up next. "I mean, not that it's much of a surprise. Those guys always have our backs."

They sure did. Adrian had been forced to work damn hard on multiple occasions in order to avoid being captured by Bravo and the Delta team in question.

If he hadn't known any better, he would've thought the two teams were one. As it stood, the two groups were a united front, both working for the greater good.

"Not to sound like a broken record"—Adrian looked at Ryker—"but why are we just now hearing about this?"

"Because I only just sent Delta down there this morning."

"Down where?"

"Colombia"

Several men in the room grumbled their dislike for the South American country. It didn't seem as if any of them had ever had a good experience there.

Join the fucking club.

"I didn't say anything at first because all I have to go on so far is a tip by a local asset we've used in the past. Knowing how important this op is, I wanted to wait for Ghost to get back with me. He's supposed to confirm he's actually at the suspected location, as well as trying to find out whether or not Jenna really is there."

"Just like they did for us when Elle was taken," Gabe muttered low.

"Precisely," Ryker confirmed. "Once we've nailed down Ortiz's location and that he's with your girl, those guys will move in and—"

"The fuck they will." Adrian limped toward the other man again. "If Jenna's there, I'm going in."

Ryker's gaze fell to his wounded leg before rising back up. "And what do you intend to do, limp your way past his guards? Use your damn head, Adrian. You're injured. I know you're used to going balls to the wall with stuff like this, but there's no shame in sitting this one out."

"This isn't up for discussion, Jason. I'm going. And since you so beautifully pointed out already, I no longer work for you. That means I don't have to ask for your blessing."

"You can't be serious," the Homeland agent scoffed.

Adrian's determined gaze lasered in on the other man's when he said, "As a fucking heart attack."

Ryker started to argue further when the burner phone began to ring. Putting a sudden halt to the conversation, all eyes went to the device still lying next to Nate's computer.

Adrian snatched it off the table and answered it, putting it on speaker for everyone to hear.

"Who the hell is this?"

A smug, accented voice came through the phone. "Am I finally speaking to the infamous Adrian Walker?"

"Yeah, asshole." A muscle in his jaw twitched. "I'm Walker. Your turn to share."

"You don't know? I assumed my father's ring would have given you the answer."

Bingo.

Adrian shared a look with the other men. "Matais Ortiz. Cesar's hidden gem."

The man chuckled. "My father had to hide me because he knew monsters like you existed."

"Oh, I'm the monster?" Adrian squeezed the phone. "I'm not the bastard who kidnapped and beat an innocent woman!"

"No. You're the bastard who tortured my father to death."

"Your father's men took my sister off the streets so he could use her for his own fucked up pleasure. Then he killed her and tossed her away like a piece of garbage."

"My father was a brilliant businessman who built an empire out of nothing."

"Your father was a sick, perverted freak," Adrian hissed. "I enjoyed every single second of pain I caused him, just like I will when I get my hands on you."

"Tsk, tsk, Mr. Walker. You really shouldn't say things about me or my father like that. Especially when my men are standing so close to Miss Shaw."

There was a slight pause before the sound of someone's fist hitting skin reached their ears. Every man in the room stiffened when they heard Jenna's muffled cry of pain.

"You son of a bitch!" Adrian spoke through a set of clenched teeth. "Touch her again, and I *swear* to God—"

They hit her again.

"Fucking stop! *Please!*" Adrian bellowed, the tendons in his neck straining from the force. Tears pricked the corners of his eyes and his gut tightened with the need to kill.

"You'll soon learn, Mr. Walker"—Matais toyed with him some more—"You are not the one in charge, here. I am."

"Fine!" Chest heaving, he temporarily swallowed his pride and hatred toward the other man. "What is it you want?"

"Oh, I think you know exactly what I want."

Adrian looked around the room to find the same look of understanding in every man's eyes.

"You want me? You've got me. But not until Jenna's far the fuck away from you."

"See, that's not going to work for me," Ortiz commented smugly. "But I'll make you a deal. You come to me. *Trade* yourself for the girl. And I'll set her free."

"Done." Adrian didn't hesitate. Didn't take time to think about it.

He didn't need to.

Jenna's weak voice broke his already shattered heart as she screamed for him to stay away and not come for her.

Sorry, baby. I love you. I have to do this.

The other men all shook their heads vehemently while silently mouthing their opposition to his response. He didn't care.

With the exception of Ryker, every man in that room had gone through similar situations with their own women. Beyond a shadow of a doubt, each of them would give up their lives in the blink of an eye if it meant keeping those women safe.

Adrian was no different.

He wasn't sure how or when it happened, but in the end, there really wasn't a choice to be made. He'd already accepted the fact that she'd never want to be with him after this, anyway.

How could she?

So if his dying meant giving Jenna the chance at a long and happy life, he'd gladly hand himself over to Ortiz. And never look back.

"Name the time and place, Ortiz," he told the other man. "I'll be there."

"Excellent." The man's sinister smile made its way through the phone. "It probably goes without saying, this invitation is being offered exclusively to you, Mr. Walker. I see anyone else on my property, the woman dies. And I'll make sure it is a slow, painful death. You're familiar with those, yes?"

You'll find out soon enough, motherfucker.

"You won't see another soul but me." Adrian spoke with a deadly calm. "And I'm a man of my word."

"I'll send you the details. And Adrian? Do try to be on time. I'd hate for my men to become bored and need something to…occupy their time."

I'll rip their hearts out through their chests and shove them down their goddamn throats.

"Save your threats and just send the fucking info. Sooner you do, the sooner your wish to kill me will come true."

CHAPTER 15

"How you holdin' up?" Gabe sat in the plush leather seat across from Adrian's.

"Me?" Adrian gave a casual shrug. "I'm fucking fantabulous."

The former SEAL rolled his eyes. "It's just us here, Walker. You can drop the whole stoic, Lone Ranger bullshit."

"Who says it's bullshit?"

Rather than respond, Gabe got quiet. Looking through the small, oval window, the other man stared at the clouds racing by but said nothing.

Adrian wasn't sure which version of the man made him more uncomfortable—silent or bossy. He looked at Gabe from the corner of his eye.

Silent. Definitely silent.

Not in the mood for a touchy-feely conversation, he took advantage of the quiet and stared out his own window. He used the time to do a mental run-through of what he knew of the plan so far and tried like hell to avoid thinking of everything he was about to lose.

After ending the call with Ortiz, the bastard had immediately texted coordinates to where he was supposedly holding Jenna and the time he expected Adrian's arrival.

With a few clicks, Nate's satellite program showed a heavily treed area located twenty miles south of Bogotá, Colombia Getting to work immediately, Nate searched the location and was able to find satellite footage of a large industrial structure.

When he dug deeper, he discovered the building was originally an assembly plant. Back in the nineties when there was a major rush in the cocaine distribution business, the place had been used as a drug smuggling front.

Since that time, the cartel that had claimed the property as their own had either died off or moved their business elsewhere. Best guess, Adrian and the others assumed Ortiz saw the building's isolated location and knew it would be the perfect place to keep his hostage.

Except she's not yours, asshole. And soon...very soon...you're going to realize what a mistake it was to even think you could touch her.

Hours later—which put the timeline of Jenna's abduction to well over three days—Ghost finally contacted Ryker with confirmation that Matais and several of his men were spotted at the place where they were headed.

Whoever Ghost's source was—Adrian didn't know, and he didn't care—had also confirmed that an American woman was being held there. A *redheaded* American woman.

It was all the proof he and the others needed.

Though Ryker was still against Adrian tagging along, he soon realized his vote was outnumbered, six to one. Gabe and the others surprised him by falling in line with the idea that he be the one to go in after Jenna.

After all, it was his head Matais wanted. Plus, the man had been pretty clear that no one else be seen but him.

Knowing there really was no other choice but to let him

face off with Ortiz, Ryker showed his concession by phoning the pilot and letting him know to have the private jet fueled and ready for a trip to Colombia.

They finally went airborne just under two hours ago.

The plan was simple. He'd go in early with the hopes of finding Jenna before Ortiz found him. Once she was safe, he and the others would rain hell down on Ortiz and his men.

On the chance that Ortiz crossed his path before he found Jenna, he'd pretend to hand himself over and hopefully buy enough time for the others to get inside and get both he and Jenna out.

Ryker had a chopper waiting somewhere close on standby. Along with the Homeland agent, he, Jenna, and the members of Bravo would use that for their extraction while Ghost and his team would trek back to the van that would be waiting at the pick-up spot.

Apparently, Delta had another op they needed to join ASAP, and the flight back to the States was in the wrong direction.

How Ryker always managed to arrange shit like this in *places* like this was beyond Adrian's paygrade. All he needed to know was that the chopper would be there when they needed it, and not a second before.

Adrian had given Ortiz his word no one else would be seen on the property. And they wouldn't.

What they would see—the very last thing the bastards would *ever* see—would be Bravo's and Delta's bullets heading straight for their heads.

Until then, he was stuck in this cracker-jack jet cruising at forty-one thousand feet with nothing to do but fucking *think*.

About how he'd fucked up.

About all the ways he wanted to make Ortiz pay for what he'd done.

About never having the future with Jenna he'd only just *begun* to imagine.

"I get what you're doing." Gabe broke the silence, tearing him away from his own, private pity party.

"Yeah?" Adrian sighed before turning to the other man. "What's that?"

"You're blaming yourself for what's happened. Making a list of all the ways you screwed up and beating your own ass for it."

Pretty damn close, but that didn't mean Adrian wanted to have a heart-to-heart about it.

"Did you need something, Dawson? 'Cause if not, I'm pretty sure your seat's over there." He pointed to the front of the plane.

Adrian knew he was being an ungrateful asshole, but if he revealed his true emotions—the anger, fear, and self-loathing threatening to consume him—he'd wind up breaking down like a fucking baby.

And that was something he would *never* do. Especially not in front of these guys.

"You don't want to talk, that's fine. I get it." Gabe pushed himself to his feet. "But you know what Jenna means to me and Elle. And I know a little about what you're going through. So all bullshit aside, you wanna talk, I'm happy to listen."

Sliding his gaze back to the window, Adrian prayed the other man couldn't see how much his supportive words affected him. He held his breath, waiting until Gabe turned his back before swallowing the painful lump that had suddenly appeared in his throat.

He'd worked solo for nearly a decade. Ryker or his CIA handler would pass along intel and instructions for a job, and he'd get to work.

Alone.

Other than when he had to check in, Adrian spent his time pretending to be what the government demanded. He'd converse with the bad guys, act like he was working for them, and then he'd do whatever was necessary to ensure they were taken down.

Either by him or another team like Bravo.

But in all that time he never had anyone to turn to. Never had someone he could just sit and share a beer with. Someone he could be *himself* around.

Thanks to Jenna, he'd found himself again. Or rather, he *thought* he had.

Thought he'd found a way out of the darkness. That he'd found someone to share the light with.

What a fucking fool I've been.

Sitting alone, he drew in a deep breath and set his mind back where it needed to be...on the mission.

He'd go in, get Jenna out of that hell hole, and do his damnedest to send Ortiz and whoever else had a hand in hurting her straight to hell. As long as she was safe, he didn't give a shit what happened to him.

"Here." Ryker seemed to appear out of thin air. "Thought you might want to look through this."

Adrian glanced down at the folder in the man's hand. "What's that?"

"Basic intel on the Delta team members you're about to go into bed with."

"I've already met them." He dismissed the agent and turned away.

"You met them when your ass was beat to hell and back, and you were focused on getting the fuck back home. Given what's at stake, I thought you might wanna know who'd have your back on this." He tossed the folder into the empty seat Gabe had previously occupied. "Read it. Don't read it. It's up to you."

With that, the other man returned to his seat at the back of the plane.

Adrian stared at the folder and mentally cursed. He fucking hated when Jason Ryker was right.

Grabbing the file, he began skimming through the contents. There was one paper for each of Ghost's team members who would be present for this particular mission. The first five were men he'd already met.

Delta Force Captain Keane "Ghost" Bryson was the afore-mentioned leader of the group and an all-around badass. Cormac "Fletch" Fletcher brought fifteen-plus years military experience to the table, and Beckett "Coach" Ralsten's eidetic memory was a fascinating asset to his team.

Graham "Hollywood" Caverly got his nickname for obvious reasons. The good-looking bastard could've easily chosen a career walking the runways instead of dropping out of planes into the most dangerous parts of the world.

Adrian flipped the page and found the last of the familiar faces contained in the file. A man Adrian remembered quite well.

Towering over them all at six-seven, Ford "Truck" Laughlin was a solid wall of muscle and brawn. The guy was a serious force to be reckoned with, and Adrian was damn glad Truck was on their side.

The other two members of Ghost's team to draw the short straw for the mission from hell were Troy "Beatle" Lennon, and a guy named Aspin "Blade" Carlisle. Adrian hadn't met them yet, but he knew enough about the way Ghost ran his team to feel confident in their abilities.

Closing the file, Adrian tossed it back over into the other seat and settled into his. Closing his eyes, he tuned out everyone and everything around him and began mentally preparing for the most important mission of his life.

He'd already lost a loved one at the hands of one Ortiz.

He'd be damned Jenna would suffer the same fate as his sister at the hands of another.

Sometime later, a deep, stern voice pulled Adrian from his meditative state.

"Listen up." Gabe stood at the front of the plane to address the entire group. "I just received updated intel from Ghost. They're holed up in a cavern about two klicks west of the old assembly plant."

"What's the game plan?" Adrian asked.

Ryker answered for the other man. "We'll land at a secured airstrip just south of Bogotá. I've arranged for a van to transport us as close as we can get to where Delta's located. Barring any unforeseen incidents, the drive should only take about twenty minutes. The off-road terrain there is spotty at best, so the driver has been instructed to drop us off a mile from the road leading to the plant. We'll trek through the trees and meet up with Ghost and the others."

"Once we reach Delta"—Gabe took over—"we'll go over the plan one final time to make sure everyone's clear on their role in this rescue mission. After that, we'll give Walker a head-start before falling in line behind him for back-up. For now, we need to use the next two hours in-flight to fine-tune what needs to happen in order to bring both Jenna and Walker out of this thing alive."

"And Ortiz?"

Adrian looked over his shoulder to Matt, who'd posed the question. "Ortiz is mine."

"Not to beat a dead horse, Walker"—Zade spoke up from his seat, catty-corner across from him—"but are you sure you're up to this? Physically, I mean?"

"I'm fine," Adrian bit out, resisting the urge to rub his aching thigh.

His leg still hurt, but nothing was going to keep him from going in after Jenna.

Fucking. Nothing.

When there were no further questions or comments, Ryker and Gabe proceeded to go over the details of the plan. Utilizing the drop-down screen at the front of the plane, they clicked through satellite images of the structure and the area surrounding it.

Through Homeland's resources, Ryker had procured current satellite views in order to obtain the most up-to-date intel they could prior to breaching the area. The fewer surprises they encountered, the better their odds of keeping Jenna safe.

The plane landed as scheduled. The men quickly set about gathering their gear and settling into the van that was waiting to take them to their drop-off sight.

Adrian couldn't help but feel gratitude toward Ryker for all he'd done to get them here. And, despite the man's objections to Adrian's participation in the mission, the Homeland agent had actually planned ahead by bringing camo gear and extra weapons for him to use.

Guess the guy isn't a complete asshole, after all. Who knew?

Once they were dressed and armed to the teeth, all seven men—Ryker included—climbed into the van and settled in for the ride.

The drop-off sight was just as described. The side of a dirt road with nothing but trees and hills as far as the eye could see.

More than ready to get the party started, Adrian hopped out of the van first, ignoring the bite of pain shooting up his left thigh.

Using it, he pushed on, keeping up with the others as they began their two-klick hike to where Delta was in place and waiting.

By the time they reached the special forces team, his leg was barking like a rabid dog, but he didn't dare let on. If these guys even suspected he was hurting, he had no doubt they'd try to re-write the plan and bench his ass.

And that sure as shit wasn't happening.

With their weapons at the ready, the men broke through the small clearing where Delta was supposed to be waiting for them. Adrian looked around but saw no one.

He opened his mouth, ready to unleash the livid beast that had grown with every painful step, but snapped it shut when seven men made their way out from behind the surrounding cover.

"Damn, Ryker." Ghost approached them first. "Never thought I'd see your ass back in the field."

"My *ass* was in the field while yours was still in Basic." Ryker held out a gloved hand for the Delta leader to shake.

"Ghost." Gabe stepped up, offering the Delta leader his hand. "We've seriously gotta stop meeting up like this."

Ghost chuckled. "No shit. It would be nice if we could all meet up over drinks instead of assholes who think it's their God-given right to kidnap women for their own sick agendas. Problem is, you take one of the bastards out, there are twelve more waiting in line behind him."

If that ain't the truth.

"We'll have that beer someday soon, brother." Gabe lowered his hand back to his weapon. "Count on it."

"How's Ellena?"

"Good." Gabe grinned like a man in love. "Really good. We're actually expecting our first child in a couple of months."

"That's great!" Ghost slapped Gabe on the shoulder. "Congrats, man."

"Thanks. I'll pass it along to Elle."

"If we could make plans for our girls' day and play catch up some other time, that would be great," Adrian interrupted the reunion.

"Sorry, Walker." Ghost turned and offered him a hand, as well. "You're looking a little better than the last time I saw you."

"Ghost." Adrian forced himself to greet the man and return the gesture. "Not trying to be an ass, but we're on a pretty tight time-crunch, so…"

Ghost's knowing gaze met his with a nod. "Understood. Real quick." He turned to his men standing behind him. "I believe you already know Hollywood, Fletch, Coach, and Truck."

Adrian gave the group of special forces badasses a tip of his chin. "Gentlemen."

"And these guys here are Blade and Beatle. They weren't able to be in on the last joint op, but just like my other men, they're the best at what they do."

Blade, who was tall with dark brown hair and gray eyes, gave the group a half-salute greeting. "Good to meet you."

Beatle's reddish hair and southern drawl made him immediately seem like the friendly type. "How y'all doin'?"

"Now that the introductions are over…" Ryker stepped into the authoritative role. "Let's go over this one last time before Walker heads out, shall we?"

For the next few minutes, the two teams and Ryker finalized their plan down to the very last detail. Once the few questions had been answered and the group came to a collective agreement on how to proceed, they were ready.

"Last chance." Gabe spoke so only Adrian could hear him. "Say the word and we figure out another way to get Jenna out of there."

He shifted his gaze to the other man and said, "There is no other way."

"We've got your back on this, Walker." Gabe locked eyes with his. "And if you and Jenna are what you say you are…

you'd better make damn sure your ass gets out of there in one piece."

The two shared a look before Adrian turned and started walking toward the far end of the clearance. Glancing over his shoulder, he addressed the entire group with what he hoped came off as a sincere request.

"Jenna's the priority. She gets out. No matter what."

"We'll get you *both* out, Walker," Ghost responded for the group. "Just keep your ass alive until we can get there. You'll be an hour early of Ortiz's schedule, so you should have the element of surprise on your side."

With a final nod, Adrian disappeared into the thick, green cover and began the three-mile hike to where Jenna was waiting.

Hang in there just a little longer, baby. I'm coming for you.

Jenna's heart was broken, and she couldn't even cry. She lay on the cold, hard floor, her hands tied together with the rope they'd used before, rather than the cuffs.

Apparently, tying her to the chair before had all been for show. Gave her more of a 'hostage effect' for the picture Matais had sent to Adrian.

It was the only reason she could come up with because, after the heated phone call, Sebastian had moved her from the chair back down to the floor.

Well the joke was on them, because at least this way she was able to lie down.

Jenna fought to keep her eyes open, terrified of what could happen if she let her guard down. As much as she wanted to, she refused to let herself fall asleep because she needed to be ready.

Adrian was coming for her. She'd heard him say as much yesterday—was that yesterday?—when Matais had called him. Despite her attempts to deter his agreement to Matais' sick plan, she'd heard the man she loved agree to trade himself for her.

Part of her had always known he'd come, but more than the knowledge of that, Jenna was starting to *feel* him.

In her heart. Her soul. It was as if Adrian was all around her, now.

Of course, it was quite possible she was finally losing her ever-lovin' mind. Dehydration, starvation, and exhaustion could do that to a person.

Maybe that's what was happening to her, now. It would explain why she thought she heard Adrian begging for the men to stop beating her while he'd been on that call.

Men like Adrian, they didn't beg. Not for anything.

I love you, Adrian.

Those four words had been running through her head on loop, over and over again. Because she knew he was coming, and when he did, they were both going to die.

Jenna's eyes started to droop closed, but she blinked them open when she heard the metal door creak open. Her heart ached with fear, terrified she wouldn't have the strength to fight against whatever was coming.

She cursed herself once again for not eating the meat and rice when Sebastian had offered it up the other day. They hadn't offered her any food since.

Sebastian had been kind enough to bring her more water. Just enough to keep her from dying.

Not that it really mattered. Hydration only prolonged the inevitable.

This is where I'm going to die.

"Rise and shine, Miss Shaw." Matais squatted down in front of her. "Time to get you ready. Your boyfriend will be here soon."

"Fuck...you." The raspy words were harsh, but the hushed tone with which they escaped ruined the effect.

"Thanks for the offer, but I'll pass." His smile turned her empty stomach. "But I'm not really into redheads. Garcia, however...he loves them. Maybe once Mr. Walker is out of the picture for good, I'll let Garcia have some fun before he kills you."

He reached for her face, as if he were going to caress her like a lover, but Jenna jerked her head just before he could make contact.

"Still the tough girl, I see. Right to the end, yes?" The bastard laughed as he pulled out a large, shiny knife.

Terror stole her words.

No! This isn't the end. It can't *be.*

"W-what are you...doing?"

"I told you." Matais cut through the rope at the center of her wrists. "I'm getting you ready for the big finale."

Relief rushed over her as he pulled her to her feet. Holding her steady with his hands on her shoulders, excitement flickered behind his evil eyes as he stared back at her.

"I've waited so long for this moment. To finally bring my father the justice he deserves. You can't possibly understand what joy that brings me, Miss Shaw."

Jenna had heard what Adrian said about Matais's father. That *he* was the man who'd bought his sister and then killed her. And this man thought a monster like that deserved justice?

A plan began forming in her mind.

It was a stupid plan. Probably the dumbest idea her mind had ever conjured up. But it was the only thing she had left.

If she allowed this man to take her to wherever he intended, she'd be used as further bait for Adrian. The man she loved more than anything would find her...try to *save* her...and end up getting killed for his efforts.

Jenna couldn't let that happen. And she damn well refused to go down without a fight. If this was her last day on Earth—if these were her very last moments—she was determined to make them count.

I love you, Adrian.

Swallowing against her desert-dry throat, Jenna drew in a deep breath and gathered what was left of her strength. Then she looked evil square in the eye.

"You're right," she rasped. "I don't understand. Because your father doesn't deserve justice, Matais." She licked her swollen lips and steeled herself for what she was about to do. "Sick freaks like that deserve to rot…in…*hell!*"

Jenna shoved the man as hard as she possibly could. She didn't have a lot of strength, but with Matais not expecting the move, he lost his balance and fell backward. His head hit the floor with a hard thud.

Momentarily stunned by the impact, the man lay there, moaning on the cusp of unconsciousness. Jenna took the opportunity to try to run but forgot to take into account how *weak* she'd become.

She'd no more gotten to her feet when she fell back onto her hands and knees beside him.

Refusing to give up, she tried again. And again. On her third attempt, she managed to find her footing—and the knife that Matais had dropped when she'd knocked him down.

A low growling sound hit her ears seconds before she felt a hand grab her left ankle and pull. She went down hard, the knife clattering to the ground as she lost her grip on the deadly weapon.

No!

Jenna screamed and kicked, fighting as hard as her weary body allowed. At one point, she felt the sole of her shoe make contact with the man's face Though she wasn't sure, she thought she heard a satisfying crunch of bone.

"Fucking bitch!" Matais yelled. His accent was strong, but she understood those words loud and clear.

It was crazy, given her situation, but Jenna felt a smile tugging at her dry and cracked lips. If this *was* her time to die, at least she'd caused her killer a bit of pain first.

With renewed energy—it was amazing what fighting for your life can do for a person—she kicked again. But this time, Matais was ready.

He grabbed her foot and twisted her leg, forcing her to roll onto her back to keep it from snapping. Crying out—which sounded more like a sick frog trying to croak—Jenna gritted her teeth and fought like mad to reach the knife lying to her left.

Catching sight of it, too, Matais climbed halfway up her body and began fighting her for the weapon. Jenna used her right hand to go for the man's eyes while she stretched the fingers on her left in an attempt to grab the knife first.

Having the same idea, Matais went for her throat. His fingers wrapped around the delicate area there and squeezed. Jenna choked and sputtered as the man struggled to regain the upper hand.

Gasping for air she could no longer get, she focused on what she *could* do.

Using as much strength as she could muster, Jenna dug her nails into Matais's face and raked them across the skin covering his cheek. The man howled and reared his head back, his strong hold easing just enough so she could slide over and grab the knife.

With her left hand wrapped around the weapon's leather hilt, she swung the blade toward him. The sharp tip sliced across his upper right arm.

Matais screamed that time, flinching backward to stave

off another assumed attack. This gave her the chance she needed.

Shoving her right shoulder into the man's chest, Jenna forced him the rest of the way off of her, making it possible for her to get away.

Scrambling to get as far from Matais as she could, Jenna felt like a hamster on a wheel as her shoes slipped several times on the concrete's smooth surface. His fingers brushed against her ankle, but she found her footing and ran.

"Come back here!"

Eat shit, asshole!

She made it halfway to the door before Matais's hard body hit hers, knocking them both back down onto the floor. The air left her lungs in one loud woosh, and fire spread through her scalp as he grabbed hold of the hair and yanked her head backward.

Jenna didn't have time to react before Matais slammed her forehead into the unforgiving floor, sending her straight into a black abyss.

CHAPTER 16

"Walker, you copy?" Gabe's voice filled Adrian's right ear as he made his way to the edge of the trees.

"Copy." He kept his voice low. The nearly undetectable ear coms they were all using—compliments of Ryker—were state-of-the-art, picking up even the slightest of sounds. "Approaching the property line, now."

"Roger that. We're half a klick behind you. Ghost and I are coming in from the west, and Beatle, Blade, and Nate are covering the north. Hollywood and Zade will make their way around the east side of the structure, and Ryker, Kole, and Matt will be coming up from the south."

They'd have the place surrounded. Adrian just hoped it would be enough.

"Just remember the plan," he reminded them. "Wait for my signal before engaging."

They'd better remember the fucking plan. Jenna's life depended on it.

A sliver of gray caught his eye as he made his way through the final stretch of foliage. "I see the assembly plant, now," he relayed to the others.

The two-story, cinderblock building was covered in cracked and broken windows and those vines that overtook anything that stood vacant for too long.

"Jesus," he muttered. "Looks like something out of a post-apocalyptic sci-fi flick."

"Watch a lot of those, do ya?" Nate teased.

Adrian's immediate comeback was, "Sure do. With your mom."

Several oohs and oh-shits came through the coms, followed by Zade's amused, "Dude. Did Walker just *mom*-joke your ass?"

Adrian almost let himself smile. He guessed working with a team wouldn't be completely horrible.

Too bad I probably won't get the chance after this.

Not that he wanted to die, but Adrian wasn't a fool. Not about this. He was walking into the hornet's nest and his closest backup was a mile and a half behind him.

As long as Jenna survives. That's the only thing that matters.

Shaking that shit off, Adrian drew in a breath, readied his gun, and stepped over the tree line onto the abandoned building's property.

Despite the objection coming from his left leg, Adrian refused to show any sign of weakness in front of Matais or his men. He forced his gait to become steady as he crossed through the knee-high grass.

"I see two men standing guard by what looks to be the building's main entrance. There's another guy, maybe two, the south side. I'm far enough over, I don't think they can see me, but I can't see the north or east sides at all."

"The most recent satellite footage showed two on each side of the building," Nate informed them. "It's safe to assume that hasn't changed."

"Agreed," Ryker joined in on the conversation. "All we can do is follow the plan and make adjustments accordingly."

"Uh…isn't that pretty much what we do on every op?" Matt asked with obvious jest.

"Ah, come on, Turner. Cut Ryker some slack." Gabe's deep voice rumbled in response to Matt's teasing. "It's been a minute since he's dusted off his boots to play with the big boys."

The banter at Ryker's expense continued until Adrian found himself in the sights of one of the guards by the front entrance.

"Look alive, boys," he spoke while barely moving his lips. "It's time to party."

"Stop!" The guard who'd noticed him pointed his long rifle in Adrian's direction. The man next to him followed suit.

"Easy, fellas." Adrian raised both hands, even the one holding his pistol. "Your boss is expecting me." He made a show of glancing at his watch and making a clicking sound with his tongue. "Damn. Guess I'm early. No worries. I'm sure Matais won't mind."

Thankfully the building was large, and the entrance was a good distance from the north and south ends. Adrian didn't think the guards in those areas could hear them.

"Yeah, asshole?" The second guard—a mouthy fucker—sneered at him. "And who might you be?"

"Name's Walker. Adrian Walker. Perhaps you've heard of me."

Both men blanched at the sound of his name. Damn, he never got tired of seeing that same *holy shit* look on supposed tough-guys' faces.

The fact that most people in this business knew of him and his reputation came in mighty handy.

"That's right, boys and girls." Adrian continued walking toward them with a pasted-on smile. "Take a good look. Hey, we could even take a selfie together. Show all your friends on the playground tomorrow. You'd be the most popular kids in school."

"Jesus, Walker," Matt's voice filled his ear. "God complex, much?"

Just playing the part, Dawson. Always playing the part.

Despite the fact that these two idiots were clearly grown men, one of the dipshits actually started to smile. As if the idea of a selfie with the world-famous assassin was tempting.

The other one, however, smacked his partner in the chest and stepped forward. "That's far enough. I'll come to you."

"Sure, man." Adrian stopped moving. "Whatever tickles your curly hairs."

The one guy snickered while the more serious one continued to approach him with caution. As expected, the guard took possession of Adrian's pistol then proceeded to pat down his cargo pants and other combat attire.

Also not a surprise, the asshat took the extra mags Adrian brought, along with the gun on his hip, his ankle, and the small knife tucked into his boot.

What the man didn't find—what he *wouldn't* find—was the KA-BAR duct taped to the inside of his button-up camo shirt.

Now, if all he was wearing was the shirt, then sure. The knife would be an easy discovery. But Adrian was wearing a vest, which of course, the guy also took.

But as it always went with untrained assholes like these, the guard assumed once the visible weapons and vest were gone, their captive was left essentially helpless.

They never thought to pat down the front of the shirt whenever he wore a vest. Not once.

Fatal mistake, boys.

Schooling his expression, Adrian allowed himself to be led to the door. Since the one man's hands were filled with the vest and weapons, it was up to the other guard to open the door. Leaving both men vulnerable to an attack.

Moving lightning fast, Adrian reached into the collar of his shirt, pulled his knife free, and jabbed it into the neck of the man who'd frisked him. The other man had only just started to turn toward the commotion when Adrian did the same to him.

Both men dropped dead where they stood.

Wiping the blood from his blade onto his pants, Adrian let the teams know, "Two down. That leaves six assholes for you guys and one for me."

"Good work." Ryker's go-to compliment came through loud and clear. "Now move fast, Walker. Ortiz will be watching for you, and if he finds the men you just killed before you find him—"

"Yeah, yeah," Adrian cut the man off as he retrieved his weapons from the dead man's hands, putting them back in their rightful place. "Not like I'm poppin' my cherry here, Ryker."

"Make sure it's not."

"The fuck is that supposed to mean?" He checked his immediate area for threats and found none.

"Just that this op is different than your others because it's personal. Just want to make sure you keep your head in the game."

"My head's right where it needs to be, dickhead." Adrian entered a huge, open space.

"Walker's right," Gabe spoke up with a surprising show of support. "The guy knows what the hell he's doing, Jason. Let him focus, yeah?"

The silence that followed was the only agreement they'd get from the Homeland agent. Shaking it off, Adrian recentered his thoughts and made his way across the factory's main area.

Earlier while on the plane, they'd been briefed on the layout of the building, so they'd know what to expect. Looking around, he saw exactly what he thought he would.

Windows lined all sides of the main floor. Most were broken or altogether missing.

The floor was cracked and covered in inches of dead and decaying leaves. The ceiling, which also appeared to be made of concrete, was being supported by several thick, stone pillars running from one end to the other along the center of the open space.

Definitely something out of an end-of-the-world movie.

A cockroach scattered across Adrian's path, giving him an idea.

During their ride from the plane to the van, he'd over-heard Ghost's teammate commenting on how he hoped there weren't a lot of bugs out this time of day. Apparently, the guy fucking hated them.

So naturally he couldn't resist.

"Hey, Beatle," he whispered softly. "You're gonna love it in here. Lots of huge, juicy bugs."

"Not cool, man," Beatle grumbled. "Not fucking cool."

The others chuckled in Adrian's ear, but he was too busy crouching down to avoid being seen by the guards at the back of the building to join in.

"Heads up. Just spotted the two guards walking along the east wall. I repeat, two targets confirmed along the east wall."

"Copy that," Gabe let him know he'd received the message.

Adrian looked up ahead, spotting exactly what he hoped he would. "I have visual of the lower staircase. Heading there, now."

Waiting to make sure he was in the clear, he stood and quickly made his way over to the top of the staircase. His heart pounded beneath his shirt as he thought of seeing Jenna again.

With each step, he had to force himself not to wonder what condition she'd be in once he located her. With every beat of his racing pulse, he had to push away the fear and dread threatening to consume him.

And above it all, Adrian had to refrain from feeling the hope he knew he shouldn't have that she'd somehow find a way to forgive him for all of this.

Stay focused, Walker. For Jenna. She needs you now, more than ever.

The voice in his head sounded a lot like Ryker's. Nevertheless, it was right.

Shaking his personal shit off, Adrian regrouped and kept his head clear as he moved. His gut told him he was on the right path, and he'd find her—and hopefully that bastard, Ortiz—soon.

They'd studied the picture Ortiz sent of Jenna with a fine-tooth comb. Other than the light from the flash, there appeared to be little to no natural light in the place where she was being held.

That, along with the echoing voices he'd noticed as he spoke with Ortiz, led them to believe she was being held on the building's lower level.

In the basement.

"Approaching the stairs, now," he relayed to the other men. "No sign of Ortiz."

"Keep your eyes open, Walker," Gabe reminded him. "We'll be there soon, but until we get there, you're on your own."

"Copy that. Might lose signal once I'm down here."

"It's no different than any other op," Ryker tried his hand at encouragement. "You got this."

No different, my ass.

Still, the man was right. As long as he relied on his training, he should have no problems finding Jenna. And Ortiz.

His leg screamed with each descending step, but Adrian pushed on until he stood in front of a door located at the bottom of the stairs. Turning the handle, he blew out a silent breath of relief when he found it unlocked.

The space he walked into was almost pitch-black, so he pulled the tactical light Ryker had given him from the pocket at his thigh and pushed it on.

The LED bulb illuminated a good chunk of the area, showing a long hallway with several doors on each side.

"Well that's not creepy as fuck," he muttered. When he got no response, Adrian tested his coms. "Dawson? Ghost? You copy?"

He was met with silence.

Shit. Well, he was used to flying solo. Like Ryker said…it was no different than any other op.

Keep telling yourself that, buddy.

And he did. With every step he took down the terrifying hallway. With every door he opened, expecting the worst but finding nothing.

Adrian told himself the same thing over and over until he almost believed it to be true. Then he heard it.

The sound was slight and hard to place. While Adrian couldn't be sure, he thought it was almost like someone was trying to move a chair across the smooth floor.

Jenna!

Doing his best not to give himself away in case Ortiz was somewhere close, Adrian went to the source of the sound. It was a room on his right, in the dead center of the hallway.

He stood outside the door, his heartbeat rushing past his ears as he tried to listen with intense focus. He heard it again.

It was her. It *had* to be her.

Adrenaline pumped through his body with impressive

speed. His heart was *hammering* now, and he actually took a precious second to gulp down a calming breath before putting the flashlight away and switching to the mounted light on his pistol.

Curling a gloved fist around the metal handle, Adrian kept his gun steady as he used the handle to give the door a gentle push.

He inwardly cringed when the rusty hinges squealed in protest, but he continued on.

The space was much larger than the other rooms he'd cleared, and at first, he thought this room was empty, too. But then the beam from his light crossed over something near one of the back corners, and he knew.

His lungs froze inside his chest as he swung the light to the spot where it had just been. Adrian's heart leaped into his throat when he saw her.

She was tied to the chair like before, but her mouth had been duct taped. Blood covered part of her forehead and right temple, and she was squinting away from the light. But she was alive.

"Jenna!"

Everything else seemed to vanish. His thoughts of killing Ortiz. The other teams. *Everything* but his primal need to go to her and make sure she was okay.

In a combination of running and limping—because his leg hurt like a sonofabitch—Adrian skidded to a stop just before he ran *into* her.

"Baby?" He moved the light to the side to avoid blinding her. "Oh, thank God!"

Wide, terrified eyes met his. Bruised and *swollen* eyes that made him want to kill. Jenna was shaking her head and trying to tell him something, but the tape made it impossible to understand what she was saying.

"Hang on, sweetheart." He squatted in front of her.

Shoving his gun into his waistband, he pulled out the knife he'd used before. "I'm going to cut you loose, and then I'll get the tape."

His blood boiled at the sight of her raw and bloody wrists. The jagged cuts looked to be infected, which only added to the rage threatening to overpower him. But first things first.

Cut her loose, get her out, kill Ortiz and every other asshole who helped him.

In. That. Order.

"There." His blade sliced through the last of the ropes. "Now the tape. It's probably going to sting, but it's better if I rip it off quick."

Before he could lift his hand to her, Jenna was yanking the silver strip from her lips herself.

"You can't be here!" Her voice came out gravelly and rough. "You have to leave!"

"We will, baby. I'm going to get you out of here right now."

He stood straight and carefully pulled her to her feet. She wobbled a bit, but he held on tight. Refusing to let her fall.

"No." Jenna shook her head. "You don't understand. He's going to kill you. You have to leave me here and *go!'*

She was damn near hysterical, and Adrian's heart ripped in two hearing her beg him to leave her behind to save himself.

Not in a million fucking years.

"Can you walk?" he asked, his eyes scanning the rest of her dirty and disheveled frame.

He knew she had to be hurting, and her sunken cheeks and dark circles under her eyes told him she hadn't eaten or slept for shit in several days.

Save her now. Kill Ortiz later.

"Not fast...enough." She sounded weak and looked even weaker. "Please, Adrian. Just...go."

Adrian was careful of her bruises when he cupped her face with both hands. Taking seconds they didn't have, he locked his gaze with hers and said, "There is no way in hell I'm leaving you here, got it?"

She looked like she wanted to cry, but no tears fell. With a slow, jerky nod, Jenna finally agreed to go with him.

"Good girl. Here's what we're going to do. You and I are going to walk out of this room and go down the hallway to our left. There's a door at the end that leads to a staircase. That's going to take us out of here, okay?"

"Then w-what?"

Damn, she sounded weak.

"Then you and I are going to go home and lock ourselves away. I'm going to make love to you over and over again, and then we'll—"

"That sounds like a wonderful plan," a voice behind him spoke up. "Too bad it will never happen."

A mental string of curse words rang through his head. He never should've kept his back to the door. A fucking rookie mistake that a man with his experience *never* should've made.

Jenna's entire body jolted beneath his touch, and he could feel the utter terror vibrating through her. Her fear became his motivation to act, because he was more than ready to put an end to all of this.

Once and for all.

"Stay behind me, baby." Adrian turned to face his enemy. "Matais, I presume?"

"The son of the man you slaughtered." Matais Ortiz stepped forward. He held a gun in his hand, and it was pointed straight at Adrian's heart. "Do be so kind as to drop the knife."

Speaking of knives, Adrian couldn't help but notice the

blood on the man's right arm. He thought about asking what happened...then remembered he didn't care.

"I'm here, just like I promised."

Adrian set the knife down slowly. He used that time to quickly do the math in his head and determined the others should be joining them any time.

"Let Jenna go, and you can do with me what you want."

"No!" Jenna tried stepping forward.

He stopped her with an outstretched arm and a shake of his head. Tried to, anyway.

"No!" The stubborn woman moved out of his reach and around his arm. "I won't let you sacrifice yourself for me."

"Not your choice, sweetheart."

"The hell it's not!"

After everything she'd been through, that fire he loved so much was still there.

"You're willing to die for this man?" Matais looked puzzled as he moved the gun toward Jenna. "It is because of him that you are here."

Adrian ground his teeth together but kept his cool. He knew Matais was trying to get a rise out of him. Goad him into losing control so he could win this sick game.

Not gonna happen, asshole.

"I don't care." Jenna tilted her chin a bit higher. "I won't let you kill him."

"I'm sorry to disappoint you, Miss Shaw. But I'm afraid you won't have a choice."

Ortiz smiled wide as he pulled the trigger, shooting Jenna in the abdomen at point blank range.

CHAPTER 17

"No!"

The animalistic roar tore from the deepest depths of Adrian's soul as he watched the woman he loved fall to the ground.

Without any thought of his own safety or well-being, he rushed to her side and fell onto his knees.

"A-Adrian?" Fear and pain consumed her emerald eyes.

He covered her wound with both hands. Her blood poured out over his fingers.

Oh, God!

"Jenna?" His voice cracked. "You're okay. Y-you're going to be okay."

"Do you really want the last thing she hears from you to be a lie?" Matais mocked him.

"Shut up!"

"I have a very good aim, Adrian. I did not want her death to be quick, therefore I did not shoot at a major organ. However, given your situation and our location, she will be dead within the hour. Two if she's lucky."

"Shut the fuck up!"

"H-he's…right." Jenna's throat worked as she swallowed. "S-sorry…"

"No!" He shook his head and pressed harder. "You are *not* dying. Not today."

His heart *hurt* from his fear of losing her.

"On your feet, Adrian," Ortiz spoke again.

"Jenna? Baby, open your eyes," he ignored Ortiz and focused on Jenna.

She was starting to let her eyes fall shut, but at the sound of his voice, she lifted her lids and looked up at him. The spark of fire he loved so much was fading. Even the greens seemed somehow muted in color.

"That's it, sweetheart. Keep those eyes open for me, okay? Please, baby. You've got to stay with me."

"Now!" Ortiz pushed the barrel of his gun against the back of Adrian's head. "The time has come for this to end."

Yeah, asshole. It sure as fuck has.

Leaning down, Adrian made a show of hugging Jenna as if to say goodbye. God, he *prayed* this was not goodbye.

He whispered words filled with encouragement and promises. Words he meant to the very depths of his soul.

While he spoke what he prayed were not the last words she'd ever hear him say, Adrian used the moment to his advantage, removing the smaller knife he'd returned to his left ankle earlier.

Expertly concealing the move, Adrian slid the weapon into his sleeve as he leaned down and pressed his lips to Jenna's.

"L-love…y-you." The feathered words barely reached his ears.

Tears burned the corners of his eyes, his heart racing frantically between his ribs. "I love you, too, Jenna." Did she know that? He hadn't actually told her that before now. "I love you so much."

"On your *feet!*" Matais yelled, his patience clearly gone.

"Please hang on, baby. For me." With another soft kiss, Adrian replaced his hands with hers and stood.

"It is time for justice to finally prevail, don't you agree?" The man's words were laced with excitement.

Adrian turned to face him, unprecedented fury smoldering just beneath the surface. "As a matter of fact, yes. I do."

"The choice was yours, you know." The man stared back at him with the same arrogance Cesar had. "The second you went after my father, you chose your fate. You chose her death."

Ortiz glanced toward Jenna, giving him the perfect window to act.

Adrian surged forward. In one fluid motion, he used his left forearm to knock the bastard's hand—the one holding the gun—to the side while simultaneously reaching over and transferring the knife into his right hand.

Eyes wide with shock, Matais fought to bring the gun back around. Adrian was much stronger.

With his fingers wrapped around the man's wrist, he twisted hard, snapping the bones clean through.

"Ah!" Matais bellowed in pain.

Adrian shoved his knife into the man's heart. "I warned you." His tone was a low, lethal growl. "I told you I would kill you for touching her. Like I said"—he twisted the knife—"I'm a man of my word."

"P-please," Matais begged for his life.

But that life was already gone.

"Go to hell." He pulled the blade free. "And tell your fuck of a father I said hello."

Matais gasped his last breath, his blood pouring from his chest as Adrian let go of him. He crumbled to the ground in a lifeless heap.

Adrian didn't waste another second on the dead man. Instead, he rushed to Jenna's side.

Her eyes were closed, her head lolled to the side.

Baby, no!

He felt for a pulse, damn near bawling when he found one. It was faint and thready, but it was there, all the same.

Scooping her up, Adrian fought through the pain in his leg and ran. He needed to get back to where his coms would work so he could tell Ryker to get the chopper in place.

"Hang on, Jen." He spoke to her as he ran. "You're going to be okay. Just a little longer, baby."

Her blood covered them both, but Adrian ignored it and continued on. Yanking open the door at the end of the hall, he ran up the stairs and through the open area with the pillars, talking to the guys as he went.

"Target is down!" he yelled. "I repeat, Ortiz is down!"

"Damn glad to hear ya, brother!" Ghost's voice came through crisp and clear. "Perimeter is clear. Moving inside, now."

"Jenna's been hit!" He huffed as he ran. "Get that fucking chopper here, now!"

"Shit. How bad?" Gabe's worried voice broke through.

"Gut shot. Lower right abdomen. She's—"

A bullet whizzed by his head. The damn thing was so close Adrian felt its heat as it passed.

"What the fuck?" he yelled as he moved behind one of the pillars. Holding Jenna close to his chest, he curled his body around her as best he could. "We're taking fire!"

"Hang tight, Walker," Ryker responded. "I've got the shooter in my sights."

Chunks of their concrete shield flew off as a second bullet struck.

Jesus. "Today would be good!"

"Just need him to move another inch to the left... and...there."

Glass shattered as Ryker's bullet traveled through a partially intact window before lodging itself into the target's head.

"Thanks." Adrian blew out a breath and started running toward the building's entrance. "We're coming out, so if there are any other surprises I should know about, now would be the time."

"That was the last straggler," Ghost assured him. "Prick must've been hiding out in one of our blind spots."

"We got an ETA on the chopper?" He'd no more asked the question when he heard the comforting sound of a helicopter's blades in action.

Thank God.

Carrying the most precious cargo he'd ever hauled, Adrian burst through the doors and out to the grassy area he'd first crossed when coming here. From his peripheral vision, he saw the other men filtering toward the designated landing zone.

The chopper landed several yards away, and Adrian pushed his bum leg to its limits to get Jenna there.

Gabe met him at the opened side of the bird.

"How bad?" The worried man asked a second time as they worked together to load her into the bird.

Adrian shook his head. "She's been unconscious for a few minutes and has lost a shit ton of blood. Ortiz...the bastard said he didn't aim for anything vital. He, uh..." His voice broke, but he cleared his throat and tried again. "He wanted her to die slowly."

Gabe's face turned red, the vein in his forehead bulging at the thought of what that fucker Ortiz had done to their girl.

As the others waved the Delta men a quick thanks and

farewell, Adrian kept his eyes on the one good thing to ever come into his life.

The bird took air, and they began their trip to the airstrip. Once they boarded Homeland's jet, the pilot would be instructed to fly them as fast as possible back to Gulfside Harbor, which happened to have the nearest stateside hospital.

Adrian slid down to the floor and settled himself at Jenna's side.

Taking her limp hand in his, he willed her to live. Since Matt was the medic of the team, he set about packing her wound with a specialized clotting agent Katherine Turner—a crazy-smart scientist who was also Matt's wife—designed for the U.S military.

The powder drastically slowed the body's response to wounds, allowing for longer timeframes between extractions and care, which was why the military had paid Matt's better half big bucks to continue researching and fine-tuning her formula.

There was a time, back when Adrian had been working undercover, that he'd aided in Kat's abduction for a man of foreign political power in order for the man to attempt to steal the formula.

As was his plan, though they didn't know it at the time, Bravo team and Delta had worked together to get Kat and her formula back safely. Knowing that same formula was helping keep the woman he loved alive was something he couldn't really wrap his mind around right now.

"Damn." The man he once served with frowned.

"What?" Adrian's heart stuttered. "What's wrong?"

Without looking up, Matt continued working on the IV. "She's severely dehydrated. Bastards couldn't have given her much to drink since bringing her here. Looks like she hasn't eaten in days, either."

The man's words had Adrian's nose burning and Jenna's prone image blurring. He watched her closely, blinking away his tears as he swallowed a giant knot down his throat.

"She's tough." Gabe put a hand to his shoulder and squeezed. "She'll get through this."

He wasn't sure who the other man was trying to convince more.

Please, God. Let him be right.

Adrian prayed that silent prayer to a god who'd most likely given up on his sorry ass a long damn time ago. And he *continued* praying.

Because a world without Jenna Shaw wasn't a world he wanted to live in.

After what felt like the longest flight of his damn life, he and the others finally landed back at the private airstrip just outside Gulfside Harbor. They'd used their time in the air to clean up and change back into their civilian clothes.

Adrian hadn't wanted to leave Jenna's side for a second, but the others finally convinced him to use the plane's miniscule shower and change so he wouldn't scare the doctors off when they got to the hospital.

Matt had managed to keep Jenna stable and her IV fluids flowing. He'd cleaned and dressed the gash on her forehead and had given her what he described as a super-dose of antibiotics often used on gunshot victims.

Once again, Ryker had come through for them by arranging for an ambulance to be standing by when they landed, as well as an SUV big enough to accommodate them all.

Following the emergency vehicle, they'd raced to the Gulfside Regional where Jenna was whisked off to surgery to remove the bullet and hopefully repair the damage.

That was four and a half hours ago.

Since then, he'd been stuck in this private but suffocating

waiting room with Ryker, Gabe, and the other Bravo Team members constantly trying to reassure him that Jenna was going to be okay.

Not that he didn't appreciate their positive vibes, but fuck. The guilt of what she'd been through was eating him alive from the inside out, and every second that passed was worse than the moment before.

I need to get out of here.

Adrian spun on his heels and was heading for the door. He needed to go into the hallway...the parking lot...someplace where he could fucking *breathe*.

Gabe stepped into his path.

"Hey, you okay?"

"Yep." He nodded, hoping like hell the guy bought the bullshit lie and let him pass.

"Listen, Adrian. I can tell you really care about Jenna. And as much as it burns my ass to admit it—"

A tired-looking man in scrubs walked into the room, effectively cutting Gabe's presumably supportive speech short.

"I'm looking for the family of Jenna Shaw."

"That's us," Gabe informed him.

Everyone gathered in close to hear what the man had to say.

Giving the group a suspicious glance, the doctor hesitated a moment before accepting Gabe's word and continuing on.

"All right, well...Miss Shaw is out of surgery and on her way to recovery."

"And?" Adrian took a step closer to the other man. "How is she? She's going to be okay, right?"

She had to be okay. He wouldn't accept any other outcome.

"Miss Shaw lost a lot of blood," the man began. "But the compound that was applied on the flight here no doubt saved her life." Once again, he assessed the men in the room. "It's unlike anything I've seen before."

"And you won't see it again, I assure you." Ryker stepped forward. "Homeland Security Agent Jason Ryker." He shook the doctor's hand. "The compound in question is property of the United States Military. Its contents and formula are patented and classified, so I'll need you and your surgical staff to sign non-disclosures as soon as you're able."

The surgeon blinked. "Uh…sure. Okay."

"Can we focus on Jenna, please?" Adrian scowled at Ryker. "Doc, you were saying?"

"Yes, um…as I was saying. Miss Shaw lost a lot of blood, but thanks to the treatment she received in transport, she didn't reach critical levels. Still, we went ahead and gave her a few units to help her body replenish and start healing at a more normal rate."

"What about her injuries?" he asked with bated breath. "Did the bullet…did it damage anything significant?"

"Most of the damage was in the muscular tissue between the bottom of the right kidney and the top portion of the large intestine. Somehow, every major organ was avoided when the bullet struck. I've never seen anything like it."

I have a very good aim, Adrian. I did not want her death to be quick, therefore I did not shoot at a major organ.

Rather than giving Jenna a slow, painful death as Matais had intended, his precision aim had helped save Jenna's life.

Take that, you sick fuck.

"Miss Shaw also has a concussion that will be monitored during her stay here," the doctor continued. "Also, we've continued the course of IV antibiotics to fight off possible infection from both the gunshot wound and the cuts on her wrists."

Adrian's stomach turned thinking about the wounds he'd

seen on her delicate skin. Wounds that would most likely scar.

Just more proof of how fierce and determined the woman was. Of how *hard* she'd fought to get herself free.

"So you're saying…"

"With rest and proper care, I believe Miss Shaw will make a full recovery. She's a very lucky young woman."

A collective sigh filled the room, but Adrian was too busy trying not to lose it in front of everyone to join in.

"You hear that?" Gabe slapped his shoulder. "Told you our Jenna would never give up that easily."

Our Jenna.

Adrian swallowed a ball of dread. He thought she was his. Had convinced himself she belonged to him. But now…

How was he supposed to face her ever again? The very thought of seeing the hatred and betrayal in her eyes when she looked back at him…

As strong as he was, that was something he knew he couldn't handle.

"Can we see her?" Gabe asked the surgeon.

"Since she'll be in recovery for a while, I'll allow one of you to go back. But only for a few minutes."

"Walker?"

He blinked and turned toward Gabe. "What?"

"The doctor said one of us can go back and see her." The former SEAL grinned. "Figure she'll want to see your ugly mug first."

"Oh uh…no. You go ahead."

Gabe's brow furrowed. "You don't want to see Jenna?"

More than anything.

"I do, but you've known her a hell of a lot longer than I have. And, like you said before, she's your family. Besides"— he rubbed the tight muscles at the back of his neck—"I'm sure Elle's on pins and needles waiting for a detailed update from you, so...it's better if you go in there first."

"Okay." Gabe's gray eyes assessed him a little too closely. "If you're sure."

"I'm sure."

With a nod, he said, "I'll come get you to switch out when I'm done."

Adrian forced a smile. "Thanks."

He watched Bravo's leader leave with the surgeon. The others took turns shaking his hand and expressing how happy they were to hear Jenna was going to be okay.

When the conversation died down a bit, Adrian excused himself to go to the restroom. Picking up on his mood, Nate stopped him just before he made his escape.

"Seriously, man. You doing okay?"

"Yeah." At least he would be if they'd leave him the fuck alone and let him leave. "Why?"

"I don't know. You just seem...different."

"Just tired," he told the other man.

It was the truth. He *was* tired.

Tired of innocent people getting caught up in the crossfire he always seemed to be a part of.

"I know our situations are different, and lord knows I never thought I'd offer this to you, but"—Nate shrugged—"you ever want to talk. I can be a pretty good listener."

One corner of Adrian's lips curled slightly. "Thanks, Carter. Appreciate it."

"No problem. Hey, when you get back from the bathroom, you wanna hit the cafeteria for some mediocre coffee?"

"Sure," he lied smoothly.

And then he walked away.

CHAPTER 18

The smell of bleach was the first thing Jenna noticed when she regained consciousness. There were muffled voices in the background from a TV show she didn't recognize, and every so often, someone would turn the page of what she assumed was a book.

Her head pounded, and there was a pain in her right side. Not sharp and burning like before. More of a dull, tight ache like she'd pulled every single muscle there.

But she hadn't simply pulled a muscle. She'd been shot.

This wasn't like the last time she'd woken up in the hospital. This time, Jenna remembered every single minute of what had happened. Right up to the point where she'd blacked out.

She'd been kidnapped and held in a dark and musty basement. Was nearly starved and had been given the bare minimum of the water her body had desperately craved.

Adrian had come for her, and she'd been shot.

Even in her medically altered state, Jenna could remember the inferno ripping through her body as the bullet from Matais Ortiz's gun tore through her flesh. And she remembered the rage and fear in eyes belonging to a man who feared nothing.

Adrian had *begged* her to keep her eyes open. To stay with him. And she'd tried so damn hard to hold on.

Everything after that was a blur, but if she was in a hospital, that meant he'd gotten them out. She was finally away from that monster, and she was safe.

I love you, too, Jenna. I love you so much!

She smiled, remembering Adrian saying those sweet, sweet words. Of course, he could've only said them because she'd said it first, and he'd thought she was dying.

But she didn't think so.

Adrian Walker loved her. He *loved* her. And she couldn't wait to hear him say it again.

Peeling her eyes open, her lids rose and fell in an unhurried pace as her eyes adjusted to the bright light.

The first thing Jenna saw was the clock on the wall at the foot of the bed. That and the small whiteboard informing her nursing staff she was NPO, which meant she couldn't consume solid or liquid foods yet.

Figures. I go from one place that won't let me eat or drink to another.

Smiling at her own dark humor, Jenna opened her eyes again. This time, she kept them open.

Turning to her right, she found machines that beeped and tubes that ran from the machines to her body. Swallowing against the worst case of cotton mouth she'd ever had, Jenna turned her head to the left and found a set of wide, hopeful eyes staring back into hers.

"Hey, stranger." Elle smiled at her from the white, plastic chair.

Not the eyes I was hoping to see.

"Hey." Jenna's voice was rough and hoarse. She hoped Elle

couldn't sense the disappointment she felt that Adrian wasn't here.

Setting the book in her hands onto a nearby tray, Elle scooted forward in the chair. Her large, round belly making the move less graceful than it normally would've been.

"How are you feeling?"

"Like I've been shot. What about you?" She motioned weakly toward Elle's growing baby bump. "You look like you're about to pop."

Her friend also had dark circles under her eyes and looked like she hadn't slept in days.

"Is that a fat joke?" Elle raised a playful brow. "Because pregnant women are extremely hormonal, and I'd hate to have to hurt you after you just had surgery."

Jenna smiled, then realized there were tears swimming in her friend's eyes. "Hey." She tried to push herself up in the bed, but a sharp pain in her side kept her from going very far. "Don't cry. I was only kidding. Your belly isn't big. In fact, you barely look pregnant at all."

Through her tears, Elle burst out laughing. "Liar."

She grinned, grateful her emotional friend was smiling again. "Hormones, huh?"

"You have no idea." The other woman wiped her cheeks dry. "Of course, it doesn't really help to find out my best friend's been kidnapped by a dead drug lord's son and then get the call that said friend has been *shot* by the maniac."

Even as she said the chastising words, Elle was scooting closer to the bed and grabbing her hand.

"You scared the shit out of me." Her friend swallowed hard. "Gabe, too. We thought we were going to lose you."

Her heart broke for her worried friends. "I'm sorry I scared you."

"You should be." Elle squeezed her hand. "But the doctor says you're going to be fine. You have a concussion, too." Her eyes rose to the source of Jenna's headache. "The nurse said you didn't need stitches, and the cut in your forehead is close enough to your hairline, the scar probably won't even be noticeable."

After what she'd been through, a scar on her forehead was the least of her worries.

Unable to wait a second longer, Jenna drew in a breath and asked, "Where's Adrian?" She glanced at the closed door. "Is he with Gabe?"

Because she'd noticed Elle's husband wasn't in the room, either.

An odd look crossed over Elle, but it was gone before Jenna could figure out what it meant.

"Gabe went to make a call, but he'll be back any minute. He's going to be so happy you're awake. I swear, that man has been climbing the walls since I got here. Before I got here actually. And oh, my gosh. You should've seen his face when I walked into the hospital waiting room. He was not happy about me driving all this way by myself in 'my condition.'" The rambling woman used air quotes. "Like being pregnant is some sort of debilitating disease or something."

"Elle—"

"But then he hugged me, and I knew I'd made the right decision to come here. He was so worried about you. He thinks of you as a sister, you know. And I knew he was going crazy wondering if you were going to be okay, and—"

"Elle—"

"I can't wait to see his face when he walks in here and realizes you're awake."

"Ellena!"

Her friend blinked. "What?"

"You didn't answer my question."

"Yes, I did," Elle's nervous chuckle was uncharacteristic to say the least.

"No, you talked about Gabe. I asked about Adrian."

"You asked if those two were together, which means you asked about Gabe, which is why I talked about Gabe."

"You're avoiding."

Elle's dark brows scrunched together. "I am not."

"Please." She rolled her eyes. "You're an expert in the field, and I practically invented the skill." When Elle remained silent, Jenna became seriously worried. "He's okay, right? Adrian's okay?"

She couldn't believe she hadn't thought to ask that question before now.

The last thing she remembered was seeing his handsome, worried face leaning over hers as he kissed her and told her he loved her. He'd whispered soft, sweet words to her, and then he and Matais had started fighting.

She lost consciousness after that and then woke up here.

Jenna had assumed since she was here and not in that horrifying basement that they'd both gotten out of that place and away from Matais. But now…

Fear for the man she loved had her dizzy with worry. What if Adrian was hurt? What if he wasn't the one who got her away from the monster and brought her here? What if…

"Adrian's fine," Elle assured her. "At least…we're pretty sure he's okay."

"You're *pretty* sure?" Jenna fumbled to find the controls on the bed before raising herself up. "What does that even mean? Where is he?"

Biting her bottom lip, it took a few seconds for Elle to make eye contact with her again. When she did, the look in her eyes said it all.

"We don't know."

Her stomach tightened. "How can you not know where Adrian is?"

"Listen, sweetie." Elle wrapped *both* hands around hers.

"The important thing is he found you and brought you back to us. And that man who hurt you...he won't ever hurt anyone else, ever again. That's all that really matters, right?"

Like hell it is. "You're doing it again."

"Doing what?"

"Avoiding the answer to a very simple question. Adrian brought me here and then, what? He just vanished?"

"Walker didn't vanish." Gabe entered the room with two to-go cups and an even deeper scowl than usual. "The selfish son of a bitch took off."

Took off?

"He...left?" Jenna couldn't believe he'd do something like that. Not again. Not after what they'd shared together. "Where did he go?"

Because maybe she was overreacting. Maybe Adrian didn't abandon her like they were making it sound. Maybe something important came up, like another job with the CIA or Homeland. Or maybe...

"Nobody knows."

Gabe's blunt answer left her heartbroken. "How long has it been since he—" her rough voice cracked, and Jenna blinked against her tears.

"Day and a half." Elle's husband looked back at her with anger and a bit of gut-wrenching pity. "Bastard split as soon as I came back to see you in recovery after your surgery. I got back to the waiting room, and he was gone."

Jenna pulled in a long breath to help keep her emotions at bay. "He didn't, um..." She cleared her throat. "He didn't tell *anyone* where he was going?"

"I'm sorry, Jen." Ellena's gaze filled with sympathy that turned her stomach. "The guys said Adrian told them he was going to the bathroom and then he just...left."

He didn't even wait for me to wake up?

Gabe shook his head, his strong jaw clenching tight. "So help me, when I find that piece of—"

"Gabriel!" Elle scolded her husband. "We talked about this, remember?"

Jenna's gaze bounced between the husband and wife. "Talked about what?"

"My wife wants to make excuses for the asshole, when the truth is pretty damn clear. Walker didn't give a shit about you, or the team, or anyone else but himself."

"That's not true." The words were out of her mouth before she could stop them.

"Really?" Gabe glanced around the room. "Do you see him here? Because I don't."

"He's not selfish." He'd risked his life to save her. "Something must've happened. He must've had something important to take care of."

"You," Elle's husband bit out sharply. "His ass should be here taking care of you."

Jenna could take care of herself. That wasn't the issue.

"What happened?" Jenna demanded to know. "After I was shot, I mean. I remember a little, but not very much."

"According to Walker, Ortiz shot you and then Walker fought with Ortiz. He ended up stabbing Ortiz in the heart and killing him."

Okay...so Matais Ortiz was dead. That was good news. Very, very good news.

But there was still a lot left she didn't know, and something in the rest of the story may be a clue as to where Adrian went or why he left the way he did.

The urge to know what sent him running was strong. Fierce. So Jenna looked at Gabe and said, "Tell me everything."

Twenty minutes later, Jenna knew it all.

After Ben Campillo was murdered, she'd been taken to

Bogotá Freaking Colombia. A fact that blew her mind. Apparently, Adrian went nuts when he found out she'd gone missing, and he'd even signed himself out of the hospital against medical advice to help search for her.

She couldn't believe she'd forgotten to ask about his leg. Couldn't believe the crazy man had gone to Colombia on a rescue after having just been shot.

But Gabe said the man was relentless in his insistence he be the one to go in after her. That, until he pulled another disappearing act, he thought the man might actually love her.

He does love me. I know he does.

"What about the other men with Matais?" She had to ask. "Their names were Sebastian and Garcia. Garcia was the one who shot Chief Campillo."

That was one memory she wished she hadn't kept.

"Ryker sent a team in to take care of the scene. I just got off the phone with him. He said they ID'd each of the ten men helping Ortiz. Sebastian Herrera and Garcia Lopez were two of the names he mentioned."

"There were *ten?*"

Gabe nodded. "Ryker's guys also found a black purse with your wallet and ID in Sebastian's apartment. He sent me this." He held up his phone to show her a picture of the items. "He's going to send it to me so I can get it back to you."

"Oh, my god."

Jenna couldn't believe what she was seeing. It was her purse and wallet, all right. Her old purse and wallet...the ones that had been stolen when she was mugged last month.

"What?" Elle looked worried. "Jenna, what is it?"

"Those were taken from me when I was mugged a few weeks ago."

"*What?*" Gabe and Elle both exclaimed at the same time.

"It happened in the parking garage at the hospital." Jenna licked her lips. "I know I should've told you, but I didn't want you guys to worry. It wasn't even that big of a deal, really. All they got was my purse and wallet, but…" *Holy shit.* "There were two men. I didn't even connect the mugging to what happened here, but now…" Jenna looked to Gabe. "Are you saying Sebastian and Garcia were the same men who attacked me in San Diego?"

"I'll look into it to be sure, but yeah. I'd say they were."

"Why?"

"Walker." Gabe stared back at her. "Ortiz needed a way to get to him, and we believe his men were watching Adrian for a while before he came to Gulfside Harbor. Those men targeted you because at some point, they realized Walker had a thing for you."

"A *thing?*"

It's more than a thing. Whether anyone else accepted it or not.

"Gabe, I'm thinking the tea you brought me is probably cold by now," Elle pointed to the drinks still in Gabe's hands. "Will you do me a favor and go get me a fresh one?"

The big guy frowned and held it out for her. "It's still plenty warm."

"The baby would like a fresh one." Elle was anything but subtle when she shot her husband a look. "*Please.*"

Picking up on his wife's blatant hint, Gabe tossed the two full cups into a nearby trashcan, gave Elle a quick kiss on the cheek. "I'll take my time."

Elle was silent until the door shut behind him before speaking again. "I think what Gabe was trying to say was—"

"I know what he was trying to say, Elle." Jenna shrugged. "He blames Adrian for what happened."

"You don't?"

"Of course not! What Ortiz and his men did wasn't his fault. Hell, they shot him, too."

"That's what I told Gabe." Her friend nodded. "Deep down, he knows that, too."

"Uh, I think your psych radar might be off a smidge because your husband's acting like he's out for blood."

Elle chuckled, her entire belly moving in synch with her laugh. "My *radar* is just fine. And so is Gabe." She drew in a long breath and blew it out. "He was just really scared for you. And to be honest, I think he's also little hurt Adrian left without saying goodbye to him. Although, lord knows he'll never admit it."

"Now I *know* your radar's off."

"Gabe was really affected by what happened to you, honey." Elle got serious. "We all were. But given what Gabe said about the way Adrian reacted when you were shot... Jenna, no one was more torn up by what happened than he was."

Jenna's heart hurt for the misguided man. "If that's true, then why isn't he here?"

With a sigh, Elle settled back into her chair. Resting her hands on her belly, she said, "No one here blames Adrian for what Ortiz did, except Adrian."

"That's ridiculous. He shouldn't blame himself for any of it."

"Adrian was already convinced that he was unworthy of love before any of this even happened."

Jenna's brows turned inward. "How do you know that?"

"Psychiatrist, remember?" She pointed to herself. "And you forget that I spent quite a bit of time with Adrian a while back. Even then, I could see the impenetrable walls he'd built around himself.

Jenna had seen them, too. In the beginning. But little by little, she'd chipped away at them until finally, she made her way through.

Then all hell broke loose.

"That man, Ortiz…" Elle continued. "He took you and nearly killed you for no other reason than to make Adrian suffer. You almost died in his *arms*, Jen. That would be hard for anyone to deal with, but for a man like Adrian Walker? I mean…look at how Gabe handled things when we lost our baby. He left for three *years* because he blamed himself for what happened. Adrian leaving…it's his way of protecting you."

"Well, it's a stupid way," Jenna grumbled.

"Yes." Elle laughed. "Yes, it is."

Jenna took a moment to process everything her friend had said. While she didn't agree with his line of thinking, she could absolutely see Adrian torturing himself for the actions of another.

She'd seen it when he spoke about his sister. She could tell right away that he blamed himself for not finding Bree in time to save her.

Now the stubborn assed man was doing it again. Only this time, it was because of her.

"What do I do?" She looked to Elle for guidance.

Elle patted her leg through the blanket and said, "Give him time."

"You saying that as a friend or my psychiatrist?"

"Both." Her friend, the psychiatrist, smiled.

"Okay." Jenna nodded. She'd give Adrian some time.

But not too much.

Because one thing she'd learned from all of this was that life was short. And if you waited too long to go after the thing you wanted, you may end up losing it, forever.

CHAPTER 19

Adrian was losing his buzz. That magical, fuzzy, floaty sensation that had kept him from thinking too much. From *feeling* too much.

That simply won't do.

Not bothering to peel himself from the lawn chair that had been his go-to spot for the past six weeks, Adrian reached down next to where he sat and grabbed the empty bottle nestled snuggly in the sand.

Through the tinted lenses of his aviator sunglasses, he stared out into the rolling sea as he held the bottle into the air and waggled it back and forth.

His signal to the private bartender that came with this private section of the beach, which came with the middle-of-nowhere room he'd rented on a week-by-week basis.

It was the perfect place to hide away. From people. From his non-existent future. From himself.

At night, though…damn if the nights didn't get to him. No matter how many beers he consumed or how many times he told himself to forget her, the fiery redhead he'd fallen in love with still haunted his dreams.

But at least she was safe.

From his past. From his enemies. And from his perpetual destruction of all things good and pure.

Damn, I really need that next beer.

Adrian started to wave the bottle again, tempted to holler up at John…or Joe…or whatever the guy's name was who got tipped too damn much, when the man appeared.

Stepping into his sunlight, a large shadow covered Adrian's sweaty body. The affect was soothing and cool.

He didn't want soothing. He wanted pain. He *craved* it.

"You're blocking my sun," he grumbled without sparing the man a glance. "Just take this and leave the other one down there. I'll add another tip when I settle up for the night."

His server said nothing. He also didn't take his bottle.

"Hello…" Adrian prompted him rudely. "You gonna take this sometime today?"

The man took the empty bottle from his hand.

About fucking time.

"Just leave the other one and go."

The sun returned in full force as the man stepped aside.

Alone again, Adrian closed his eyes and drew in a breath. He knew he was being an asshole, but he couldn't seem to help it. The anguish he'd been living with since walking out of that damn hospital had made him this way.

No, you *made you this way when you ran off like a little bitch. Again.*

Refusing to respond to his annoying inner self, he blindly reached for his newest drink. His fingertips met nothing but sand.

Opening his eyes, Adrian had just started his search for the misplaced bottle when a fountain of fresh beer rained down over his head. The cold liquid was a shock to his heated system, and he jumped up like a wild man to try to retreat from its path.

"What the fuck?"

He swiped a palm across his dripping face, knocking his baseball hat off his head and to the sand by his feet. The hat had helped block some of the fresh brew, but the position Adrian had been lounging in had left most of his face exposed to the attack.

"What the hell is your problem, man?" He rubbed beer from his stinging eyes. "Know what? Doesn't matter 'cause you are *so* fucking fired."

"Yeah, I'm pretty sure you don't have the authority to fire me. Or anyone else, for that matter."

Adrian froze because, shit. That was *not* the voice of the man who'd been bringing him endless drinks these last few weeks.

"Dawson?" He licked a drop of beer from his upper lip. "What the hell are you doing here?"

"Funny. I came all this way to ask you the same question."

The man was dressed in a U.S. Navy t-shirt and a pair of khaki cargo shorts. And he looked pissed.

"It's none of your goddamn business." He walked back over to his chair. "Sorry you wasted a trip."

Adrian made a move to sit down, but his ass met sand because Gabe had just *pulled* that chair out from underneath him.

"Jesus." He stumbled to his feet and dusted himself off. "What is your fucking problem?"

Gabe glared. "You're seriously going to stand there and ask me that? I've known you as a lot of things, Walker. But not once did I ever see you as a fucking coward."

The words didn't hurt as their owner had intended. Mainly because Gabe wasn't saying anything Adrian didn't already know.

"Go home, Dawson." He turned his back on the other man and started walking toward the water's edge.

"She's fine, by the way!" Gabe hollered after him. "Not that you bothered to ask."

Adrian stopped in his tracks but kept his eyes glued to the water in front of him. His gut turned inward, and his back teeth clamped together. He hadn't asked because he didn't want to hear it.

He didn't want to know that Jenna had moved on without him. Even though she had every right to.

It was why he'd left in the first place. To give her a chance to be free of him and the shadows that would continue to follow him. A chance to live her life without fear of his enemies coming after her—again—because of him.

A chance to be happy and fall in love with someone normal and safe.

So while he was relieved as fuck to know Jenna was, in fact, okay, Adrian didn't want to know anything more. Knowledge like that, it hurt too damn much.

And like Gabe had so kindly pointed out...he *was* a fucking coward.

"I'm glad," he told the other man.

"Are you? 'Cause the way I see it, you don't give two shits about Jenna."

Adrian closed his eyes and took deep breaths in through his nostrils. Losing his temper wouldn't change anything, so why bother exerting the effort?

"Not gonna deny it? So I guess I was right about you, all along, huh?"

He's goading you. Just ignore him, and he'll go away.

"All that talk about how much you cared about her. About how she was yours and you'd do anything for her. Why spout off all that bullshit and put on a fucking show like you gave a damn when she clearly means nothing to you."

"She means everything to me!" He lost the battle and spun on his bare heels. Storming his way back over to the other man, Adrian released six weeks of pain and anger. "I left because I do care. You saw what happened to her! You know that shit's on me!"

"That shit's on Matais Ortiz and no one else."

"Bullshit!" He moved into Gabe's personal space. "She was targeted because of me."

"True." Gabe nodded. "Still not your fault."

"How can you say that? Hell, I was the one who personally handed her over to Ben. A man who was working for the other fucking side!"

"He wasn't."

"What?" Adrian pulled back. "Of course, he was. Nate found proof of—"

"Carter found proof of two incoming phone calls to Campillo, yes. But Jenna said the only reason he helped Ortiz's men was because Ortiz had threatened Ben's wife and daughter if he didn't."

"And she believed him?"

"Yes." Gabe nodded. "She did. She said he seemed extremely remorseful, spouting off that he didn't have a choice. That he had to protect his family."

Sonofabitch. "So Ben handed her over, and they killed him, anyway."

"He was a witness."

Adrian's heart felt heavy for his friend. For the family the man left behind. But still…

"Doesn't matter. It all leads back to me, which makes everything that happened my fault."

"Jesus Christ, Walker. I mean, I've seen pity parties before…hell I've thrown enough of my own to last a lifetime. But there comes a time when the party ends and real-life resumes. Question is what is that life going to look like for you and Jenna?"

"She'll be fine without me."

"Is that what you think? Damn, brother. You are dumber than you look if you believe that shit."

"It's true. Jenna's strong. A hell of a lot stronger than me."

"Well, yeah." Gabe shrugged. "We all know that. Just like I know Ellena can handle a fuck ton more than I ever will."

Adrian frowned. "Meaning?"

"Meaning, those women of ours? They're tough as nails when they need to be. Problem is, you're putting Jenna in a position to be strong when, right now, *she's* the one needing someone to lean on."

His heart thumped against his ribs. "I thought you said she was okay."

"Physically, yeah. She's almost completely healed. And to anyone else, the rest of her seems to be moving on just fine, too. But I know that woman. So does my wife. Jenna's hurting, Adrian. And you're the only person who can make it stop."

"I can't face her, Dawson." He rested his hands on his hips and shook his head. "I wouldn't even know what to say."

"Hello, tends to get the conversation going."

Smartass.

"How could she ever look at me the same again?" It was a question he'd asked himself over and over again since he found her in that damn basement. "Every time she sees my face, she's going to remember what happened to her…and why."

"Or." Gabe rubbed the muscles at the back of his neck. "She'll look at you and see the man who was willing to put his own life on the line in order to save hers. A man who, for reasons I will probably never understand, she fell madly in love with despite his violent past and perceived flaws."

In a rare moment of vulnerability, Adrian let his guard down enough to ask, "What if she can't see me like that?"

"Then at least you'll know. You'll be free to come back here and waste the rest of your life drinking imported beer on a fucking beach with no one but a male server to talk to."

Maybe it was the alcohol still in his system, but Adrian felt himself huffing out a chuckled breath.

"Let me guess. Ellena sent you down here after me?"

"No, actually." Gabe licked his lips and looked out over the water. "She thinks I'm on a job. Coming here was all my idea."

"Yours?" That bit of news shocked him. "Why?"

The other man brought his lens-covered eyes back around. "Because I've been exactly where you are now. I blamed myself when Elle was hurt by a former teammate who wanted me to suffer. He came after her a few years back because he was pissed at me. She, uh…she ended up having a miscarriage as a result."

"Shit."

"Yeah."

Adrian waited a beat before asking, "What did you do?"

"I left." He stared back at him. "Walked away, just like you did. And I spent the next three years miserable and alone before I finally came to my senses."

He hadn't known that part of Gabe and Elle's story. Or how much he and the man who'd once been his enemy had in common.

"What made you go back to her?"

A muscle in the other man's jaw twitched. "I almost lost her for good."

Just like I almost lost Jenna.

"I don't get it. You were pissed as hell when you found out she and I had gotten close. Why the sudden change in heart?"

"She loves you, dumbass," Gabe growled. "Why the fuck

she chose you will forever remain a mystery to me. But for whatever reason she did, and she deserves to be happy." He huffed a breath. "Never thought I'd say it, but so do you."

Drawing in a cleansing breath, Adrian pretended to be interested in a bird flying across the blue sky before returning his focus back to Gabe. "You really think she'll take me back?"

"Only one way to find out." The other man smirked. "Although, if I were you, I'd plan on doing a shit ton of groveling. You do know how to grovel, right?"

Not really. "Can't be that hard. Besides, I've got the entire flight from here to California to figure it out."

Dawson's smirk turned into a full-blown smile. "There's the cocky fucker I know. Come on." He slapped a hand to Adrian's shoulder. "Let's go get your shit packed up and get the hell home."

Home.

It wasn't a word he'd ever truly known. Not even when he was a kid.

But if Gabe was right, and Jenna somehow found it in that big heart of hers to forgive him for being such a jackass, Adrian thought he might just be ready to have a home—and a life—of his own.

And he wanted to share them both with her.

Jenna was done waiting.

Going back through each of her bags, she double checked to make sure she had everything she needed. She'd made a list last night before she started packing, but she had to be sure.

The appointment with her doctor this morning had gone

well. Her body was healed enough to resume normal activities, which meant she had the green light to fly.

And once she stepped onto that plane, there'd be no turning back.

Zipping her bags closed, she hauled the load down the hallway to her apartment's front door. There was a slight twinge in her side, but nothing she couldn't handle.

It was the pain in her *heart* she needed to do something about.

After going back through the apartment to turn off all the lights and close the drapes, Jenna went into her bathroom for a final once-over before she left.

Her subtle makeup was noticeable but natural, and the decision to leave her hair down had definitely been a good one.

The shiny red locks fell over her shoulders in waves, creating a striking contrast with the silky white tank top she'd chosen to wear. From the waist-up, she appeared conservative-yet-stylish.

But from the waist down...

Jenna smiled. The green skirt she bought for the occasion fit her like a second skin. With a hem that stopped mid-thigh, the mini wrap-around tied together at her hip.

It was just this side of scandalous, and for what she had planned...it was perfect.

Checking her watch, she turned off the bathroom light and headed for the door. The last time she'd made a hasty decision like this, she'd ended up kidnapped and shot.

Neither were experiences she cared to repeat, but she also wasn't going to sit around on her ass waiting for a certain man to finally grow a pair of balls and face her.

With her purse on her shoulder and her keys and bags in her hands, Jenna turned off the last of the lights, opened the door, and...nearly ran into a wall of muscle.

Startled, she chuckled nervously. "Oh! I'm sorry, I didn't…"

The air all around her vanished. Every molecule of oxygen sucked dry by the man standing before her.

He was dressed in a pair of well-worn jeans and a dark gray t-shirt. Nothing fancy or new, but damn if he didn't look like he'd just stepped off a runway.

His dark hair was a bit longer than before, and there were a few new, lighter streaks from where the sun had kissed it.

The skin on his face and neck was tan. His cheeks, forehead, and nose almost pink from *too* many ultraviolet kisses. And his eyes…

Those gorgeous, tortured eyes were lined with creases that made her heart hurt. Worry had put those lines there. Worry and pain.

With his hands shoved into his pockets, Adrian stared back at her as if he wasn't really sure what to say. Or if he should even be here at all.

Finally, after what felt like forever, he offered her a small smile and a rough, "Hey."

Jenna's insides tingled. Like always, her body reacted instantly to the deep timbre of his sexy voice.

She was still so busy trying to wrap her brain around the fact that he was actually *here*, a full minute passed between them, and she hadn't said a single word.

"I, uh…" He glanced down at the bags and cleared his throat. "I probably should've called first."

"It's fine." Jenna finally snapped out of her shock-induced trance. "I mean, I was just about to leave, but—"

He forced another smile. "Right. I'll get out of your way."

Adrian turned and started to walk away.

Seriously?

Jenna had a half a mind to let him go. To leave him

dangling on the hook he'd left inside her a little longer. But she didn't.

"You want to come inside?" she hollered before he got too far to hear. "I can make us some coffee."

He stopped in his tracks and spun around. With another quick glance at her suitcases, he asked, "You sure you have time?"

Jenna shrugged. "I have a few minutes."

Waiting a beat, he slowly began walking back toward her. She purposely kept her eyes on his, refusing to focus on the way his shirt stretched over his broad shoulders and chest. Or how his strong thighs worked against his denim with every step.

She turned and started to pull her wheeled suitcase behind her, but he picked up his pace and grabbed the handle.

"Let me get that for you." He lifted it with zero effort.

His warm hand brushed against hers, sending a shock-wave of electricity through her system. Jenna's eyes dropped to the bulging biceps and taut forearms, and...

Damn it, Jenna! You weren't supposed to look.

Shaking off her momentary failure, Jenna stepped back into her apartment and shuffled to the side to give him room.

"Here okay?" He motioned toward the open area to the left of the door.

"Sure." Jenna gave him a tight smile, and...nope. She would not—would *not*—look at his fine ass when he bent over to set the suitcase down.

Aaaand...she looked.

Her mouth watered and her inner muscles clenched.

Good lord, woman. Do you seriously have no self-control with this man?

No. No, she did not.

Adrian stood upright and turned to face her. Praying she'd schooled her expression in time, Jenna slid her purse and carry-on off her shoulder and set them on the floor next to her feet.

He stared back at her, his eyes even more guarded than when she first met him, but there was something else there this time. A nervousness that didn't fit the man she knew him to be.

"You look good." His heated gaze fell on the hem of her short skirt.

"Thanks." Jenna smiled inwardly. "You, too." *Better than good.*

God, she hated the awkwardness that was between them, now. She and Adrian had shared a lot of things, but this sort of egg-shell politeness had never really been one of them.

"Listen, Jen. I—"

"What are you—"

They both began speaking at once.

"Sorry." He offered another polite smile. "You were saying?"

"No." Jenna shook her head. "You're the one who came all this way to see me. You go."

That's right. Remind him that this particular impromptu visit was his idea.

He'd made the first move, so now it was on him to say what he'd come here to say.

Adrian licked his lips again, and *mother trucker*, if she didn't want to grab him and put those wet lips on hers.

"Okay." He drew in a deep breath and let it out. "I spoke to Ryker this morning. He contacted the FBI after taking care of things in Colombia. Thanks to you, they started an official investigation into the disappearance Stella Gallagher. Nothing's turned up yet, but he assured me they *will* continue to look."

"That's...wow." Jenna blew out a breath. "That's great."

"Yeah. It is."

Seconds passed without a word spoken between them before she asked him, "Is that the only reason you're here?"

"No." He shook his handsome head then said, "I screwed up."

No shit.

Jenna crossed her arms and raised a brow. "Just so we're clear, which particular screw-up are you referring to? Leaving me in that hospital without so much as coming to check on me first, your latest vanishing act...I mean I don't know. It just seems like there's so many options to choose from."

Looking really uncomfortable—like crawl-into-the-nearest-hole uncomfortable—Adrian ran a hand over the scruff on his jaw and sighed.

"You have a right to be pissed. I know that. I also know that a simple apology doesn't even come close to making up for leaving the way I did. But I *am* sorry, Jenna." He swallowed. "More than you'll ever know."

The misplaced guilt he was feeling poured off of him in waves. Jenna wanted to go to him. To hold him and tell him it was okay.

But it *wasn't* okay. And she needed to make sure he understood that.

"You hurt me."

She was blunt and brutally honest. And the way he was looking back at her said she'd cut him deep.

"That was the last thing I ever wanted to do." He started to take a step toward her but stopped. "I need you to know that."

"Then why did you?" Jenna took the step for him. "Why did you ghost me like that? Again?"

She already knew the answer, but if they had any chance of moving past this, she needed him to say the words.

"I was scared."

Holy shit. He actually said them.

Jenna blinked, but kept her composure. "Of what?"

"Losing you." His eyes locked with hers as he finally took that step forward. "I've been alone for so long, I guess I forgot how to let someone in. Hell, I have no idea how to even *be* in a relationship, which I used to be perfectly fine with. But then I met you." He sighed again. "I don't know what you did or how you did it, but you became a part of me, Jenna. The very *best* part. And when I almost lost you…" Adrian rolled his lips inward and shook his head. "Everything you went through. All the pain. The fear. Nearly fucking dying. All of that shit happened because of me."

Damn. He was *so* close.

"All of that shit happened because Matais Ortiz was a sick, twisted freak like his father," she reminded him.

"I know that." He pointed to his temple. "In here. But here?" He patted his chest. "Baby, the pain and fear I felt watching you bleed out right in front of me is still there. I've been living with it every single day since I left."

"You think *I* don't feel those things?" Jenna moved a few inches forward. "That I don't have nightmares where I see myself dying in your arms? I see you and Matais fighting almost every time I fall asleep. Only in my dreams he shoots *you* instead of me."

"I'm sorry."

"Quit saying you're sorry and tell me why you left!"

"I told you." He frowned. "I was scared."

"Not good enough." Jenna shook her head as his image began to blur. "People get scared all the time, Adrian. But they don't just take off the way you did. You left without a single fucking word. You went off on your own without any thought to the people you left behind. Like you didn't give a shit about me, or Gabe, or anyone but yourself."

"I left because I wanted to protect you!" Adrian's deep voice bellowed. He stepped closer, his voice rising with every syllable. "I have enemies, Jenna. Real ones with real power. Enemies with more money than God and countless ways to get to you. I almost lost you once because of something in my past, and I'll be damned if I let anything like that ever happen to you again."

"Then why bother coming back?" She yelled, throwing her arms to the sides and let them slap against her legs. "If all you wanted to do was say you're sorry, you could've done that over the fucking phone."

"I wanted to see you!"

"Why?"

"Because I want to fucking marry you!"

The room went silent. The world stopped spinning, and Jenna almost certainly stopped breathing.

"You what?" she whispered softly.

The *oh fuck* look on Adrian's face was priceless. "I...uh..." His Adams apple bobbed as he worked his throat "Shit. I didn't mean to just blurt it out like that."

"But you meant it?" She held her breath and waited.

"Yeah." His shoulders shook with a silent huff. "Yeah, I fucking meant it."

Oh. My. God.

Adrian closed the gap between them and cupped her face with his hands. "I love you, Jenna. I love you so much I thought I needed to let you go. I thought it was the only way to protect you. But the thing is, I don't *want* to live without you. I tried. I really did. But I gotta tell you...it fucking sucked."

Jenna chuckled as his image blurred from her unshed tears. She wrapped a hand around one of his thick wrists. "I love you, too, Adrian. But if this is going to work you have to accept the fact that you can't protect me from every single threat the world has to offer."

"Sorry, baby. I'm not really wired that way." He stared down into her eyes with purpose. "But I promise I'll try to get there. Might take a while, though. Say…fifty years."

Her chest swelled and her heart soared. "Fifty years, huh?"

"Give or take."

Jenna blinked, sending silver streaks down her flushed cheeks. "You really serious about this whole marriage thing?"

Adrian smiled. Pulling a hand from her face, he slid it into one of his front pockets. When he pulled it back out, he was holding the most beautiful diamond ring she'd ever laid eyes on.

A free-fall of tears poured down her face. "Oh, Adrian."

"This serious enough for you?" His lips curled into the same smartass smirk she'd grown to love.

Jenna gave him a watery smile. "I think we could make that work."

"Let's make sure, shall we?" Adrian lifted her trembling hand and slid the simple platinum solitaire onto her left ring finger.

It fit perfectly. As if it had been created just for her.

"It's beautiful."

"You're beautiful." He cupped her face again and pressed his lips to hers. "So what do you say? You wanna marry a former traitor-turned-government assassin?"

"No." Jenna shook her head. "I want to marry a former Marine who's spent the last several years risking every-thing, including his own happiness, to help keep our country safe." She rose to her tiptoes and kissed him again. "I want to marry the man who's risked his life to save mine." Another kiss. "Twice." And yet another. "I want to wake up every single day next to the man I've been praying would come back to me ever since I woke up in that damn hospital."

Guilt filtered into his eyes again. "I'm sorry I left you."

"Kiss me and we'll call it even."

With a smile that took years off his face, Adrian put his hands at her waist and hoisted her into his arms. He *did* kiss her, then. And she kissed him back...all the way to the bedroom.

Hours later, they were still lying in her bed. Content and perfectly sated.

Before, after Adrian had left, she'd felt empty. Like she only had half of herself. But after making love to her—twice —Jenna realized she was finally whole again.

"Shit." Adrian propped himself up on one elbow.

"What?"

"Your trip. I never asked where you were going. Do you need to call someone? Let them know you're going to be late?"

Ah, yes. That.

"Nope."

"You sure? If it was important..."

"Oh, it was very important." She told the truth. "The most important trip I've ever planned, actually."

His expression fell a little, and Jenna could tell he felt guilty. She should probably feel bad about stringing him along the way she was.

But she didn't.

"Jenna, I don't want to stand in your way. If you need to go to...wherever you were headed, I'll wait. As long as it takes."

Her heart thumped. "As long as it takes, huh?"

Okay, now she *did* feel a little bad.

"For you? Hell yeah." Concern marred his beautiful features. "Why? Where were you going when I showed up?"

Jenna smiled. "To find you."

"Seriously?"

She nodded. "I knew Nate would find you if I asked. So I was going to fly to Texas, find his place, and wait until he did. Then I was going to hop on a plane to wherever I needed to go in order to find you."

Her plan clearly amused him. "What would you have done once you did find me?"

"Knock some sense into your stubborn ass."

"Yeah?" He rolled them over, so he was on top of her. "And if that didn't work?"

"I was going to kiss some sense into your stubborn ass." Jenna grabbed his toned cheeks and squeezed.

"That why you put on that sexy as fuck skirt? To seduce me into listening to reason?"

"Did it work?"

He rubbed his hardening cock against her core. "You tell me."

They both laughed, but Adrian's smile soon fell as he got serious. "You would've gone through all that trouble just to find me?" He seemed genuinely confused. "Why?"

Ah, babe. We still have so much work to do with you, don't we?

"Why do you think?" Jenna brought a palm to the scruff covering his jaw. "I love you, Adrian Walker. Every single part of you. And if you ever doubt that again, I swear to all that's holy, I will kick your ass from here to that beach you were hiding out on."

His gaze narrowed. "How did you know I was on a beach?"

"You sure as heck didn't get this tan hiding away in a cave."

He grinned as he leaned down, pressing his lips to hers. His tongue invaded her mouth in the most delicious way imaginable, and when he pulled back, their heavy breaths mingled together as one.

"I love you, Jenna Shaw." He brushed some hair from her eye and tucked it behind her ear. "And I will keep loving you every day, for as long as I live."

EPILOGUE

Six months later...

"Doesn't matter how long you stare at that thing. Your ugly mug ain't gettin' any prettier."

Adrian turned away from the mirror to face the smartass who'd just walked into the room. "Fuck off, Dawson."

Dressed in a matching tux—minus the white rose—Gabe shoved his hands into his pockets and smirked. "That any way to talk to your best man *and* the guy giving away the bride? Better face facts, Walker. I say the word, this wedding doesn't happen."

Like hell.

"You do anything to ruin this day for Jen, I'll gut you like a fucking pig and bury you in the cemetery behind the church."

The two men stood like that, facing off in the back room of the small country church Jenna had chosen until Adrian finally caved.

Unable to deny how ridiculously happy he was, he lost

the staring contest and grinned. "Thanks again for doing this." He held out his hand for Gabe.

The man who may as well have been Jenna's blood brother gave him a good, strong shake. "Never thought I'd say this, but I wouldn't miss this day for the world."

It was amazing how a couple of years could completely transform a person's life. In that time, the two men had gone from enemies, to guys who tolerated each other when they absolutely had to, to damn near best friends.

Of course, the women in their lives played a pretty big hand in that.

Unlike most, Elle had been rooting for him and Jenna almost from the start. But even though Gabe had been the one to drag his ass off that beach and back into Jenna's arms, the overprotective bear had still made it clear that his respect where Jenna was concerned wouldn't come easy.

The fact that Gabe was getting ready to stand up with him *and* walk Jenna down the aisle...Adrian was pretty damn sure he'd finally earned it.

"The girls ready?" he asked as a sudden trickle of nerves ran down his spine.

"Who do you think sent me in here?"

Pulse racing with anticipation, Adrian turned back to the mirror to check his hair and tie one last time. Seeing that everything was still in place as it should be, he filled his lungs to capacity before exhaling at a slow, steady pace.

"You're looking a bit nervous. Sure you want to do this?"

He met the other man's gaze in the mirror. "I've never wanted anything more."

Gabe smiled and squeezed Adrian's shoulder. "Good answer. 'Cause you know, if you were thinking about running off again, I'd have to hunt you down and kill you."

"You could try." Adrian turned back around with a smirk.

"But you won't have to. I've spent my whole life running, Dawson. I'm ready to slow things down a bit."

"Just don't get *too* slow," Gabe teased. "After all, Bravo may need a special consult now and again."

The two men started for the door. "Consult, huh? That mean you're offering me a job?"

"Fuck no." Gabe chuckled. "But rumor has it, McQueen might be."

Adrian didn't say anything, but he and Jake McQueen—owner and head of R.I.S.C.—had already had a conversation over the phone the other day.

The man *had* offered him a job working with both Alpha and Bravo teams, as well as consulting on specialized jobs with the security company's up and coming Charlie and Delta teams.

McQueen had given Adrian time to consider the offer, which was good because he hadn't mentioned it to Jenna yet, either. Logistically, there was a lot to work out, and she'd been busy planning the wedding.

He'd tell her about the offer soon, but for now, he wanted to focus on the new life they were starting together.

The music began playing, and Adrian knew that was their cue. With one final nod, the two men walked out the door leading to the front of the church.

Standing at the spot he'd been shown during last night's rehearsal, Adrian watched as Gabe walked away, toward the large double doors at the back of the church.

Jenna's behind those doors.

Thrown by the flurry of butterflies flapping around inside his gut, he tried—and failed—to force his lungs to breathe normally.

He was a former Marine. A hitman for hire. He'd *killed* people before, for fuck's sake. But not one of those things had ever made him feel as nervous as he did in this very moment.

Get a grip, Walker. You're about to become the luckiest bastard alive.

As usual, the tiny voice in his head was right. For reasons he'd never understand, Adrian had been given a second chance with the only woman he'd ever loved.

Proof that God *hadn't* given up on him, after all.

He'd been right there all along. Watching over Adrian and placing him in the exact right place at the exact right time. Just when Jenna had needed him most.

The big man upstairs had also gotten him here, in *this* exact moment. Waiting to take her hand.

The large doors opened, and Ellena began walking forward. Wrapped snuggly in her arms was the cutest baby girl Adrian had ever seen.

With Elle's smile and Gabe's eyes, Adrian couldn't help but think of how screwed the man was going to be when little Emma was older, and the boys started coming around.

Actually, it was the *boys* Adrian felt most sorry for. Those poor kids had no idea the level of fatherly wrath that awaited them.

Elle approached the front of the church with their honorary flower girl. She looked up at Adrian and gave him a wide, approving smile before taking her place next to where Jenna would soon stand.

The music changed and the small crowd stood. With his nerves and excitement on point, he glanced around at the people who'd come to witness the special day.

The bride's side held people Jenna knew from work and a few close friends. Some he'd already met. Some he hadn't.

The opposite side of the aisle—the groom's section—held the members of Bravo Team and their significant others, along with Ghost, his wife, and a few other couples from the Delta Force team.

Jake McQueen, his wife, and their daughter had also made the trip for his and Jenna's big day. So did Jason Ryker. Not surprisingly, the Homeland agent was flying solo.

These were his friends. His adopted family.

With absolutely no reason to, and despite all the shit he'd put them through, this group had taken him in as one of their own. For the first time in his life, Adrian was filled with a sense of acceptance.

As he waited for his bride, Adrian's gaze fell across the other men and women on his side.

Nate and Gracie sat in the front pew. One of Nate's arms was wrapped around Gracie's shoulders, his other hand resting lovingly on his wife's growing belly.

Next to them were Matt and Katherine. The two couldn't seem to keep their eyes off of each other, and Adrian understood why. Last month at a Bravo Team barbeque—one Adrian and Jenna had been invited to—Matt had announced that he and Kat were *also* expecting their first child.

Behind them in the next pew back were Zade and Gabby, and Kole and his wife, Sarah.

Every couple on that side of the church—including the ones from Delta Team—had gone through the same sort of hell he and Jenna had. And they'd survived.

More than that, they'd come out stronger than ever before, which only solidified what Adrian already knew.

No matter what life threw at them, he and Jenna were going to be fine. *Better* than fine. They were going to be deliriously happy.

And he couldn't fucking wait.

Speaking of happy...

His soon-to-be wife had just started walking down the

aisle. Her hand clung to Gabe's arm as they slowly made their way toward him.

Adrian's breath hitched when he got his first good look at her. She truly was the most beautiful woman he'd ever seen.

Carrying a bouquet of white roses, Jenna smiled at the guests as she and Gabe passed by. Her hair was pulled up in some sort of loose-fitting style that allowed several loose curls to fall naturally from the studded crown holding her veil.

The lace dress she'd chosen hugged her body snuggly, flaring out mid-way down her thighs. The delicate hem brushed the carpet as she walked.

Adrian swallowed his tongue as his eyes focused in on the neckline. It was sexy yet modest. A sleek line that ran across her chest and off her delicate shoulders. The small train in the back added just the right amount of traditional beauty.

Just when Adrian didn't think they'd ever get there, Jenna and Gabe reached the end of the aisle. They stopped directly in front of where he stood.

The minister instructed the guests to be seated, and then went on to say some other things. But Adrian didn't hear a single, solitary word.

He was too busy looking into a set of emerald eyes brimming with more love than he deserved. Selfish bastard that he was, Adrian was going to grab hold of that love with all he had and never *ever* let it go.

"Who gives this woman to this man?"

He blinked when he heard Gabe proudly say, "I do."

With eyes that appeared to be suspiciously wet, Gabe gave Jenna a sweet kiss on her cheek before following tradition and placing her hand into Adrian's.

Under his breath so the preacher wouldn't hear, he warned, "Hurt her, and you're a dead man."

"I'd rather eat my own bullet," Adrian whispered back as he took his bride's hand and held it tight.

She smiled up at him and the rest of the world vanished.

Someday he'd try to remember the words they both said. The precious vows they'd repeated. The songs that were played.

But for now, in this moment, all Adrian cared about was that Jenna was here. She was safe and protected.

And she'd chosen him.

"By the power vested in me by the State of California, I now pronounce you husband and wife. You may—"

Adrian kissed his bride. Behind him, he heard Gabe's deep rumble of laughter just before the entire crowd joined in.

He didn't care.

He simply held Jenna close and poured every ounce of love he had into their first kiss as husband and wife.

"God, I love you," he whispered against her soft lips.

Her green eyes sparkled with joy. "I love you, too."

Adrian kissed his wife again. He didn't know what he'd done to deserve someone as perfect as this woman, but she was his. And he was hers.

Always.

Click below to purchase your copy of Rescuing Gracelynn today!
https://amzn.to/2KOap0o

AFTERWORD

Dear Readers,

Thanks so much for reading *Rescuing Jenna*. This was the first story I've written as the ending to a series, and I have to admit, I'm sad to see Bravo Team go. That being said, I'm happy each couple finally found their HEA, and who knows…maybe Gabe and the guys will pop up again, sometime. (*wink wink*)

I hope you've enjoyed this team and their stories as much as I've enjoyed creating them. If this is the first Bravo Team book you've experienced, I hope you'll go back and read the others.

XOXO ~
Anna B.

ALSO BY ANNA BLAKELY

Bravo Team Series

Rescuing Gracelynn

Rescuing Katherine

Rescuing Gabriella

Rescuing Ellena

Rescuing Jenna

R.I.S.C. SERIES:

Book 1: Taking a Risk, Part One (Jake & Olivia's HFN)

Book 2: Taking a Risk, Part Two (Jake & Olivia's HEA)

Book 3: Beautiful Risk (Trevor & Lexi)

Book 4: Intentional Risk (Derek & Charlotte "Charlie")

Book 5: Unpredictable Risk (Grant & Brynnon)

Book 6: Ultimate Risk (Coop & Mac)

Book 7: Targeted Risk (Mike & Jules)

Book 8: Savage Risk (Eric & Riley)

Book 9: Undeniable Risk (Ryker & Sophie)

Book 10: His Greatest Risk (Series Finale)

Want to read Kole & Sarah's story for FREE?

Click below to sign up for Anna Blakely's newsletter and receive your *FREE copy* of *Unexpected Risk-A Bravo Team Novella*

https://dl.bookfunnel.com/u3zicn7yhu

*Unexpected Risk was originally released as part of the Because He's Perfect charity anthology. It is now only available through this link, and brings you Kole & Sarah's trying experience while dealing with shocking news and a malevolent stalker.

ABOUT THE AUTHOR

Author Anna Blakely brings you stories of love, action, and edge-of-your-seat suspense. As an avid reader of romantic suspense herself, Anna's dream is to create stories her readers will enjoy and characters they'll fall in love with as much as she has. She believes in true love and happily-ever-after, and that's what she will always bring to you.

Anna lives in rural Missouri with her husband, children, and several rescued animals. When she's not writing, Anna enjoys reading, watching action and horror movies (the scarier the better), and spending time with her amazing husband, four wonderful children, and her adorable grand-daughter.

FB Author Page: facebook.com/annablakely.author.7
Blakely's Bunch (reader group): https://www.facebook.com/
groups/354218335396441/
Instagram: https://instagram.com/annablakely
BookBub: https//www.bookbub.com/authors/anna-blakely
Amazon: amazon.com/author/annablakely
Twitter: @ablakelyauthor
Goodreads: https://www.goodreads.com/author/show/
18650841.Anna_Blakely

facebook.com/annablakely.author.7

twitter.com/ablakelyauthor

instagram.com/annablakely

amazon.com/author/annablakely

There are many more books in this fan fiction world than listed here, for an up-to-date list go to www.AcesPress.com

You can also visit our Amazon page at:
http://www.amazon.com/author/operationalpha

Special Forces: Operation Alpha World
Christie Adams: Charity's Heart
Denise Agnew: Dangerous to Hold
Shauna Allen: Awakening Aubrey
Brynne Asher: Blackburn
Linzi Baxter: Unlocking Dreams
Jennifer Becker: Hiding Catherine
Alice Bello: Shadowing Milly
Heather Blair: Rescue Me
Anna Blakely: Rescuing Gracelynn
Julia Bright: Saving Lorelei
Cara Carnes: Protecting Mari
Kendra Mei Chailyn: Beast
Melissa Kay Clarke: Rescuing Annabeth
Samantha A. Cole: Handling Haven
Sue Coletta: Hacked
Melissa Combs: Gallant
Anne Conley: Redemption for Misty
KaLyn Cooper: Rescuing Melina
Janie Crouch: Storm
Liz Crowe: Marking Mariah
Sarah Curtis: Securing the Odds
Jordan Dane: Redemption for Avery
Tarina Deaton: Found in the Lost
Aspen Drake, Intense
KL Donn: Unraveling Love
Riley Edwards: Protecting Olivia

PJ Fiala: Defending Sophie
Nicole Flockton: Protecting Maria
Alexa Gregory: Backdraft
Michele Gwynn: Rescuing Emma
Casey Hagen: Shielding Nebraska
Desiree Holt: Protecting Maddie
Kathy Ivan: Saving Sarah
Kris Jacen, Be With Me
Jesse Jacobson: Protecting Honor
Silver James: Rescue Moon
Becca Jameson: Saving Sofia
Kate Kinsley: Protecting Ava
Heather Long: Securing Arizona
Gennita Low: No Protection
Kirsten Lynn: Joining Forces for Jesse
Margaret Madigan: Bang for the Buck
Trish McCallan: Hero Under Fire
Kimberly McGath: The Predecessor
Rachel McNeely: The SEAL's Surprise Baby
KD Michaels: Saving Laura
Lynn Michaels: Rescuing Kyle
Olivia Michaels: Protecting Harper
Wren Michaels: The Fox & The Hound
Annie Miller: Securing Willow
Kat Mizera: Protecting Bobbi
Keira Montclair, Wolf and the Wild Scots
Mary B Moore: Force Protection
LeTeisha Newton: Protecting Butterfly
Angela Nicole: Protecting the Donna
MJ Nightingale: Protecting Beauty
Sarah O'Rourke: Saving Liberty
Victoria Paige: Reclaiming Izabel
Anne L. Parks: Mason
Debra Parmley: Protecting Pippa

Lainey Reese: Protecting New York
KeKe Renée: Protecting Bria
TL Reeve and Michele Ryan: Extracting Mateo
Elena M. Reyes: Keeping Ava
Deanna L. Rowley: Saving Veronica
Angela Rush: Charlotte
Rose Smith: Saving Satin
Jenika Snow: Protecting Lily
Lynne St. James: SEAL's Spitfire
Dee Stewart: Conner
Harley Stone: Rescuing Mercy
Sarah Stone: Shielding Grace
Jen Talty: Burning Desire
Reina Torres, Rescuing Hi'ilani
Savvi V: Loving Lex
Megan Vernon: Protecting Us
LJ Vickery: Circus Comes to Town
Rachel Young: Because of Marissa

Delta Team Three Series
Lori Ryan: Nori's Delta
Becca Jameson: Destiny's Delta
Lynne St James, Gwen's Delta
Elle James: Ivy's Delta
Riley Edwards: Hope's Delta

Police and Fire: Operation Alpha World
Freya Barker: Burning for Autumn
B.P. Beth: Scott
Jane Blythe: Salvaging Marigold
Julia Bright, Justice for Amber
Anna Brooks, Guarding Georgia
KaLyn Cooper: Justice for Gwen
Aspen Drake: Sheltering Emma

Alexa Gregory: Backdraft
Deanndra Hall: Shelter for Sharla
Barb Han: Kace
EM Hayes: Gambling for Ashleigh
India Kells: Shadow Killer
CM Steele: Guarding Hope
Reina Torres: Justice for Sloane
Aubree Valentine, Justice for Danielle
Maddie Wade: Finding English
Stacey Wilk: Stage Fright
Laine Vess: Justice for Lauren

Tarpley VFD Series
Silver James, Fighting for Elena
Deanndra Hall, Fighting for Carly
Haven Rose, Fighting for Calliope
MJ Nightingale, Fighting for Jemma
TL Reeve, Fighting for Brittney
Nicole Flockton, Fighting for Nadia

As you know, this book included at least one character from Susan Stoker's books. To check out more, see below.

SEAL Team Hawaii Series
Finding Elodie
Finding Lexie (Aug 2021)
Finding Kenna (Oct 2021)
Finding Monica (TBA)
Finding Carly (TBA)
Finding Ashlyn (TBA)
Finding Jodelle (TBA)

Eagle Point Search & Rescue
Searching for Lilly (Mar 2022)
Searching for Bristol (Jun 2022)
Searching for Elsie (Nov 2022)
Searching for Caryn (TBA)
Searching for Finley (TBA)
Searching for Heather (TBA)
Searching for Khloe (TBA)

Delta Team Two Series
Shielding Gillian
Shielding Kinley
Shielding Aspen
Shielding Jayme
Shielding Riley
Shielding Devyn (May 2021)
Shielding Ember (Sept 2021)
Shielding Sierra (Jan 2022)

SEAL of Protection: Legacy Series
Securing Caite (FREE!)

Securing Brenae (novella)
Securing Sidney
Securing Piper
Securing Zoey
Securing Avery
Securing Kalee
Securing Jane

Delta Force Heroes Series
Rescuing Rayne (FREE!)
Rescuing Aimee (novella)
Rescuing Emily
Rescuing Harley
Marrying Emily (novella)
Rescuing Kassie
Rescuing Bryn
Rescuing Casey
Rescuing Sadie (novella)
Rescuing Wendy
Rescuing Mary
Rescuing Macie (novella)
Rescuing Annie (Feb 2022)

Badge of Honor: Texas Heroes Series
Justice for Mackenzie (FREE!)
Justice for Mickie
Justice for Corrie
Justice for Laine (novella)
Shelter for Elizabeth
Justice for Boone
Shelter for Adeline
Shelter for Sophie
Justice for Erin
Justice for Milena

Shelter for Blythe
Justice for Hope
Shelter for Quinn
Shelter for Koren
Shelter for Penelope

SEAL of Protection Series
Protecting Caroline (FREE!)
Protecting Alabama
Protecting Fiona
Marrying Caroline (novella)
Protecting Summer
Protecting Cheyenne
Protecting Jessyka
Protecting Julie (novella)
Protecting Melody
Protecting the Future
Protecting Kiera (novella)
Protecting Alabama's Kids (novella)
Protecting Dakota

New York Times, *USA Today* and *Wall Street Journal* Bestselling Author Susan Stoker has a heart as big as the state of Tennessee where she lives, but this all American girl has also spent the last fourteen years living in Missouri, California, Colorado, Indiana, and Texas. She's married to a retired Army man who now gets to follow *her* around the country.

www.stokeraces.com
www.AcesPress.com
susan@stokeraces.com